"As usual for Ms. Wine, historical facts are masterfully woven into her story, giving it authenticity seldom found in historical romances…a must-read."

—*Night Owl Reviews,* Top Pick

"An absolute delight! You will forever be astounded as well as gratified by reading Mary Wine's Highlander series. Scottish Medieval fans are sure to be in awe."

—*My Book Addiction and More*

"Entertaining and engrossing…Mary Wine weaves a tapestry of a tale with adrenaline-pumping action, sweet and spicy love scenes, a touch of humor, and a twist and turn here and there."

—*Long and Short Reviews*

"Wine's rip-roaring ambushes and beddings make for a wild ride through fifteenth-century Scottish eroticism."

—*Publishers Weekly*

"Wine's crisp writing, intricate plot, and deep insights into clan politics make for a fun and satisfying read."

—*Booklist*

"An exciting, sexy tale…action-packed, suspense-filled historical romance."

—*Romance Junkies*

Also by Mary Wine

Hot Highlanders
To Conquer a Highlander
Highland Hellcat
Highland Heat

The Sutherlands
The Highlander's Prize
The Trouble with Highlanders
How to Handle a Highlander
The Highlander's Bride Trouble

Steam Guardian
A Lady Can Never Be Too Curious
A Captain and a Corset

A SWORD FOR HIS LADY

MARY WINE

 sourcebooks
casablanca

Published by Sourcebooks Casablanca, an imprint of Sourcebooks,
Inc.
P.O. Box 4410, Naperville, Illinois 60567-4410
(630) 961-3900
Fax: (630) 961-2168
www.sourcebooks.com

Printed and bound in Canada.
MBP 10 9 8 7 6 5 4 3 2 1

One

London, July 1189

RAMON DE SEGRAVE IGNORED HIS GROWLING BELLY. The dawn was just beginning to break, the horizon turning pink as fingers of light stretched across the land, chasing off the shadow of darkness. The mosaic glass window in the front of the sanctuary began to glow with the light stretching across the pews and himself, driving away the chill of night.

A firm hand landed on Ramon's shoulder, gripping it with increasing strength until Ramon abandoned his focus and looked up.

"You've done your duty, my friend. Let us go tend to the more mundane chores of life. Such as breaking our fast."

Because he was still on his knees, Ramon turned his head and ducked his chin to offer deference to his king. Richard the Lionheart chuckled and slapped him on the back.

"Come, Ramon, enough piety for one night," the king insisted. "You and I are the only ones still here."

There was a note of disappointment in Richard's voice, but Ramon was more interested in the flicker of approval in his king's eyes. It was hard enough to come by, which left no room for Ramon to pity those who didn't earn it. Richard was not a man easily impressed—it was a quality Ramon admired about his king.

Ramon stood, his knees protesting with shooting pains because he'd been on them all night. It was a small discomfort compared with the surge of achievement moving through him.

Ramon looked at the window again. "It is just now dawn, Sire."

"And you are ever a man to be just, even when those who wish to share the same honor I bestow upon you do only the minimum required of them." The king nodded, dark circles ringing his eyes belying the fact that he had also spent the night in the sanctuary. The cross he wore over his robe was something the king held sacred. Richard had earned the right to wear it, just as any other knight under his command, by performing the required nights of devotion on his knees and lending his sword arm to the Crusade.

The king grinned as they walked through the doorway and left their duty completed behind them.

"So, my new baron, now that you have taken your noble title with humility, what is next?"

Ramon lifted one eyebrow in response. "One night of prayer is hardly something I would call humility. I did not expect you to bestow such an honor upon me, Sire."

"Which is why I did it." Richard made a slashing motion with his hand. "You have earned the honor.

I wish half the men who serve me understood as well as you what nobility truly means. They plead with me for honors and station, yet cry their excuses when it is time to follow me into battle."

"Aye, Sire…honor is earned."

"That it is, my friend."

Richard spoke loudly, his voice echoing off the stone that made up the hallways. Servants lowered themselves the moment they heard the king coming, most dropping their gazes in reverence. For this was the king. The man so often talked about but rarely seen inside his own realm. Ramon kept pace with his king, accustomed to the bold way Richard continued talking to him, without a care for who might be listening. Such was the nature of the king. He often led charges himself and was known for walking among his soldiers to hear what they had to say when they felt at ease. He was a man who craved being immersed in life.

And craved controlling it.

Richard clapped his hands, the sound echoing between the walls. "It is time to discuss what I need of you."

Ramon held back a frown. They entered the main hall and several servants dropped their plates in surprise. The king strode determinedly toward the dais that held his table and chair while his personal servants hurried to attend him. There was always a crowd of men waiting for the king to notice them. The king's scribe followed them on silent steps with his assistants holding rolled parchments.

Ramon waited until they seated the king. It wasn't an easy task, controlling the urge to ask the question that was gnawing at him. The king glanced at his scribe, but summoned Ramon forward instead. Ramon took the seat next to the king.

"There is no question of what I am going to be doing, Sire. I shall accompany you on the Crusade."

Richard was back in England only long enough to call up a new army, which he planned to march on Jerusalem.

"This Crusade is necessary to wipe my past sins away, but I must strip every resource out of this country to outfit my army."

Servants began to place the first meal of the day in front of them. Bowls of steaming porridge were set down and, since it was the king's table, there were also bowls of fresh summer fruit, a small pitcher of cream, and even costly lumps of sugar. The king frowned.

"Take the luxuries away." He flattened his hand against the tabletop. "We have come from praying the night through and will greet the morning with a meal befitting the humility every Christian soul should observe while our holy city is held captive by the Moors."

The servants hustled to obey, and Richard winked at Ramon. "We'll need a reason now to celebrate, my friend. Tonight we shall feast in honor of your coming wedding."

Ramon ground his teeth. Richard laughed, tilting his head back and roaring at the ceiling.

"You should see the look on your face, Segrave! I swear you look like a beardless lad facing a bride who is old enough to be his mother...yet still eager for the consummation."

"The look on my face is born of a man's experience with marriage." Ramon didn't flinch in the face of the hard glare Richard sent him. That steadfastness gained him a grunt of approval from his monarch. "Forgive me, but I would keep my own counsel when it comes to choosing a bride. On that matter, I suggest you confine your opinions to who is in your bed."

A servant looked up, her eyes wide with shock. The king slapped the tabletop with mirth.

"You know something, Segrave? I am going to miss having your honesty by my side. Too many of these knights are greedy bastards at heart. They fear to tell me anything that might upset my delicate disposition."

Ramon's lips twitched. "You haven't a delicate bone in your body, Sire."

Richard took a fresh round of bread and tore it in two. The king bowed his head and offered up a prayer of thanks. The scent drifted on the morning breeze, making his mouth water, but Ramon remained focused. The king was in a controlling mood; his own empty belly could wait. Once Richard made a decision, it was set in stone. Even ones he made while breaking bread.

"I would accompany Your Majesty on the Crusade as I have done for the last decade. To serve you is my greatest honor, and the only life I know."

Richard bit off a chunk of bread and chewed it before answering. "Aye...aye, and that is exactly why I need you to remain here in England." Another section of bread disappeared into the king's mouth, so Ramon had to wait to hear the king's reasoning. He didn't care for the tension that knotted his neck.

"The Welsh persist in their rebellion against me, while my own brother covets my throne in this miserable country." He stopped and pointed at Ramon. "I need you to stabilize the government here, which is why I elevated you to the station of baron. My dear brother John will have a barons' council here to keep him in his place. You will be one of those men, Ramon. One I can rely on to rule justly and keep the law. You will be a member of the highest council in this kingdom."

The king nodded and wiped his lips with a cloth lying on the table.

Ramon frowned. "I am a knight. I belong beside you."

"Now, you are a baron," Richard declared firmly. "A new duty with an even greater challenge. You will rule according to the law, not by drawing your sword."

Ramon was forced to hold his tongue. Richard didn't miss the effort it took to not argue.

"Make no mistake, living in England will be a battle worthy of a knight such as you. You won't be sitting by the hearth and warming your backside." The king chuckled ominously. "But to secure this country, you will need a property that is positioned just right." Richard lifted his hand and snapped his fingers. His scribe was well accustomed to waiting for the king's command, and quickly brought forward a rolled parchment. Richard pushed aside the dishes in front of him and spread out the paper.

"Here, along the Welsh border, is Thistle Keep. It is owned by a young widow." The king turned his head and grinned at Ramon. "But she has no way to defend her land because her garrison owes me service. I sent for them three days ago."

Ramon wanted to argue, but there was a look in his king's eyes that he recognized too well. Richard was set on his plan to leave Ramon behind in England. The country was riddled with unrest and Ramon's loyalty was unquestionable. It was a compliment, even if it was one he did not covet.

"If it is your will that I remain here to keep order, I shall, Your Majesty, but I do not require a wife to do so."

"Are you truly afraid of one lone woman, Ramon?"

Richard chuckled at the deadly look Ramon gave him in response. He tapped the parchment with his index finger.

"Look closer."

Ramon peered at the map, his irritation growing. "The lady has a great deal of marshland. It is little wonder she is unwed. That land is useless." Hence, the widow was poor.

"But her people are fat and her taxes paid."

Ramon frowned and Richard nodded. "That widow is clever. She's managed to turn her marshes into a breeding ground for geese. I need those feathers for my archers, and I need the keep held against the Welsh."

"Two things that can be accomplished without marriage."

The king flattened his hand on the parchment. "You are the bravest man I know, but I swear at this moment, you tempt me to call you a coward."

Ramon stiffened, but the king waved his hand in

the air between them. "Fine then, I am not ordering you to wed the widow, but I need that land secured. She has no knights, they are marching with me. Her land is coveted by her Welsh neighbor, so I am sending you to fortify Thistle Keep with your men. What you do with her personally is your choice. Yet if it were me, I would want to know more about a woman who can manage her estate so well on her own. She is no timid miss, you may be certain of that." Richard looked at the map once more and stabbed a finger at a section of land bordering the widow's. "This land belongs to the crown. It will be yours."

The king's tone told Ramon that the matter was decided.

"Thank you, Your Majesty."

"I know you are not pleased. Give it time. Go and meet the widow, see if she raises your…interest."

Richard chuckled. Ramon tilted his head and grinned at his king. "A pleasant enough task."

The king nodded.

"The land I've bestowed on you is good crop land, but there is no keep and no timber or stone to build one. Yet it will farm well and be an excellent addition to Thistle Keep if you see the logic in wedding the widow."

"A good suggestion."

His words were given grudgingly, carrying a little too much relief for his own taste. Richard didn't miss either emotion. The king sighed.

"Think ill of me if you like, Ramon de Segrave, but my own position would be more secure if I had sons. It is time for both of us to trust enough in a woman to beget a few heirs. There's something for you to dwell upon on your march to the borderland. Besides, that widow has geese, and I need more feathers. Her flock is the only one for twenty miles. I don't know how she managed to send me so many feathers and still keep her geese. See if you can discover her secret."

Ramon stood up and bowed. "As you command." He meant it sincerely. Serving his monarch had always been his primary goal. He turned and struggled to mask the distaste for his king's order.

Women were not to be trusted.

He'd learned that lesson through bitter betrayal. He was not interested in wedding again so another wife might place the horns of a cuckold on his head. Being disgraced once was enough.

Yet such an opinion left him without a true direction for the first time in his life. He had always been a knight, always looked forward to riding for the Crusade. In truth, he had spent little time in his wife's company. It was simply the way life was.

But not anymore. Which left him looking toward the future in wonder.

His captain raised an eyebrow when Ramon joined him at the edge of the high ground, where Ambrose had been forced to wait by the king's personal guard. Together, they descended the steps of the high ground and left the king and his court behind.

"Pleased, are you?"

Ramon shrugged. "In truth, I am not certain."

Ambrose St. Martin cut him a questioning glance.

"It appears we will be riding for the bordering land,

to meet the widow residing at Thistle Keep. Richard is leaving me here to keep the peace and hold the border against the Welsh."

"And wed."

Ramon shrugged. "That part was not a command."

Ambrose chuckled softly. "With Richard, suggestions are best minded."

Ramon felt his temper strain. "Aye."

It was a solid truth and he'd be wise to remember it. There was also truth in the fact that his land had no keep, which meant his men would be exposed.

Yet…a wife?

He might wed her and secure the land as his own. Such was the common practice for a knight such as himself, having spent so many years in the service of his king. There were plenty of knights who had pillaged their way through the same service, but he was not one of them. The Code of Chivalry forbade it, and his honor was the only thing that meant something to him.

Marriage was one thing he might consider to increase his holdings without tarnishing his honor. Richard was correct in saying it was time to consider having sons, and the widow, Isabel of Camoys, would be a good match. United, they would have an estate that might provide everything they needed, but only if he decided to risk marrying the woman. The men that were needed to secure her land might also be the means for her to shame him with when she took a lover from among his ranks. Everything he had earned over the last ten years would crumble because his men would see him as too weak to control his wife.

He ground his teeth and chided himself. It was

unjust to think badly of the lady. There was dishonor in that.

His mood lightened. Actions always were the better means to judging a matter or a person. In fact, now he was intrigued. His first wife had been a woman who enjoyed court. Isabel was busy running her land. By the condition of her land, she was not lazy.

Yes, that was indeed intriguing.

"Why are you smirking?" Ambrose demanded.

"Richard told me to meet the lady and decide if she raised my…interest," Ramon explained. "I am thinking I am going to enjoy this particular royal dictate."

༄

The ground shook.

Isabel looked up and found herself staring into the eyes of the three other women working at the stillroom table with her. Their eyes were wide and seeking, looking at her to assure them there was nothing to fear from the horses approaching.

Isabel wanted to soothe their concerns, but she could not. The times were uncertain and the sound of approaching riders was not welcome; she had no household knights to defend those looking to her for protection.

Inheriting her husband's land had lifted the burden of being under the rule of another from her shoulders, but in its place was the responsibility of protecting everyone who lived on her land.

Truly, she had never thought freedom might come with such burdens.

"Likely knights on their way to join the king,"

she offered to those watching her. "They will pass through."

She dusted her hands across the apron she wore to protect her over robe and went toward the front of the keep. The hallways were dim, in spite of it being full daylight, because they were long and the sun's rays didn't penetrate beyond a few feet.

It was chilly too. The stone that the keep was constructed from hadn't yet lost the bite of winter. It lingered in the center of the passageway, urging her forward to the inviting spring weather.

But the view from the keep's steps was not pleasant. The rumbling sound grew without the thick walls to muffle it. Thistle Keep was placed on high ground, which gave her an unobstructed view of the road.

Isabel's throat tightened.

Twin columns of mounted knights were riding toward her. The sunlight flashed off the surface of their armor; even their horses wore metal faceplates. They were clearly full knights, men who were seasoned by battle and hardened by rigorous training. She struggled to maintain her poise. The harvest had been poor the last two years, and King Richard was focused on gathering supplies for his Crusade. Behind the knights there were more mounted men and even more on foot. There were archers in their ranks as well, confirming that this was not some random group of pillaging raiders. They were an army. The columns stretched out too far into the distance to be anything that might be considered good. These men rode with a purpose, and what concerned her were the wagons with them. Wagons they would likely expect to fill with food.

She needed everything she had to provide for her people. There was nothing to spare.

The dust rose as they drew closer, and she could make out the crest on the flags the lead knights flew. A raptor with a baron's coronet in blue against a white background.

A baron. That meant even more trouble. A baron was a noble and only answered to the king.

"What do they want?" Mildred asked from behind her.

"They will pass through," Isabel said quickly, not caring for how much her words sounded like a prayer. A desperate one at that. She straightened her back, forbidding herself to be afraid.

There was no time for childish emotions. She was the lady of the keep and duty was calling her.

Mildred scoffed at her, but Isabel raised her chin and refused to lower it. Dust teased her nose as the knights pulled their stallions to a halt in front of her. The animals pawed at the ground and shook their heads while the armor their riders wore shifted, filling the air with the sound of metal clanking against metal.

"I seek the Lady Isabel of Camoys."

A chill raced down her spine but Isabel maintained her position. The knight who had spoken lifted one gauntlet-covered hand to raise his visor. His hair was dark and his eyes the color of midnight. He peered at her, his gaze as hard as his breastplate.

"I am Isabel." She fought the urge to twist her fingers in the fabric of her over robe. Thistle Hill did not even have men training to become knights because the king had summoned all of them for his Crusade.

No boy over the age of twelve was left, unless she counted those wearing sackcloth in the church. That left only her courage to protect the people looking to her as their lady.

Maybe she should have ordered the keep barred instead of coming out to face the riders. Dread twisted through her belly. It was not just her fate that hung on her decisions, it was every soul who lived on her land. Barring the door would have left all their food unprotected. She stepped forward.

"I am Baron Ramon de Segrave."

He raised one hand into the air, with his palm flat and his fingers pointed skyward. The men riding with him responded quickly, the air filling with the sounds of them dismounting.

Isabel gasped, feeling control slipping from her grasp. "How may I assist you, Lord de Segrave?"

Her hope that the man might have a simple request died as he swung his leg over the back of the horse and lowered himself to the ground. Her belly twisted as she noted just how imposing a man he was once he was braced on his feet. He gave the stallion a firm pat but his eyes remained on her. Piercing and sharp, his gaze cut into her in spite of the distance between them. He was a hardened man, one built for war.

"His majesty has sent me to discover why you withhold your geese from him."

Isabel stiffened. "His Grace does not need my geese, only their feathers, which have been sent each season as is required of me."

The baron closed the distance between them. Isabel fought the urge to retreat because even though she stood on the top step, the man looked her straight in the eye.

Something strange fluttered through her belly.

Something completely misplaced.

Yet surprising, nonetheless. She felt as though her heart skipped a beat.

Which was, of course, ridiculous.

"His majesty requires more feathers for the archers he is preparing to march to the Holy Land."

Isabel's temper stirred. "There is not a goose for twenty miles beyond the borders of my land because the king had them slaughtered. My flock must not have the same fate. I need my geese alive to nest or there shall be no feathers next season."

The number of men behind the baron drove home the fact that she could do very little against them if she failed to convince the baron that her geese should live to procreate. She swallowed her anger. Logic was her only weapon and she needed her wits to wield it.

"I see you and your men are set to join the king. There are some feathers in my storerooms for this year's taxes. I shall fetch them."

She didn't wait for the man to answer, but hurried off toward the long storage buildings that ran alongside the keep. Mildred kept pace with her, muttering beneath her breath as they opened the door to the storerooms and heard one of the merlin falcons flutter its wings when the sunlight disturbed it.

Isabel reached for one bird without thinking, her fingers trailing over the smooth back of the animal in a familiar motion.

"Be at peace, Griffin."

Her hand was suddenly grasped, the baron's fingers closing all the way around her wrist. He lifted her arm away from the hawk in one swift motion.

"Even hooded, a raptor is dangerous, lady." His voice was thick with reprimand and his eyes flashed with his displeasure. "Your father should have taught you better than to touch one."

Isabel lost the battle to rein in her temper. "My father is the one who instructed me upon the art of falconry. I am every bit as confident with Griffin as any man might be."

She reached out and stroked the hawk once again, keeping her rebellious gaze on the baron's. His eyes narrowed.

"Then it is a good thing your father is dead, for I would have words with him about teaching a woman the art of falconry. Such is a duty for a man."

His voice held all the arrogance she expected from a baron—well, from a *man*. Perhaps it was a sin, but she did not miss having to answer to a husband.

"Since the king requires all my men, the duty of running this land is mine and I see it done well. There are the feathers. God's peace be with you."

Ramon de Segrave didn't turn. Instead, one of his dark eyebrows rose. He clearly didn't care for her tone, but she had more important things to do than court his favor. He studied her with his dark gaze, and something shifted in the air between them. A gust of heat that had nothing to do with the changing season and everything to do with how close Ramon was to her. She shifted back, losing the battle to remain poised.

"Do you argue against your place, lady? Is that the

reason you wheedled your way into being taught to handle a hawk?"

She drew in a harsh breath. "There was no wheedling involved, my lord. You are presumptuous to assume women only use sniveling to gain what we need."

"Need, madam? Admit you only sought the status the hawk would bring you when it was perched on your arm." Determination edged his words. His opinion shouldn't have mattered, but her pride flared up.

"There are many here who look to me in these hard times. I have learned the tasks necessary to make sure my land feeds my people."

He frowned at her. Isabel wasn't sure if it was her tone or her words that displeased him, most likely both. He was a knight and a baron. The church preached that it was her place to be humble in his presence, but she could not seem to recall that as she was forced to suffer his arrogance.

She pointed once again at the baskets the feathers were carefully stored in.

"Rats steal goose eggs. Hawks eat rats. My flock of geese is large because I fly Griffin over the marshes to hunt the rats. It keeps the vermin out of the stores as well."

His eyes narrowed as he contemplated her. Her belly fluttered again, which was preposterous because there was no reason she should worry about pleasing him.

And yet…that sense of heat shifted between them again, and she noticed just how black his hair was. Like the deepest winter midnight.

Enough!

"Clever lady. You use reasoning well. Interesting."

His lips twitched. Something flashed in his eyes that sent her back a step in spite of her resolve to remain unmoved by him. There was a sense of command in him that seemed woven into the very fiber of his soul. She could have sworn she felt it, like heat radiating off coals.

He turned his attention from her and looked at the baskets. Isabel was grateful for the moment of privacy because she was sure her face betrayed how unsettled she was.

She wanted him and his army gone. The sooner the better.

Maybe *needed* was a better word.

You shall not think in such a manner…

Her poise was crumbling, deserting her in a fashion that she had never experienced. It was so unsettling, she was nearly breathless.

"I hear the king leaves soon on his Crusade, and that he has even taken to wearing the cross on his robe."

"He has." Ramon de Segrave stared back at her. This time he lingered over her features, his gaze slipping down her body with a slow, sweeping motion that sent heat to her cheeks. It was unseemly for any knight to look at a lady in such a way, but it suited his nature.

Excitement twisted through her like too much wine during a winter feast.

"Enough." Her mouth had gone dry. "Your gaze is overly bold for a knight embarking on the Crusade, my lord."

His lips twitched. "When you greet me with your head uncovered, you should expect such."

His chastisement stoked her temper. "The day is fine and warm. Whilst working inside, I had no need of a veil. This is not court, where efforts are devoted to vanity instead of the work necessary to begin planting. I dress to suit my duties."

She raised her chin and refused to lower her head with shame. He pressed his lips into a firm line, but she could see him weighing her words. Judging her.

Wasn't that the way of men?

"I bid you good travels." She lowered herself in one swift motion that erased the amusement from his expression. The baron quickly moved into her path, almost too fast for how much armor he wore, blocking the doorway with his large body.

"His majesty has bestowed the title of baron upon me for service by his side, and given me the duty of making sure his kingdom is secure while he is away. Specifically, this borderland. I am also your neighbor now; the land to the south of your estate is mine." His expression became impossible to read, drawing her closer as she sought some understanding of what he intended. There was something brewing in his eyes, something that twisted her insides with anticipation.

She stepped back from him and his eyes narrowed.

"That land has been deserted for two generations. There is not even a manor house still standing, for the Welsh burned it."

"Which is why the king has seen fit to suggest I wed you. Together, our land will become an estate the Welsh will find they cannot raid."

Her throat tightened until she couldn't squeeze even a breath through it. Her temper flared up. She had held these lands countless days and toiled long hours to provide for their inhabitants. Everything was a credit to her own dedication. Yet to Ramon de Segrave, it might all so easily become part of the spoils.

"When hellfire rains down from heaven, and not one moment before, shall I stand at the church door to wed you."

She hurried down the length of the store house and out another doorway, every muscle in her body quivering.

From her anger, no doubt.

You lie...

She ground her teeth together.

Perhaps, yet it was only a small dishonesty, for she was angry too.

Aye, a tiny dishonesty, for she would be damned to hellfire before admitting she quivered for Ramon de Segrave.

Or any man.

❧

"She has spirit, that one. And pride," Ambrose St. Martin remarked from beside him. Ramon reached up and pulled his helmet off his head before answering his second in command.

"Yet it is earned. So not completely misplaced."

"Earned or not, she'll not take easily to being bridled."

Ramon offered his friend a shrug that sent his shoulder armor clanking against his breast and back plate. The sound echoed inside the storeroom, so he stepped outside.

"My first wife played the part of a submissive spouse very well. I discover myself wondering if I do not prefer Isabel's honesty. However misplaced it may be. She does not veil her lies with flutters of her eyelashes."

Which roused his curiosity. Her scent lingered, teasing him with thoughts he'd long banished. Or at least confined to the sort of woman he might make agreement with for her favors.

Ambrose took the helmet from his lord, but there was a dark frown lingering on his lips. "There are others you may wed for a better plot than this cursed marsh keep."

"What is your quarrel with the match?" Ramon asked. In truth, he needed to be reminded why marriage was something he disliked, for the sight of Isabel had somehow clouded his thinking.

Ambrose looked him straight in the eye as he spoke. There was a confidence in the man Ramon admired, thus why they were friends and not just knights who shared only the bond of the chivalric code.

"Her nurse told me she survived the fever that claimed the lives of her father, brother, and husband. She appears set on running this estate. You may not last longer than her husband did."

"I am more concerned over her ability to cloud my thinking when it comes to marriage."

Ambrose stiffened. "Perhaps you are simply trying to serve Richard and his whims, as you ever have done."

"Perhaps."

Ambrose drew in a stiff breath. Ramon ground his teeth. "Yet I discover my interest stirring. She stood up to me. With clear purpose and spirit. It is my own failing that allows such traits to undermine my thinking on the matter of wedding."

Ambrose raised an eyebrow, his lips curving knowingly. "Have you fallen at last to the sweet song of the gentle sex?"

"Spare me your taunting, Ambrose." Ramon considered the number of bundles in the storeroom. It was nearly full and the harvest was not yet finished. "Richard was correct when he said her people were fat and that this land needs defending. There is much here worth stealing, including the lady herself. When the Welsh hear her garrison is gone, they will come for her, because she is an heiress and they will think to expand their territory while the king is away."

Ambrose conceded the point with a nod. "Yet the lady herself is far from biddable." His gaze strayed to the merlin. "She will argue against the place you mean to set her in."

"Her marriage was very brief; there are rumors it was never consummated."

Ambrose stiffened. "Then she is guilty of falsehood."

"Not so, for she has yet to speak upon the matter. It was her father who took possession of her husband's holdings by using the marriage documents. A daughter must be obedient to her sire."

Ambrose nodded. "Yet I still believe you are more interested in pleasing Richard. Be careful, Richard will not be the one who must suffer that female in his bed."

Ramon chuckled. "It is the thought of her in my bed that has changed my thinking. It makes wedding more enticing, I admit."

Ambrose's face lit with surprise before he burst out laughing. Ramon growled at him, but his fellow knight only bent over with his mirth.

"'Tis grateful I am for such understanding," Ramon said.

Ambrose cleared his throat but didn't quite erase the smirk from his lips. "Age has caught you at last. Before long, you'll be casting out your wisdom to young squires as you recount your days of glory. That lady will put the bridle on you."

He choked on the last word, a fresh round of amusement claiming him. Ramon shot him a glare that only made the knight choke a few more times as he tried to rein in his enjoyment.

"I've a fine memory, Ambrose," Ramon warned before stepping back into the storeroom and looking around with a critical eye.

Isabel of Camoys had been passed over by many of Richard's knights in favor of women who had land that wasn't so close to the rebellious Welsh, who refused to accept Richard as their rightful king.

"One thing is for certain, we need to set the men to building structures that are large enough to defend this keep." He scanned the open road in front of the store houses.

Ambrose didn't look pleased. "Should you not decide upon the matter of wedding the lady before improving her land? The men will expect their pay from you, and your land stands vacant. You need to plant your own fields to provide for them."

Ramon grinned and reached out to slap the man on the shoulder. His armor clanked as he did so.

"Richard wants this land secure. I cannot leave it in this condition and keep my word to the king." Ramon drew in a deep breath. "It will not be long before the Welsh hear Richard has departed with all his knights."

"And the lady?" Ambrose insisted. "What will she do to earn our men's labor?"

Ramon heard his man grumble, but his squire ran forward and took the helmet away from Ambrose. The distraction gave Ramon the opportunity to consider the lady in question. She was slender, which indicated Isabel did not take more for herself than she gave to others. Her honey blond hair, a color that suited her blue eyes, was braided in a long plait that hung down her back, but several locks had worked their way loose around her face to confirm she had not been sitting idle while her people toiled.

Both were sound reasons to consider wedding her. He scanned the keep and storerooms, frowning at the way they stood wide open to attack. There weren't even wooden walls to help fend off invaders by closing a gate. Only the keep and the outer buildings. Her father had clearly been a trusting fool, for the Welsh had a king who would happily take whatever he might while Richard was off on the Crusade. They were fortunate Richard was intent on crusading, or the Welsh would find themselves conquered in short order.

Much like Isabel of Camoys. It had taken only a ride up to the steps of her keep to secure her. She had looked back at him, her eyes narrowing. Something stirred in him, tightening inside him as he contemplated the stance she'd taken up on the steps of her keep. She'd taken the high ground, and the look on her face told him she intended to try and hold it.

He liked that trait. It spoke of courage.

Heat stirred in his loins.

A very unexpected reaction. She was no great beauty and wore no gown worthy of a poet's quill. Yet there was fire in her gaze; in truth, he would have sworn he felt the heat radiating off those flames. No meekly lowered lashes for Isabel of Camoys. She fully intended to hold her ground.

Yet she had no hope of evicting his men without his agreement. She was defeated, yet stubbornly standing in the doorway to bar the way.

The facts should have put him in a better humor. But he found himself dissatisfied and on edge. The source of his discontent was simple to identify. Isabel of Camoys challenged him, and he found her a worthy opponent.

His fatal weakness…

❧

London

Jacques Raeburn was irritated.

It wasn't the fact that his king wouldn't grant him a private audience that agitated him. It was the smirks on the lips of the other men surrounding Richard the Lionhearted, because they knew what Richard was doing.

Jacques took a drinking bowl from his squire and drew off a slow sip before handing it back.

Patience.

It would not be the first time he needed persistence to gain what he wanted. Jacques remained with the king, making sure his monarch noticed him watching, because there was one thing that Richard truly was at heart, and that was arrogant. Richard believed himself worthy of Divine approval and, therefore, the devotion of men. The truth was, he enjoyed power as much as the next man. Stroking his ego would win Jacques what he wanted in the end. Finally, Richard lifted his hand and waved him forward, past the other knights and nobles trying to gain the king's attention.

"I wish to speak of Isabel of Camoys, Sire."

"I did not expect you to be pleased by the elevation of Ramon de Segrave, but I will not placate you by giving you the same reward," Richard informed him the moment they were closed behind thick oak doors.

"You mistake the cause of my reason for seeking you out, Your Majesty."

Richard looked unsure. "Then tell me what put that frown on your face."

Jacques hooked his hands into his belt. "Isabel of Camoys was wed to my kin."

The king frowned. "I did not know such."

"Her late husband was a bastard son of my father's, but blood nonetheless." Jacques watched the king absorb the implications of his statement. "My father has charged me with wedding her and recovering the land she gained through her marriage. I seek your permission to do such."

Richard grunted. "You've explained your dark

brooding, Raeburn, but I will not take back what I have given to Ramon."

"Did you order the lady to wed him?"

The king took a long swallow from his drinking vessel before answering. "No, I did not. As a widow, she has the right to choose."

Jacques felt his mood lightening. "May I offer Ramon competition for the lady?"

The king chuckled and sat back in his chair. "So long as it is fairly done and without bloodshed. I need Ramon to keep this country loyal while I am in the Holy Land."

"I would need to be on equal footing to make it an even match."

The king pressed his lips together. "An agreement could be reached."

There was a glint in the king's eyes Jacques recognized too well. Richard was focused on his Crusade and England was a poor country. The king was determined to wring every piece of gold out of its inhabitants. If Jacques wanted to please his father, he'd have to buy his noble title from his king, since Richard knew he wanted it now.

He resented that.

Jacques felt anger burn through him for the slight Richard was dealing him. Ramon wasn't the only one who had ridden beside his king for years, yet Richard denied Jacques the same reward.

But did it truly matter? Jacques lowered himself in submission to his king, shifting his focus onto what mattered.

A knight owed his allegiance to his blood kin. He'd

please his father, as a son was bound to do by God's command. Isabel of Camoys, by the will of fate, had land that belonged to his family.

He vowed to gain it back.

෴

"My lady, they are making camp."

Alyse ran into the keep with her eyes wide. She pointed toward the doorway behind her. "Wagons have come, an entire line that is still arriving, and they are putting up tents."

The other women gasped, several of them muttering prayers. But Isabel knew it was going to take more than heaven's mercy to be rid of Ramon de Segrave. Men rarely changed their agendas to please a woman. But the tension in her shoulders was eased by the fact that the army in front of her keep would surely be a deterrent to any invaders eyeing her storerooms.

Marriage to the baron was too heavy a price to keep the security his men might provide. Let him stay. The Welsh wouldn't need to know his reason, only see that his army was present.

There. She had found the blessing in the day at last. But she felt less than satisfied.

"The baron claims he is planning to remain." There was no hiding her irritation and Alyse drew her hands up in front of her mouth.

Isabel pressed too hard on the herbs she was grinding and they scattered across the tabletop, some of them even rolling onto the floor. She made a soft sound beneath her breath that wasn't very polite. The others stared at her and she felt guilt color her cheeks for her lack of discipline. Allowing her temper to ruin anything was unacceptable.

She drew in a stiff breath. "He claims the king has recommended me to him for marriage."

Just saying the words enraged her further. With a huff, she left the table. That gained her more shocked looks from her maids, but she couldn't seem to remain still. Her blood felt as though it were rushing through her body too quickly, and her heart was beating as though she had been running.

Such was all she needed. A man who unsettled her.

"You cannot refuse the king's will, my lamb."

Isabel turned on Mildred so quickly her robes flared away from her ankles. "The man wants to wed me because the king gave him the land on our southern border. He is only looking to increase the size of his holding and secure it with my keep," she muttered with a wave of her hand. "He'll soon tire of waiting on me to accept him. A baron will want a biddable wife."

"Maybe you should be the one getting tired of being alone. You're young enough yet to have children of your own."

Isabel felt her eyes widen.

Children.

Fate had truly dealt her an unkind blow in making it so none of her husband's efforts in their bed resulted in children. A babe would have made his callous touch far easier to bear.

"Aye, young enough…still," Mildred tempted her.

"Shall I simply trust Ramon de Segrave's word about what the king has said? It's possible he is naught more than another rogue baron intent on pillaging us while the king is focused on his Crusade. I have only his word that he owns the estate south of us." She would be wise to doubt the man. Many an heiress discovered herself wed to a man who wanted her property and had nothing of his own. "For all we know, his men have not been paid and he'll be wanting my silver too."

"The baron has an army with him to enforce his will upon us." Mildred reached out and stroked Isabel's arm. "There is naught to do but bend to his demands. Better to bend than to be broken."

Isabel scoffed at the woman who had raised her. "I detest marriage."

Mildred made a low sound of warning. "Methinks you shall like being the man's leman even less, and with his men here, there is no one to force him to wed you, should he decide to take anything he desires." There was a note of harsh reality in Mildred's tone.

But experience had left a bitter taste in Isabel's mouth. *Loathe* was too kind a word for how she felt about being beneath a man. "He shall not have my inheritance if he does not make me his wife."

Mildred laughed but it was not a cheerful sound. "He occupies Thistle Hill, and with the king leaving for the Crusade, no one shall be here to force him to relinquish it, except perhaps invaders from Wales. I believe we will fare no better under their rule." Mildred's expression turned solemn. "You are still young enough to conceive. He can breed a bastard on you and inherit through his child when he acknowledges it. You know it happens, just as I do. There is no king to run to for mercy, only the barons' council."

"Which he sits on." Her mouth went dry.

Isabel discovered her attention drifting toward the doorway. The double doors were open, to let the fresh spring air into the keep. She moved forward and scanned the activity filling the yard. The baron's men weren't wasting time. Wagons pulled up and were immediately emptied. Large canvas pavilions were being raised, and she could see the blacksmith setting up a makeshift shop.

All of it was done with an ease that spoke of numerous repetitions. She stared at the anvil the blacksmith was leveling on top of thick wooden blocks. Ramon de Segrave had come to stay, bringing everything his army needed to sustain it. A blacksmith was as essential as water to knights.

She spotted the baron and felt a shiver go down her back. A page removed Ramon's chest armor and he stood up, rotating his arms in large motions once he was free of the protective breast plate. He was a full head taller than most of his men, and his shoulders were packed with thick muscle.

She contemplated him, debating the sensation swirling through her belly. Did she find him pleasing?

"You cannot go your entire life dreading a man's touch simply because your husband was a harsh man," Mildred said.

"He was a brutal man, Mildred, and speaking kindly of him only makes me distrust your words, for you knew it full well." Mildred inhaled sharply. Isabel felt a stab of guilt for her harshness; life was difficult enough without bitter words. Still, she could not lie. "I am no longer a child who needs to be sheltered from life's unpleasant realities. Ramon de Segrave is a man of war. I have no reason to be happy to wed him. Besides, shunning men works very well for nuns. And every married man who has left for the king's Crusade has left a wife alone."

Mildred made a low sound of disapproval that drew Isabel's gaze to her. "Forgive me, Mildred, I speak harshly today." Or at least in a tone that wasn't respectful. That was shameful and stoked her temper. She didn't want any man to needle her so greatly that she forgot how to be kind to those she considered family.

"Your husband was a harsh man, but I've warned you time and again not to let that make you bitter." Mildred shook her head. "Some men are mean-hearted, but you have been blessed by his passing, so do not dwell on it."

"You speak wisely." It was a polite, polished response. One that left her feeling hollow.

Mildred grunted. "Don't be thinking I am impressed by that meek response."

Isabel couldn't resist the urge to smile. "Why? Because you were the one who taught me how to use such bland courtesies?"

"Precisely."

Isabel's smile grew larger. Mildred shook her head.

"I warned your father that Bechard was a poor choice of groom for you and that you were too young for the marriage celebration. You fear the duties of a wife now, as I warned your father would happen."

Isabel pressed her lips back into a hard line. Even the memory of her husband was enough to sour her disposition. "As you said, let us not dwell on him. My father wanted the alliance and it was a good one." She looked at Mildred. "That is not the reason I will refuse to wed Lord de Segrave."

"Then what is, Lady Isabel?" Ramon said.

Isabel gasped and jerked her attention toward the baron. He was still ten paces from her and yet his expression told her he had heard her very clearly. "For I am most curious to discover the root of your discontent."

The gravel beneath his feet crunched with every step he took. He lifted one hand and pointed at Mildred. "Leave us."

There was solid authority in his voice, and Mildred lowered herself immediately and left. Isabel had to fight the urge to offer the man the same courtesy because such manners had been drilled into her since childhood.

Indeed, her husband had enjoyed every meek and humble display she had offered him. Mean-hearted was not a harsh enough term for the man who had so often taken delight in humiliating her.

Ramon de Segrave stopped in front of her, his gaze sharp and seeking the answer to his question. Isabel raised her chin. Honesty was something men valued. She would be direct.

"I do not care for the marriage bed," Isabel said.

Her words shocked him. She saw it in his eyes. She watched the dark orbs, feeling the weight lift from her shoulders until something new flickered in the dark depths of his eyes.

Something unmistakably sinful, yet strangely enticing.

"Your husband's failing. I promise to prove more attentive to your…desires."

Her mouth dropped open. She snapped it shut and felt her cheeks burn. "Stop your boasting."

No man had ever spoken so brazenly to her. She gave him a reprimanding glare but only received a soft smirk in response. Or was it a smirk? She peered more intently at his mouth, trying to decipher his expression.

Why had she never noticed how soft a man's lips seemed? Her own tingled with anticipation.

Enough!

"It would be best for you to take the feathers to the king and ask him for another bride. I am not a virgin."

"Neither am I." There was a hint of arrogance in his tone.

Her pride finally flared. "Obviously you are not, since you boast so brazenly about your skills in the bedchamber." Her eyes widened when she realized what she was discussing so calmly, but Ramon de Segrave chuckled at her audacity. "Go and find your amusement elsewhere. I have no liking for your company." She could never admit she found him enticing.

He lifted a hand to silence her. "But we have spent so little time in each other's company. Your judgment is rash."

"It is sound." She knew she was being impolite. She blushed at the thought, but if it sent the man away from the idea of wedding her, it was worth the guilt. Let him think her a shrew.

He lifted one foot and set it on the bottom step.

"What are you doing?"

One of his dark eyebrows, and his entire body, rose as he climbed another step. Something new was flickering in his eyes. Hard, male determination.

Her belly twisted.

"I am entering the keep." His tone made it clear he knew he was invading her home.

"No." She fought back her breathlessness. "You shall not."

She backed up, but forced herself to stop in the doorway.

"Why not, my lady?"

He climbed another step and she felt her knees quiver. It was an insane reaction, one that shocked her with its intensity.

"You do not belong in the keep. This is my home."

He frowned but climbed another step to stand on even ground with her. Isabel lifted her chin trying to maintain eye contact.

"I need to fully assess this structure, and I plan to begin doing it now. You may stand aside or I shall remove you from my path. The choice is yours. Yet lifting you might speed along our introduction, so perhaps it is best."

"I said nay." She stamped her foot because she didn't know what else to do. Her temper flared with a need to argue. She didn't want him to think she was impressed by his size.

She should have lowered herself and gracefully glided out of the doorway. It was the only response the code of chivalry afforded her, but she couldn't force herself to do it. She didn't feel in control of her emotions; they were scattering like autumn leaves.

Her heart accelerated. He was pressing closer, watching her, gauging her reactions to him. She'd never felt so exposed. Never felt like any man took so much notice of her. He reached for her, his expression full of promise.

"No one enters this keep without bathing." She spat the words out in a rush and had to pull in a deep breath because her lungs burned. Relief flowed through her, for she had found a valid argument to use.

The baron's expression didn't change, but he made a sound that betrayed his irritation. His face was a hard mask that didn't tell her what he was thinking. His hands were clenched around his wide leather belt, his knuckles turning white. She was trapped in the doorway. Retreating inside the keep was her only option.

"Take yourself off to the bathhouse, my lord baron." She was brazen.

His eyes narrowed as her stern words hit him. He suddenly grunted, amusement returning to his eyes. "Very well, lady, since you wish to offer me your hospitality, I accept."

She stared at him, uncertain of the flicker burning in his dark eyes. This wasn't a man who knew defeat, and the muscles in her neck tightened when his lips twitched into a smug grin once again.

An expression that was full of victory.

"I shall enjoy having you bathe me, Isabel. It is certainly a good place for us to begin to learn more about one another." A gleam appeared in his eyes that sent a shiver down her body. "You will certainly learn more about my…ability to pleasure you once we are wed."

"I did not offer to bathe you myself," she said in a horrified whisper.

He stepped closer, capturing her wrist in a grip that surprised her with its gentleness. Instead, she felt their connection, so much that she couldn't form a single sensible thought. Logic had always offered her salvation in the past. Before Ramon de Segrave. But now it crumbled away, leaving her at his mercy.

And the mercy of her own traitorous flesh.

"You claim you are no maiden, so it is only customary for you to attend me since you are the lady of this keep." His voice lowered. "Or perhaps you would prefer not to act as a lady. In such a case…I will be most pleased to dispense with ceremony."

He tugged her forward. She put up her hands and pressed against his chest. His mail tunic was hard but she shivered as though her palms rested on his flesh.

His features changed, becoming more sensual. When his eyes met hers again, there was a spark in them that sent a twist of excitement through her belly.

"I admit, sweet Isabel, I find the idea of dispensing with the church's dictates on civilized behavior rather fitting when it comes to your argument against marriage. I will be most happy to prove my worth to you."

Her eyes widened and her mouth went dry. For a moment, she was torn. Something inside her leaped toward the promise of sampling forbidden things. Those whispers she'd heard in the dark shadows where lovers met, the ones she'd always been too conscious of her duty to venture into.

The ones her marriage had proved so bitterly wrong…

He stroked her inner wrist, his fingertips sending ripples of delight up her arm.

A feeling of heat licked its way through her insides, urging her toward recklessly needling the baron further…so he would put his hands on her…and she'd reach for him…

"The bathhouse, then. I shall attend you there."

A warm hand cupped her chin. She gasped, shivering as she felt the heat of his skin through his leather gauntlet.

How long had it been since a man had touched her?

Was that the reason her body was so full of impulses that she found it difficult to think?

"I find myself doubting your word, Isabel." His fingers moved gently along the side of her jaw while his gaze cut into her. "You claim to be a woman of experience and yet you blush like a maid. Were you a wife or a bride?"

She stiffened, lifting her chin from his grasp. "A wife. Although I found the title of *possession* more appropriate. I had a place among my husband's playthings. To be used or toyed with at his leisure. You cannot expect me to resume such a position when I have a choice."

For all her fascination with him, Ramon was like any other man. He would expect her to perform to his satisfaction or suffer his displeasure.

"What I expect, lady, is not to be judged guilty of another man's crimes."

She drew in a deep breath and lifted her arms so that his grip on her wrist was clearly in sight. "Do you not even now make it clear your will shall become mine?"

He released her. For a moment, she was disappointed. But he reached out and stroked the surface of her scarlet cheek.

"Do you not blush, lady? Is that not the sign of inexperience?"

It was a sign of something she wasn't willing to admit.

"I never claimed to be experienced, Lord de Segrave. My marriage lasted less than a season. What I said was, I am no longer a virgin."

He withdrew his hand and stepped back, his hands returning to his belt. There was a hard look on his face, but he offered her a single nod in agreement.

"Well then, lady, I shall await your hospitality at my bath." His eyes narrowed. "I assure you, you will be more experienced when you finish tending to me."

"And I assure you, my lord baron, you shall not be so pleased with your victory."

❧

"The brute," Mildred said softly from her hiding place. She emerged from behind the door frame. "He enjoyed baiting you."

Isabel snorted, not caring that the sound wasn't genteel. "That is the nature of a man, to gain what they crave. A wagon full of barley or a wife, men seem to see little difference."

Mildred frowned. "I'll attend him with you."

"Nay," Isabel responded. "I am not afraid of him, nor shall I have him thinking I cannot find the courage to look upon him in naught but his skin. He has nothing I have not seen before. Best to settle this matter of whether or not I am interested in sharing a bed with him now."

She refused to be intimidated. The brute wanted his back scrubbed? Well, she may not have much experience when it came to the marriage bed but she knew how to put a shine on a clod of dirt if need be. He'd not be so pleased with himself when she was finished. Her attention settled on Mildred's covered head.

"Let me have your wimple."

Mildred clicked her tongue but there was a glint of merriment in her eyes. "Careful now. Play games with that man and I fear he'll not be satisfied until he has bested you. Knights who become barons often do not know how to admit defeat."

"Neither do I." Isabel spoke confidently. "We'd all have empty bellies if I were given to shying away from situations that appeared too difficult to manage. Or that the rest of the world felt only a man could manage."

"Right you are about that, my lamb."

Isabel unwrapped the cloth that shrouded Mildred's head. Isabel fit the cap over her own hair, and Mildred helped tuck Isabel's braids into the back of it as Isabel pulled the tie closed to keep her hair completely inside the cap. There was a second piece that was little more than a square of linen, folded in half and sewn to the top of the cap. Once flipped back from her face, it fluttered down to hide every inch of her neck.

"We cannot have the baron displeased with my lack of modesty."

Mildred pressed her lips into a firm line to conceal her amusement. "Certainly not."

Isabel lifted the front of her robes and walked down the steps before she lost her nerve. She embraced her temper, which had flared from having her duties interrupted by Ramon's demands.

It was a bath, nothing else. A courtesy the lady of the manor performed for honored guests.

That was all.

If the man wanted to bare his body in her presence, fine. She wouldn't be impressed, not a bit. Men so often considered their members to be something a woman enjoyed seeing, but Ramon de Segrave was bound to be disappointed if he thought the sight of his cock might sway her position on wedding him.

You certainly were interested in him.

Isabel muttered beneath her breath as she got closer to the bathhouse. She was a fool.

Her husband had delighted in showing off his erect member before demanding her submission. She was obviously quite correct in her conclusions about Ramon. The man was exactly like her late husband.

Yet, he was correct about her condemning him for crimes he hadn't committed.

Guilt made her stop. She stood for a moment and listened to the sound of the baron's men making camp.

It was welcome.

She could not deny it brought a sense of relief. Tonight, her people would sleep soundly, knowing there would be no raids.

Well, she still wasn't interested in wedding the man. But she was willing to admit that there were some benefits to the baron being here. Such was logical thinking—something which had served her well.

Now all she needed to do was find logical reasons for rejecting the baron's proposal.

The bathhouse was at the end of one of the long store buildings. With the warm spring weather, the window shutters were open. Isabel had to add wood to the hearth and push it into the ash to touch the coals, because no one needed a fire during the day at this time of year. The sound of the river rushing by filled the long room, and she could hear several women singing as they washed clothing. It was a short walk outside the bathhouse to the stone embankment her father had built to keep the water from changing its path by eroding the bank during the spring melting of snow.

The river rushed up to the edge of the stones, and there were long poles for lifting buckets of water. Women used the surface of the stone walkway for scrubbing clothing, and the strong scent of lye soap lingered in the air. The soap kept the mold from growing on the stones and making the surface slick. The stone wall allowed the river close but kept the rushing current from eroding the land that the bathhouse was built on.

Long troughs leaned up against the outside wall. Isabel lifted one and fit it into a standing trough that was near the edge of the wall. She would haul the water up from the river and dump it into the trough so that it would run into the bathhouse through the window. For bathing in the spring, it made the chore much easier. In winter, she would have to haul buckets of snow.

She walked back into the bathhouse and pushed the large kettle into the flames of the fire. It was always hanging off a large hook, ready to be heated. The flames licked at the drops of water on the exterior, making them sizzle.

"Lady?"

She turned to find two youths holding a bathing tub that was far larger than any Thistle Hill had.

"The baron's tub, lady. Where would you like it?" one of the boys asked.

She lifted one hand and pointed toward the open window. "Put the foot beneath the end of the trough."

The window cell was notched to keep the trough steady and the boys looked at it once they had set the large tub down.

"That's a clever design," one of the boys remarked. "Must save wear on the hands for sure." They continued talking to one another as they left. Isabel frowned at their backs, annoyed at the way they had left her to the task of bathing their lord. Her irritation doubled when she remembered that it was Ramon de Segrave who had decided she would be the one washing his back.

Along with several other intimate duties, if she wasn't clever enough to outwit the man.

Isabel walked closer to the tub and looked at it. It was quite large, but she realized that Ramon de Segrave would have had to sit with his knees against his chest in the tubs that she had to offer. She frowned—the tub was confirmation that he had come to her land with the intention of staying.

If he had gained the king's favor, she would have to wed him.

That thought sent a chill down her back and she didn't care for the weakness that was seeping into her. She was already thinking of yielding and it simply wouldn't do. Moving quickly, she tried to use the chore of filling the tub to dispel her dark mood. She'd learned to stay busy so as not to dwell on the fact that she hadn't cared for her husband's touch, because the more she thought about it, the worse she dreaded sunset.

A hiss came from the hearth and the water she had left to heat. It was boiling over the sides of the kettle. Reaching for a length of iron that had a hook on the end, she used it to pull forward the arm holding the kettle so she might grasp the handle. She poured it into the tub and set more water for heating.

"How curious to see you wearing a wimple now that we are in private." A shiver crossed her back and rippled down her body. The man's voice was like a sliver of a summer midnight, when the cool breeze was a welcome thing. Something you wanted to sink into and be wrapped in. Isabel bit her lip to contain her gasp. She resisted the urge to reach up and touch the veil that now covered her head.

"There was no reason to wrap my head when I was working in the keep with only my women about." She gave him a stern look. "And I certainly cannot have a baron disappointed with my conduct."

The baron pulled off one of his leather gauntlets, tugging on each fingertip until he removed the garment. Her gaze lingered on the bare skin of his hand for a moment that seemed far too long.

"You are already contradicting yourself, Lady Isabel."

The baron's dark eyes moved to the edge of the linen that she had wrapped around her hair. The bathhouse suddenly felt small with him here. He moved across the space between them and reached out to finger one lock of hair that was stubbornly curling outside the fabric. "For I find this moment quite pleasing."

This time her gasp was quite loud. She jumped back, retreating from his touch.

"Your hair is quite comely, Isabel. You have set me the challenge of seeing it again. I enjoy a challenge."

She sucked in a harsh breath, reality cutting through the weakness in her knees. "Of course. Such is the nature of a man. To conquer challenges."

One of his dark eyebrows rose. "You believe me shallow. And yet, if I were a man who spent his days spinning tales of what he was going to do, while never accomplishing any of those things, would you not label me something worse?"

Isabel turned away from him, guilt needling her. She dipped one hand into the water to test its temperature. There was no point in arguing with him. "Your bath is prepared."

"But I am not."

She turned back to face him and frowned when she discovered him watching her with eyes that challenged her. He tossed his other gauntlet aside and flexed his fingers. The knuckles popped, sounding too loud, her senses overly aware of every detail. He curled one finger, beckoning her forward.

"Come here and offer me your hospitality."

She was tempted to refuse him. The urge to disgrace her mother's teachings was almost too strong to ignore.

God's teeth! The man affected her intensely.

Which was all the more reason she had to face him with her shoulders squared.

He was naught but a man, and she knew what was hidden under his clothing.

"Since that is what you wish."

He was watching her, the weight of his stare feeling too hot.

"Do you wish me to tell you that I shall enjoy having you touch me?" His voice was deep and coated with male satisfaction.

She jerked her attention away from the ties that closed his tunic. "Have done with teasing me. I cannot imagine why it amuses you so much. We are strangers."

His fingers stroked across her cheek. It was a whisper of a touch, and yet she felt it as though it had been as loud as thunder cracking directly above her head.

"I intend for us to be much more intimate, very soon."

"I have not agreed to wed you, Baron de Segrave." Isabel propped her hands on her hips. "You seem to have been in the company of women who are easily impressed with a few smooth words; women who would allow you to touch them without seeking anything from you except compliments. I am not such a woman."

He crossed his hands over his chest, which made his biceps look larger. "I know full well you have not agreed that a union between us would be best. Since you have failed to use logic to make the best decision, I am employing other methods of swaying your mind."

There was a hard determination flickering in his eyes that horrified her.

"Then I owe you no hospitality, my lord, because you are not maintaining your knightly virtues."

He laughed and his features transformed momentarily into something she found quite attractive. His eyes sparkled with his amusement, reminding her of her father and the days when there had been much merriment at Thistle Hill.

"You have a romantic view of the chivalric code. It reminds me of a new squire." His smile faded. "One who has yet to endure the harsher side of being a knight in the service of the king."

"Many things are better when spoken of, than during the time they must be endured. Just as the squire learns the harsh realities of war, the bride discovers the disappointments becoming a wife yields."

"You did speak truly." His tone had hardened. "You were a wife." It gave her no solace to hear his agreement. She felt devastated. Ramon de Segrave would be far more accustomed to having his every instruction followed because the man was used to commanding an army. He was as solid as the armor he'd been wearing; even now his face was devoid of any hints to his true thoughts. She caught herself staring at him, trying to find any trace of the merriment that had been there so short a time ago.

There was none.

She looked back at the ties that laced his tunic closed, to avoid looking at him any longer. In the pit of her belly she felt a growing sense of vulnerability that sickened her. How simple it might be for him to take everything he wanted from her.

Well, she could choose whether she wanted to allow herself to be frightened of him.

She refused.

But still, the man unleashed a weakness in her. One she must never allow him to see.

The laces slid free easily, leaving his tunic gaping open. She focused on the task before her. Trying to imagine he was one of her father's friends.

A very ancient one, with rotten teeth and stinking feet.

"You will have to sit on the stool so I may remove your tunic."

He grunted and a moment later he pulled the garment over his head with one swift motion.

"You will learn that I am a man who enjoys doing some things himself." He dropped his tunic over the stool he'd refused to sit on.

"Or one that cannot stomach doing anything a woman suggests he do."

He snorted, but the corners of his lips rose into a grin. "You truly have been without a master."

Her temper flared and her hands went back on her hips. This would have earned her a slap from her husband, but Ramon de Segrave only chuckled.

"Go on, lady, I dare you to argue with me while we have no one to witness where our passions might take us."

"Temper has naught to do with passion."

"I disagree." His voice came out in a sultry tone that sent a ripple of emotion through her. "Dare you proceed and test which of us will prevail as the victor in this subject?"

He was trying to bait her once again. Isabel ordered herself to maintain her dignity and grant him no response. Reaching up, she leaned closer to him in order to reach the ties that closed the collar of his under robe. She caught a hint of his scent, and even before his bath it was clear he was not a man who allowed himself to stink.

"Why do you insist that every guest who comes to Thistle Hill bathe before entering your keep?"

"Such keeps the fleas out of our beds. I banned rushes on the floors for the same reason. The rats find the keep less comfortable than the marshes now."

She reached for the cuff of one sleeve and untied the laces. Her eyes traced the calluses on his palms that proved he was a master of his sword.

"That must make lying in bed, in only your skin, a pleasant experience."

She gasped and pulled too hard on the laces of the second cuff. They knotted and she had to pick at them while he chuckled at her.

In naught but skin? She'd never... Yet...

"You're thinking about it, are you not?" he teased her.

She jumped and bit back a curse. The cuff came loose at last.

"I might accuse you of enjoying toying with me, but I believe you would consider it a compliment," she said boldly.

She was surprised. A tingle went through her, and she enjoyed it. Bechard had never teased her. A claimed wife was nothing a man had to bother teasing.

"There, lady. Admit you are enjoying my company."

"Perhaps."

His chest rumbled with a chuckle that bounced off the walls of the bathhouse. His fingers touched her chin, raising her face so their eyes met again. It was a gentle touch, just a soft contact that wouldn't have woken a baby, but her heart hammered inside her chest.

"The idea of you in naught but skin is a pleasant one."

"A sinful one," she corrected.

"Not so." He slid his fingers beneath the tie that held the wimple closed. With a swift jerk, he snapped it.

She jumped back, but her braids were falling down her back, the wimple no longer secure. His lips curled up with victory.

"Since I have asked you to wed, it is not sinful to contemplate knowing you, Isabel."

His dark eyes dared her to continue. She reached up and pulled the ruined wimple off her head. It would be wiser to refuse him her hospitality, but part of her could not stomach the idea of retreating.

In fact, it was intolerable.

She was not a mouse.

She reached up and dug her hands into the shoulders of his shirt. With a short jerk she pulled the under tunic off him, baring him from neck to waist.

He was nothing like her husband at all.

Two

Isabel pulled in a deep breath and swallowed the lump that formed in her throat. Ramon de Segrave was muscular, his shoulders wider than his waist. He didn't have a round belly that spoke of too many fine meals and indulgence. No, he didn't resemble her husband at all.

"The look on your face is truly a compliment, Isabel."

There was heat in his tone that sent a curl of desire through her belly.

He sat down and stretched out one leg so she might assist him in removing his boot and their eyes met as she grasped it. Her insides tightened, her mouth going dry as she tugged on the boot, and she licked her lips in front of him.

"You like what you see." His statement was bold and arrogant.

"That is not—" She clamped her mouth shut before she found herself guilty of lying. The man was not worth spending time on her knees while she made recompense for the sin of speaking untruthfully.

She deposited the boot behind her and heard him

chuckling. Her temper ignited, but if she left the bath-house, the man would call her a coward.

Justly so.

Well, she wasn't having any of that.

Seems like you won't be having any of him either...

The second boot took more work to remove because she did not have her anger to aide her. She was too busy chiding herself for her immodest thoughts.

The last thing she needed was to turn wanton.

Isabel set the second boot beside the first one and turned around to discover the baron on his feet again. He wore only his leggings now and the front was filled out with an unmistakable bulge. She hesitated, another tingle of heat sliding through her belly.

"Are you crying quarter, lady?" His voice was deep and edged with the challenge she had seen in his eyes. She raised her face so he could see her determination. He wasn't the only one who knew how to cast gauntlets.

"I have seen a man's parts before." At least her tone didn't betray the rising heat inside her.

She picked up his boots and carried them toward the door so they might not be near the tub when she began using the soap. Lye could leave spots on the stained leather.

"So you have stated." There was a soft splash and she turned to discover the leggings draped over the stool and the baron settling into his tub. His back was to her and she was grateful for the moment of privacy. Yet she had to confess that she was also disappointed. She reached up to wipe away several beads of perspiration from her forehead. She wasn't working hard enough for such a response from her body, and yet her fingers came away wet.

He stretched his arms out and even wiggled his toes. "I have been wearing those boots for three days," he grumbled. "I believe I could become accustomed to some of your rules." He turned his head and looked at her over his shoulder. "Perhaps we might negotiate an agreement between both of our desires."

Isabel reached for a small pottery dish that contained the soap. She held her tongue for a moment, trying to decipher his expression. "I have never met a man who accepted a woman's will above his own. By your own words, you think I have been without a master too long."

"Without masters, we would all become beasts."

"And your master sent you here." She spoke without thinking. She scolded herself for being so familiar with the man. Eve had spoken to the serpent and look where that had led: straight into damnation.

Ramon nodded. "True. I believe Richard has faith in my ability to see the wisdom in us wedding."

Of course. A king would always expect his subjects to bend to his will.

She bit her lip to remain silent—what was the point in arguing? Such would prove that she was less loyal, or perhaps less mature. Only spoiled children argued against their place. She used a soft cloth to scoop up some of the soft soap and set the dish aside.

"I am pleasantly surprised that you use soap."

Isabel discovered herself hesitating to apply the first touch. "My father served the king and brought many useful things back with him from his time on the

Crusade. For all of their faults, the Moors know much of how to make life here on earth more comfortable."

"Aye," he agreed. "I doubt God cares for stench, even if I have ridden beside men who reject everything Eastern because it comes not from a Christian hand."

"Careful, you'll end up in the stocks with unchristian talk such as that."

He shrugged and leaned forward so she could wash his back. "I've been there before for unchristian... behavior. Likely part of the reason why Richard suggested I wed you. He fears for my soul if I do not have the church's blessing to enjoy the comfort of a woman."

"So I am an opportunity to avoid hellfire, now?"

She forced her hands forward and ran the linen cloth along the top of his shoulders. A tiny ripple of sensation raced up her arms, raising goose bumps. She ordered herself to dispense with being so aware of the man but that didn't seem to have any effect at all upon her fickle emotions. She tightened her grip so her fingers wouldn't tremble like some virgin on her wedding night.

Who's feeling the heat of hellfire now?

"I learned a few things in the east myself. Thistle Hill has need of fortification. This keep should become a castle," Ramon said.

She pulled her hands back, frustration making her crush the bathing cloth until water squeezed between her fingers and dropped down the front of her over robe.

She knew that it had to be done, yet she did not have the skill to do it. "The king calls away every man with building knowledge."

"I have such knowledge." The baron made a soft sound beneath his breath. "You could become accustomed to my presence, Isabel."

He wasn't merely making a suggestion. She heard the unmistakable ring of promise in his voice. Authority.

Well, she recalled that part of being a wife very well.

"Is that what having me bathe you is about, then?" Her voice quivered with her temper. "To introduce me to the position that is now mine by your decree?"

He continued to look out the window, giving her only his back to scrub. "We are both past the age of sonnets delivered through our servants."

"Aye, there is naught sweetly gallant about you, sir."

She turned in a swirl of her robes and made it three steps before Ramon's deep voice stopped her.

"Nor is there anything sweetly demure about you."

She turned to face him in shock. No knight spoke like that to a lady.

"Of course I am sweet, or at least kind. I did not ride to your home and tell you all that you know must change," she said, but the look in his eyes froze her. His eyes glittered with something more than determination—something partially savage. His toes no longer rested on the upper edge of the tub either. He had his feet planted firmly on the bottom of the tub and one hand gripping the side so that he might rise quickly.

"I am a man of my word, lady. My king sent me here and told me to consider you for a wife." His voice dipped low, becoming menacing.

"I doubt the king envisioned me bathing you as a means of introduction."

His lips split into a wolfish grin. "I don't doubt it. Richard needs a wife as much as I if he hopes to evade heaven's wrath."

There was a splash of water as he pushed to his feet. Water glistened down his length as he stood facing her, without any hint that being completely nude bothered him. He enjoyed shocking her. Every inch of him was solid, including the look in his eyes that confirmed what he threatened her with.

"Have you no shame?" Her voice faltered, catching as she tried to force her gaze to rest only on his face.

"None at all when it comes to winning the battle." A warning flashed in his dark eyes. He lifted one hand and motioned her back toward him. "The choice is yours, lady. Assume your duty or I will run you to ground. You may be a lady or a vixen with me."

Isabel was suddenly so angry her head hurt. Her fingers curled into fists as she toyed with the idea of leaving.

Christ! He'd likely pursue her into the yard just as he was.

The beast was bold enough, for certain.

She returned to where the bathing cloth was lying on the floor. She picked it up and looked back at Ramon to find him watching her with amusement shimmering in his eyes.

"I'll not get locked in the stocks beside you because the priests think I led you on."

"Ah, the sight of your uncovered hair…raised my passions beyond control…" he taunted her.

Raised…

Her glance slid low, down his body, until she was looking at his member.

"You'll find it is indeed…raised."

Her temper sizzled hotter than the coals on the hearth.

"Well, sit down then if you want me to finish washing you. You are too tall for me to reach your back when you are on your feet."

One of his dark eyebrows rose. "Since I am on my feet, perhaps you should wash what is within your reach." His tone was far too smug for her taste. Isabel raised her hand with the cloth clenched inside her fist.

"As…you…like…"

She punched toward his belly, but he caught her fist. His fingers curled all the way around her fist, in a grip that was solid but painless. She looked at the hold he had on her, her eyes tracing the corded muscles that ran along her forearm and up to his bicep.

The man had the strength to hurt her, there was no doubt about it.

"You have courage."

Three words had never sparked such an intense reaction inside her before. She raised her face and discovered the baron's gaze burning with approval. It spread through her like fire consuming dry straw. There was simply no way to ignore that she was pleased to have earned such praise, for he was not a man to praise the undeserving.

But her eyes narrowed as she contemplated the pleased expression on his face. "If I had wept and trembled like a frightened mouse—"

"I would have gladly granted your desire to remain unwed."

He sat down, giving her his back again. Isabel gaped and then shut her mouth.

She was so foolish…so undisciplined.

Regret burned a path through her as she began scrubbing his wide back. At least her thoughts were troubling enough to distract her from what her hands were doing. Let the man think what he would. She hadn't promised him anything. So long as she performed the duties required of the lady of the manor, Ramon de Segrave would have to respect her wishes. With her father gone, there was no one who might order her to wed except for the king. She was suddenly glad Richard was set to depart on his Crusade.

She wished him a quick journey, and that was the truth.

◆

"Do you have any skin left on your back?" Ambrose asked. Ramon's fellow knight entered the bathing area with one of his young squires following him with a stack of fresh clothing.

Ramon shrugged into a fresh under robe and smirked at Ambrose. Isabel had left him the moment she had finished washing him, since it was a squire's duty to dress his lord. Or a wife's, but he'd needled her enough for one hour.

"It is for certain I have no fleas, thanks to the lady's efforts."

Ambrose snorted. "That lady looked as though she were intent on scrubbing your skin from your bones. I would have refused to allow her near my cock as well."

"It was worth it to have her hands on me."

Ramon watched Ambrose shake his head. He

didn't care if Ambrose approved of his intention to wed the heiress of Camoys or not. A part of him found it humorous the knight didn't like Isabel.

Although discovering that emotion did not set well with him.

Marriage was a fine tool for arranging a situation to benefit all. It was not something that required emotions. All that was required was enough attraction to ensure his bride didn't leave his cock cold and useless when it came time to produce children.

His damned cock was still rock hard and drawing a curious look from his page.

"How did you find the keep?" Ramon asked.

"None of us have set foot inside the keep, because you yielded to the lady's order that we must bathe first. The men descended to the river banks, scattering the shocked inhabitants." Ambrose chuckled.

The squire was trying to stifle his laughter and doing a poor job. Ramon turned and walked toward the window until he could see the river. A good number of his men were still bare as newborns along the bank. Conversation drifted up to the window from men enjoying the moment, doing something they liked instead of the chore of making camp.

"I should imagine Lady Isabel is quite pleased to see her instructions being heeded so diligently," Ambrose choked out.

Ramon grinned. "She is likely spitting fire." He sat down so his squire could dress him. "I admit I cannot wait to see her reaction."

❧

"The man is Satan reborn." Mildred covered her face with her apron.

"Hush. If the church knights hear you, we shall have even more unwanted knights on our land," Isabel hissed. "I do not believe I can endure such." Her voice softened and she sighed when Mildred peeked at her around the edge of her apron. "Forgive me for being cross."

Mildred grunted. "I believe you are allowed to be unsettled, my lady." The older woman dropped the apron and frowned at the line of naked backsides on display. She waved her hand and turned her back on the river.

"The baron is a huge beast of a man; I agree with your refusing to wed him." Mildred nodded her head. "His member is far too thick and—"

"Do not say it," Isabel interrupted her companion. "I saw enough of the man and I wasn't peeking around the door frame as you clearly were."

Mildred shrugged, unrepentant. "A member like that means only one thing," Mildred continued in spite of Isabel's displeasure with the topic. She leaned closer and lowered her voice. "The man will have a great appetite for the flesh. Every midwife will tell you a member that thick and long is a demanding one. He'll need to spend once a night at least and likely twice with sacs such as those."

Isabel groaned and felt her cheeks burn with the memory of what Ramon looked like beneath his tunic. Mildred noticed the color immediately.

"Oh, there now. I didn't think I needed to temper my words with you. You've had a husband."

"I am not tender, simply overwhelmed at the moment. That is all." Isabel stiffened. "I've a need to find something to occupy my hands before Lord de Segrave demands more of my time."

His member was long and thick…

She tried to dismiss the image of it from her mind; there was no way to avoid thinking about how different Lord de Segrave was from her late husband. It was more than his physical attributes. The baron exuded a confidence that she could feel just by standing near him. It was this same confidence that must have helped him on the battlefield, and earned him his title of baron.

All around her, his men were raising a city of tents. A steady stream of horses were being taken over the rise so that the scent of their droppings wouldn't become intolerable. Men were taking bundles of long poles along with the animals to build corrals. A knight needed his stallion because it was the combination of his skill with weapons while mounted that made for a superior fighting man.

Overwhelmed…

She felt far more than that. Isabel tried to resist feeling beaten, but it proved difficult when everywhere she looked there were men she had no means of evicting from her land. Thistle Hill had enjoyed two seasons of peace that she had known would not last, but she still felt the sting of tears in her eyes to see it. She had dared to hope that the king would leave for the Holy Land without bothering her.

Isabel shook her head and entered the keep. It was a large structure rising four stories. The first level had been built to provide shelter from Hell's armies when the Vikings had plundered the land. A second story had followed, to hide all the valuables those Nordic raiders liked to steal.

Isabel's husband had added to the keep, wedding her so that he could use her dowry to continue building. Bechard had planned to impress the king by fortifying the border between Britain and Wales, but he'd also been intent on making sure he had a dwelling that would rival even the king's.

It was also a way to avoid riding for the Crusade.

Isabel climbed to the third floor where four large solars were located. Bechard had held court in one that was lavishly furnished with things he had brought home during his days with the king's army.

Plundered.

Isabel slowed as she neared the opening to the solar. Some might say it was beautiful but she detested the gold and silver goblets her husband had taken such joy in owning. Persian carpets adorned the floor, and three glass windowpanes made of small shapes of colored glass formed brilliant mosaics when the sunlight shone through them. Her husband had taken delight in his things while there were families on his own land in need of shoes.

She preferred the simple wooden shutters in the women's solar. She left her husband's solar behind and sought out her own. The shutters were open now and the spring air filled the large room. She caught a hint of newly turned earth and could hear the river roaring with the abundance of springtime runoff. Two girls were turning the bedding, and they nodded toward her with respect, but did not stop to offer her any formal courtesy.

Those sorts of wasteful gestures had been missing since her husband died. Thistle Hill required everyone's efforts, and it did not need a lady of the manor who was puffed up with her own vanity.

Retrieving her hawking gauntlet, Isabel retraced her steps to the first floor. She turned and crossed through the hall that was filled with long trestle tables and benches. At the far end were wide doorways to the kitchens that were built behind the keep to prevent the smoke from filling the lower floor. The cook looked up as she entered, but Isabel didn't linger. Several girls were turning pastry on the long table in front of the fire while still more chopped vegetables that had been brought up from the cellars. The vegetables were still frozen but would fill the stew pots well.

She returned to the storerooms where the hawks were perched. They would be moved to wooden structures outside when the weather was no longer frigid at night. The animals were critical to Thistle Hill; their room was kept tidy, cleaned twice a day.

"Come, my prince, we've work to do, and I imagine you are hungry," Isabel said.

Griffin lifted his wings in response to her voice, opening his beak to let out a sharp cry. His hunting instincts were keen and he turned several times, eagerly anticipating soaring free.

She pushed her hand into the gauntlet, flexing her fingers to make sure she had the protective leather all the way on her hand. When she extended her arm, Griffin stepped up without being coaxed.

She closed her hand around the length of the

leather strapping that was attached to the hawk's right ankle and carried him out into the sunlight.

She crossed the land that the keep overlooked. The sound of the geese became louder. Once she went over the high ground, the land sloped down toward a large area of marshland. It was an area many considered useless until she kept the geese there.

The birds were happy among the reeds. They built nests along the banks, and the dense growth afforded them security.

"Lady…look…we've more feathers today."

Three small girls came running up from where they had been carefully searching among the reeds for feathers. They held up their prizes, clearly hoping that she would be pleased with their efforts. Long baskets, woven in the shape of cylinders, hung from their backs to help them carry the feathers without damaging them.

"Well done, sweetings."

They were only girls, the youngest six, but they had sharp eyes and were eager to earn their way by searching the reeds every day. Not a single feather was allowed to be lost to the murky waters. Bechard had berated her for keeping the birds alive, but she had proven him wrong in a single season when she produced more feathers for the archers than he did by slaughtering his half of the flock.

"My lady, there are nests now. I counted five with more than two eggs each," the eldest girl reported.

Isabel smiled. "Did you mark them?"

The girls nodded quickly.

"Good. Off to the kitchens, for it seems that you have all earned your way."

The girls scampered off, eager for the promise of warm bread. Their ankles flashed in the afternoon sunlight as their tunics flipped about their knees. On the other side of the marsh, peasant men and their sons worked the plows, turning the fields. Bechard had always complained bitterly of how much marshland he was cursed with, but she had made it profitable. Goose feathers were the only ones used for longbow arrows. Thistle Hill paid its entire due to the crown in feathers now and there were often more to sell. That left all of their crops for winter stock. No one had gone hungry since she had taken over management of the estate.

Pride might be considered a sin, but she was proud of the life she afforded her people. For as far as she could see the fields were being readied for planting. Smoke rose from the village and women were working outside their homes, enjoying the spring weather.

Isabel looked over the marshes and heard the geese. The ganders glided across the water with their heads held high. They stretched out their necks and preened for the females who blended in with the reeds. She walked down farther, searching for the small loops of scarlet ribbon that marked where the nests were. The girls would have tied them to the tops of sturdy reeds so no one made the mistake of disturbing a nest. The goslings would be a welcome addition to the flock.

She pulled the hood off Griffin and the hawk wiggled with excitement. She gave him his freedom and he took to the air with a hard flap of his wings. She watched him soar over the marsh, his eyes searching for rodents.

At dawn she would bring Griffin out again. The

hawk would catch the rats that wanted to steal the
eggs. The hawk dove down and returned to her arm
with a prize in his talon, but she took it from him and
sent him into the air again. The hawk went gladly,
enjoying the hunt as much as filling his belly.

The afternoon was fading and the church bells began
to toll in the distance. Isabel allowed Griffin to keep his
last prize. She turned to head back for mass, leaving the
hawk happily feasting on the small rat he'd caught.

The day seemed as though it had been too long,
with too many unsettling things happening. She
walked toward the church and joined the streams of
people filling it for the service. Mildred was already
standing near the front and made room for her.

The normally quiet service was interrupted by the
sound of spurs grating across the church's stone floor.
Ramon de Segrave and his captains led the rest of
his men into the church. Their mail tunics filled the
church with the clanking sounds of metal, and the
sound of swords being left outside the sanctuary drifted
inside too. The monks froze, their faces reflecting
their surprise at seeing the church completely filled.
Everyone was pressed together, men on the left and
women on the right. The nuns remained in the hallways because there was no room for them anywhere
else. The priest had been kneeling, with his back to
the members of his congregation. He muttered the last
few words of his prayer and stood up, slowly turning
to face his flock.

His eyes widened, but he smiled too. Isabel sighed. At
least someone was glad to have the baron on her land.

She was certainly not.

❧

"The lady sits at the common table," Ambrose muttered.

"My eyes work well," Ramon said.

His fellow knight offered him a mocking look. "Even if your sense of humor does not."

Ramon grunted but grinned at Ambrose. "Am I too serious a companion for you tonight?" He stared at Isabel while his hands tore a round of bread in half. The lady had presented him with her back. It was not exactly a slight, even if he had expected her to sit beside him at the high table. Isabel broke bread with her nurse at the same tables her people ate at.

"You are serious, my lord, yet I can agree you have reason to be so absorbed in your thoughts." Ambrose plucked a section of sausage off a large serving plate with the aid of his dagger. "Considering marriage with yon prickly blossom would consume my good humor as well."

"You mistake spirit for ill temper. Isabel of Camoys is no girl, but a woman. I do not expect to find her meekly obedient. This keep would be in poor condition if she didn't have the spine to run it." Ramon lifted his goblet toward his friend in a silent toast. "I prefer her spirit to half-starved villagers who lack the strength to plow the fields for planting."

His friend leaned toward him. "Exactly my point. She is set in her ways."

Ramon found himself amused by his friend's somberness. "She is not so old. In fact, I believe her father wed her too young."

"Possibly, but that does not change the fact that she sits there, content with shunning the position of honor you have saved for her. She is discontented with the will of her betters."

Ramon winked at Ambrose. "Where has your sense of adventure gone, Ambrose? I recall many a time you enjoyed chasing a fair girl in spite of her words dismissing you."

His friend's expression lightened and he placed an open hand in the middle of his chest as he bowed mockingly. "Your praise is appreciated, even if I must warn you against the sin of envying me my skill."

"You mistake envy for judgment."

Ambrose chuckled. "Since you consider yourself so skilled at the art of seduction, I cannot wait to hear of your plans to win the fair Lady of Camoys who offers you such a fine view of her back."

"Success will require a sound strategy and unfailing persistence." He drew a long swallow from his drinking bowl before finishing his thought. "Two items I have in abundance."

Ambrose laughed loud enough to draw the attention of several people sitting at the lower tables. They considered the knights while leaning closer together to whisper their thoughts in tones that would not travel far.

Ambrose lifted his own drinking bowl. "To your quest, my lord, and may you survive to tell the tale." His eyes twinkled with merriment. "I cannot wait to be amazed."

Ramon didn't answer. His thoughts were concentrated on Isabel. She looked his way, their gazes connecting for a brief moment, but that was long enough. Her eyelashes fluttered, betraying the fact that

she was not as unmoved by his presence as her back
to him declared. A union between them was a sound
idea, even if he hadn't been set on taking a wife. She
wore another full wimple, as befitted a widow, and he
decided that it did not complement her at all. She hid
behind the rules of society when it suited her. More
importantly, she hid from life.

She was too young for widowhood.

Ramon smiled slowly as an idea formed in his
mind. With it came a rush of anticipation that
warmed him. It seemed she was able to raise more
than just his passions.

It had been a long time since a woman had done that.

For a moment, he pondered the wisdom of leaving.
The last time he'd allowed himself to feel deeply about
a woman, she'd left a scar on his heart. Isabel turned
and locked gazes with him. He felt the connection, his
passions rising.

Dangerous or not, there was no way he was leaving.
He lifted his drinking bowl to her, silently sending
along his acceptance of her challenge.

And to the victor went the spoils.

❦

"They are in good humor," Mildred muttered as she
looked past Isabel at the baron and his officers.

"Of course they are. They have taken what they
rode out to claim."

Well, not all that the man had come seeking was his.
She pressed her lips together, feeling a knot of dread
tightening in her belly. Time felt as though it were
crawling by while she waited for the baron's next move.

It's more like anticipation…

There were times she loathed not being able to deceive herself.

"Stop that frowning. The king could have sent someone worse," Mildred chastised.

Isabel felt her temper flaring again. She stood up, irritated by just how quickly Ramon de Segrave was able to destroy her poise. Just the mention of the man was enough, it seemed.

You're the one who insisted on him bathing…

Heat licked at her insides and crept into her cheeks.

She sought out her bed, grateful for the fact that her chamber was one place where she would not have to deal with the baron. But Mildred followed her, intent on finishing their conversation.

"You'll have to think about it, my lady." There was a hard note in Mildred's voice. "Barons are not the sort to be denied what they crave."

"I have nothing from the king that orders me to wed him, Mildred," Isabel muttered. Mildred pressed her lips into a hard line for a long moment as silence filled the chamber. A soft pop from the fire across the room made Isabel flinch. She happily removed her wimple and laid it on a table with a sigh. There was no garment she detested more. Having her hair smashed against her scalp drove her insane.

Mildred drew in a deep breath. "That man doesn't look like he is planning on leaving." She used a firm tone and waved the two other girls that were in the chamber toward the door. Isabel sighed when they were gone. Mildred helped her lift her pelisse up and over her head, leaving her in a thin under tunic.

Mildred didn't have to help her disrobe, but she did anyway, and Isabel was grateful for their friendship. Mildred gave the heavier over gown a few shakes before laying it carefully over the back of a chair. Isabel pulled the under robe over her head and traded it for the worn one Mildred offered her. She slept in her oldest under robes. A few mended spots and thin fabric were no concern once the candles had been snuffed out.

"You can see right through that now. The fabric will fail completely in a few more washings, mark my words."

"Well, until then it is soft and comfortable." As well as the first thing that had pleased her since the baron arrived. "I can see to myself, Mildred, go and tickle your grandson."

Mildred smiled and nodded before heading toward the door. "Brush your hair out or the fairies will come to steal your dreams and leave you naught but nightmares."

Isabel picked up the comb that was laid carefully on the long table sitting against the wall of her chamber. It was a silver one her parents had given her. In spite of how many years ago she'd received it, the comb still shimmered in the candlelight.

Isabel had been too sour with her friend today. Left alone with her thoughts, she felt guilt nip at her.

Two wide candles were set into wooden holders on the table. Their flames flickered yellow and orange. She sat on the side of the bed and pulled her hair over her shoulder, working the tie free that held it in a single long braid.

⟨≈⟩

The way to keep Ramon de Segrave at bay was to make certain the man was busy.

Isabel woke with a start as the thought crossed her mind.

Of course.

It was simple logic.

She rolled over and out of her bed, ignoring how cold the stone floor was. Her toes smarted so she hurried to get dressed. Despite the early hour, there were others stirring. Spring was a busy time—they wanted to have enough to eat during the next winter. She could hear voices floating up from the kitchen and movement in the yard.

"You are up early, Lady Isabel."

She stopped so quickly her skirts kept going and fell back against her ankles with a soft flutter. Ramon de Segrave was blocking her path, his sword in hand. His hair was tousled from the night but his dark eyes were clear and alert. He turned the sword with an expert motion and sheathed it.

Something fluttered through her insides. Something she forbade herself to take note of. But she shivered anyway.

Ramon was wearing only his breeches and a shirt, unbuttoned halfway down his chest.

You saw him in less yesterday…

She focused on his face, only to find his lips curved in a grin.

"Dare I hope you are eager to see me?"

She was shaking her head before she recalled her purpose. "In sooth, I was seeking you. Or your captain."

The baron's grin faded. "Bring your needs to me, Isabel."

He was using her Christian name on purpose. There was a glint in his eyes that dared her to take issue with the familiarity. The intimacy.

You are overly sensitive…

Perhaps she was, but Ramon was overly sure of himself.

"Since my squire has yet to rise, you may assist me."

"I think nae…"

He raised one eyebrow and his lips curved again, this time into a full, arrogant smile. He opened his arms wide, making his shirt billow and split open farther to give her a glimpse of his powerful chest.

"I will happily stay in naught, if that pleases you." He reached down and grasped the bottom of his shirt. "I did not dare to hope the needs that have you searching for me were of so personal a nature."

She jumped forward, pressing her hands against his chest to keep the shirt in place. His body was warm against her fingertips, setting off another spiral of sensation in her belly. She gasped, recoiling, but he followed her, pressing back against her and trapping her hands beneath his.

"I should like to discover more of our reactions to one another."

She tried to tug free but he stepped toward her, backing her into the wall. Her eyes widened as he planted his hands on either side of her, caging her.

"I made my position clear, my lord."

His eyes were full of promise. "As you can see, I am very good at changing your position. I suggest we try many different positions." His tone was dark and alluring but his words were a reminder of cold, hard reality.

"Aye, men enjoy putting their wives into whatever places they like."

His expression tightened. "You accuse me unjustly. One man's sins are not another's to answer for."

"You are the one holding me against the wall."

He shrugged, the motion drawing her attention to just how powerful his shoulders were. The scent of his skin drifted between them, drugging her, dulling her wits.

"And you put your hands on me first."

"Only because you were going to…to…" Her memory offered up a crystal clear recollection of what he looked like in only his skin, and her breath got caught in her throat.

He chuckled softly, lowering his head so that his lips hovered next to her ear. "I never make idle threats."

She growled and shoved at the wall his chest made in front of her. "Enough toying with me! The sun is up and only a fool wastes daylight."

"You tempt me to sin, in more than one way."

She gasped.

He grunted but moved aside. "Be pleased with me, for I am bending to your dictates."

He moved back across the floor and scooped up his tunic from where it was lying over the back of a chair. A length of wool was laid out on the floor in front of the hearth, marking where he'd made his bed.

"You are not bending to my will." She had no idea where the persistence to argue with him came from, only that she had no control over it. "You are not an idle man."

He looked at her once he'd donned the tunic. "My actions are both."

Her lips suddenly twitched and she shook her head. There was a ridiculous urge needling her to flutter her eyelashes. She'd already done it twice before she quelled the impulse.

"Why do you question me, Isabel? What reason have I given you to doubt me?"

His tone was sincere, drawing her toward him as she tried to read his expression. There was a clink as he pulled his sword belt around his lean hips and secured it. His squire came hurrying into the room when he spied his master already awake. Ramon lifted his hand and the boy skidded to a halt. The lad turned and left.

Ramon retrieved his sword from where it was lying on top of his bedding and sheathed it. His boots made soft sounds on the stone floor as he closed the distance between them once again.

"You are correct; I am not idle, nor do I care for guessing games." He stopped in front of her and stared at her. "Why have you set your mind to argue against a match between us?"

"Why have you set your mind to accept it?" His eyebrows lowered but she didn't give him time to reply. "For if it is your own holding you crave, you do not need to wed me for it. I will show you where my quarry is and you can have the stone you need to build the castle you want."

"You have a quarry?" His tone had dipped low, his eye narrowing.

Disappointment swept through her. It really shouldn't have. She should have been pleased to see him realize he didn't need her keep. Yet, the feeling persisted and settled into her chest, like a hard stone against her heart. But she nodded.

"So you see, you do not need Thistle Keep."

He clasped the pommel of his sword, staring at her from behind a hard mask. She stared back at him, letting the sight of his displeasure sink into her. This was the reality of what men were—hard and calculating. They always had a purpose.

"I would like to see your quarry, Lady."

Lady.

Of course he was formal now, for there was no reason to woo her.

So why was she not pleased?

᳀

They heard the stone workers cutting before they saw them. Isabel controlled her mare as Ramon's war horse nipped at her. The mare hurried forward, trotting down the winding road that led into the quarry. It was a huge cliff of rock; the workers pushed the moss back to reveal it. Every stone of Thistle Keep had been carved from it, and many of the buildings on her husband's family grounds too. The stone was valuable and might be sold or traded for the things her land did not provide.

Men looked up, lifting their hands to shade their eyes and see who was coming.

The baron's flag caused an uproar. Men whistled to the other men working farther up on the rock face. They began to stumble down. Many of them were older men, some were the lucky survivors of the king's last Crusade. Several limped from wounds they'd endured while fighting in the Holy Land. They staggered to the bottom of the rock face where a wagon was being loaded.

Isabel slid off her mare, but Ramon swept the area twice before dismounting. His knights were equally untrusting. Ramon looked up to see that four of his men had remained on the crest of the road where they might see any trouble approaching. But Ramon stopped and looked at the large stack of finished stone. She only sold off small amounts in order to keep her quarry secret, so the remainder was substantial.

"The king does not know you have this," Ramon said.

"I have not deceived him."

Ramon cast her a knowing look. "Yet you have not gone out of your way to let him know your full worth."

Isabel didn't lower her eyes.

"I pay my due, my lord, but make sure my people have enough to thrive."

Ramon slid his hand along the edge of a stone block. "You do, and quite cleverly too. But you would have been wed long ago if it were known you had such a prime source of stone on your land. You would have more coin in your coffers if you had sold off some of this, but that would have drawn the attention of prospective grooms."

It was true. Her cheeks colored slightly, but she didn't look away because she couldn't deny how pleased she was. "Is it so terrible to want to be seen as something more than a resource?" For a moment, she saw understanding in his eyes. It was the last thing she expected. "I suppose you know something of that position yourself. How many years did you ride with the king?"

"I barely recall a time when I did not."

She nodded, finding them oddly equal in that moment.

"Men are not the only ones who can manage an estate well."

His expression hardened. "Yet you have no means of protecting what you have."

Her chin rose, pride warming her blood. "I have a stone keep to bar against invaders. One built with stone that I discovered. No one suspected there was naught here but more marshland. I found this place and my husband ignored me because as a woman I could never know the difference between worthy stone and that which is not."

Surprise flashed across his expression. "Well done, Isabel. Well done, indeed." His lips thinned. "But why were you this far from the keep?"

She walked past him to greet one of the senior stone masons lined up and waiting for them. The older man squinted at her but reached up to tug on the corner of his wool cap.

"Do not let me keep you from your work."

The man nodded but looked past her to where Ramon stood. His squire was standing beside his lord, holding a pole with his master's tenant flag fluttering in the breeze. None of the masons moved.

Of course not. Ramon was the highest ranking person there. It was for him to dismiss those waiting.

Isabel felt her temper flare. Ramon locked gazes with her, giving her a glimpse of the unmovable side of his nature. Of course, she'd already decided that there was nothing bendable about the man. Still, the look he gave her made it clear he knew he was trampling her authority.

Men.

"Ambrose."

Ramon's captain quickly dismounted and approached his master. "Survey this site. I want to know what resources we have to work with."

Another stab of disappointment went through her, frustrating her completely.

What ailed her? The man would be gone soon and it was exactly what she craved.

Liar.

She bit her lip as she felt a tingle of heat in her belly. It worked its way lower, until it was between her thighs. Somehow, she must have sinned greatly to be so cursed now.

Yet she discovered herself fascinated by the surge of lust. Oh yes, she knew what it was, even if she had no experience with it. She glanced at Ramon, taking the opportunity to study him while he was engaged in conversation with the master mason.

The heat remained, growing stronger as her skin rippled with awareness. Her clothing felt tight, her breasts heavy. She'd tried so hard to cultivate such feeling for her husband, but had been left with nothing but disgust when she looked at him.

Perhaps she was being punished for her pride. The priest liked to remind her that running Thistle Hill was a man's duty. But she was the one who had managed it and she wasn't interested in repenting. Not a bit. She turned and found her mare. Tugging her gently over to where a rock protruded from the ground, Isabel gained the saddle and turned the animal around.

"Hold." Ramon's voice bounced off the exposed rock face, shocking her. She twisted around to glare at him.

"I have duties to attend to."

"You will not risk your person riding alone, Isabel."

Her eyes narrowed. She sunk her teeth into her lower lip to keep from spitting out what she truly wanted to say. Defiance was boiling up inside of her. A few moments more and she was certain there would be no way to contain her temper. She turned and kicked her mare into motion.

The horse took to the road easily, happy to be leaving the rocky area where there was nothing to graze on. The mare carried Isabel up the road, granting her a moment of relief as Ramon was left behind.

But his men closed in on her, coming down from their position on the point and forcing her mare to stop. She reached down to pat the side of her mare's neck.

"Allow me to pass."

One of the men shook his head, his mail shirt catching the morning light. "I cannot, lady."

"You certainly can."

The man tightened his expression, distaste in his eyes, before he kneed his horse and came toward her. Her mare tossed her head, letting out a sound of distress. Isabel grabbed at the reins, clamping her thighs around the animal to maintain her seat. Ramon's knight plucked her off the back of the mare with ease.

She squealed but landed in front of the man. Her

thigh smarted from the edge of his saddle as he spurred his horse back down the road.

"You have no right," she hissed.

The knight offered no response. He guided his horse to his master and pulled up on the reins. Isabel took her chance to be free, sliding down the side of the horse and jumping away from the powerful animal the moment her feet touched the ground.

She collided with another hard body. Ambrose had a similarly tight expression on his face. He lifted her up, with firm hands on her waist. Ramon reached out and hooked her with a solid arm, pulling her over the front of his horse.

She snarled as he sent her all the way over, until her head was hanging down and her bottom facing the sun. Ramon turned the horse and sent it into motion. The beast's powerful stride made it impossible to roll over and sit up. She was bounced right back down. Her head was bouncing with every stride, turning her stomach until she reached for Ramon's leg, clutching at it out of desperation.

Once her head stopped bouncing, she heard the other riders joining them. Their snickers were low but she heard them. Her temper boiled over. She twisted and curled up, straining her body but demanding that her muscles perform.

Ramon clamped her against his body the moment she succeeded in sitting up. His chest rumbled with a growl that twisted her insides again.

Only this time, she knew what she felt was lust.

For him.

Her temper burned hotter than she thought

possible. She shoved against his chest, but ended up having the small rings of his chain mail shirt pressed into her palms.

"Be still," he ordered.

"I shall not," she snapped, but her breath got caught in her throat when their gazes locked. There was promise flickering in his dark eyes. Promise that excited her.

The motion of the horse made it impossible to keep her distance from him. She ended up in his embrace and prey to another invasion of her senses. This time, the assault came from the scent of his skin. Her face was pressed into his neck, leaving her no option but to draw her breaths next to his skin.

He smelled good.

Christ! Was there no mercy?

The man was intent on owning her. She needed to keep her mind set against allowing him such power.

And yet, his embrace was not unappealing.

Ramon rode right up to the steps of the keep. A cloud of dust was still settling when he let her slip to the ground and followed her.

"You had no right to place rough hands on me," she snarled.

He bent over and tossed her up and onto his shoulder in response. Someone squealed as he stomped into the keep and kept going up the stairs. He carried her right up to her bedchamber before setting her down and closing the door with a kick. The sound of it slamming shut echoed down the tower.

"When it comes to your safety, lady, I have no intention of debating if it is my right or not. I am a knight, it is my duty." He set himself between her and the chamber door.

"I ride my land often. Never have I feared it." She put her hands on her hips, facing off with him. The need to put him in his place was so strong, she shook with it. "Nor do I wish to start."

"Circumstances have changed."

"Of course you believe they have." She laughed dryly, out of despair. "For you view me as something to add to your holding. So of course I must now change my thinking to suit yours."

He ran a hand through his hair, pushing it back from his face. Anger was flickering in his eyes, but he fought to control it. Seeing his effort made her bite back the next barb she wanted to fling at him.

His attention lowered to where her teeth were set into her lower lip. He gave her a tiny nod of approval and drew in a deep breath.

"Hundreds of men have returned with Richard. Hardened, fighting men who have no masters and no home. Half of those men cutting stone have the look of men who know what fighting is. They all know you are an heiress. Who could your people send out if you were taken?"

"They would never harm me. I pay their wages and give them shelter through the winter." She turned and caught sight of her bed.

Was she really having a passionate conversation with the man in her bedchamber?

She turned around and tried to fight off the sense of vulnerability sweeping through her. Temper was suddenly of no use, for it was another form of passion.

Something Ramon had promised her he would satisfy.

"Those men have brethren who are not willing to seek out honest employment. Men who will be drawn to land belonging to a widow with no garrison."

She shook her head. "I do not want to hear this. Life is full of uncertainty. There is no point in dwelling on it."

He reached out and cupped the side of her face, slipping his hand along her jawline and into her hair to hold her steady.

"You will hear it. When it comes to your safety, there will be no discussion. I will act."

His touch set off a wave of craving. It washed through her, pooling deep inside her and leaving her wanting.

Wanton…

She stiffened, trying to break away from his hold. She twisted and heard him muffle a profane word before he released her.

"I will have my way in this, Isabel. Resign yourself to it."

She turned to face him, her robes flaring out. "As I must resign myself to seeing you claim everything I have built here?"

"You cannot protect it."

Her longings died in a sizzle of icy memory. Defeat was looming over her, as great and hulking as the man in front of her. "And you shall take what you please." Tears prickled her eyes. Fighting them back was the only thing she might do.

"Yet the choice to wed is still yours."

She was still blinking away her tears, her vision

blurred. When it cleared, she studied him, trying to discover his purpose. He chuckled at her confusion.

"Do you think I lack an understanding of kindness?"

She nodded before thinking. It was a simple response, completely honest and likely to get her in trouble if she didn't control herself. Yet it was her sincere feeling on the matter.

He moved toward her again, this time stroking her cheek with the back of his hand. So simple, yet it blew across the coals of her craving for him, kindling something more.

Now, there was a sense of trust beginning to flicker inside her.

His lips lifted into a ghost of a grin. "The choice is yours." There was solid promise in his voice.

"Why?"

He withdrew his hand. "Because I was no more pleased than you when the king told me to consider wedding. I have gone to the church doors at the bidding of my parents as well. My wife found the constraints of matrimony too constricting when the king called me away. She cuckolded me and made sure my seed never took root in her womb."

She was stunned. "Why did you not renounce her?"

His jaw tightened. "Because like you, my family arranged the match, and I am a man who respects his father's word and keeps his vows. I was also away on the Crusade and understood how faith does not always satisfy loneliness."

"Did you take a leman with you?" She truly should not have asked, but she couldn't stop herself. Part of her was desperate to know.

He struggled with an answer. She witnessed the battle in his eyes.

"Not with me but I sought comfort once I learned my wife was not being faithful." He drew in a deep breath. "The Crusade is said to be a holy thing and yet it brings out the most unholy actions in men."

"And the women left behind." It was true. There would be babies born the next season and no one would question their origins.

"Richard would find himself without subjects if all kept so strictly to their vows."

Surprise held her silent for a long moment. Once more, they had things in common that she had never thought to share. Doubting a king? It wasn't done, or at least it wasn't spoken of. She had assumed he didn't question his monarch the same way she did.

She'd never thought she could find a companion in a man. It was illogical, after all. Men and women were so different.

She drew in a deep breath to compose herself. If she acted like a lady, he'd have no choice but to respect her wishes. It was safer, more predictable, and less likely to see her falling from grace.

But it's also disappointing…

"Your offer is honorable, but I must decline. Widowhood suits me well." She nodded, at last feeling like the wimple suited her, or at least served her needs. Ramon studied her from behind an unreadable mask.

His eyes darkened and his gaze settled on her lips. "The bold way you look at me says you are discontent, my lady."

"All the more reason for you to take the stone and be on your way."

He chuckled, the sound dark and promising. "And turn my back on the chance to see satisfaction glittering in your eyes after sharing a bed with me?"

"You cannot know such a thing, much less promise me...um—" She clamped her mouth shut, realizing with horror what she was discussing.

"Satisfaction?" A glint appeared in his eyes. "True." He looked at her from head to toe and her mouth went dry at the boldness. "Such a promise requires me to prove my worth to you." His voice dipped into a low growl. "I accept your challenge."

"Wait—"

He captured her gasp beneath his lips, holding her nape as he pressed a firm kiss against her mouth. He kissed her hard but not brutally, moving his mouth across hers and preventing her from clamping her lips shut.

She shivered.

She flattened her hands on his shoulders to push him back, but all she ended up doing was curling her fingers into his clothing to hold him close. His kiss was intoxicating, numbing her senses as she tried to follow his lead and return it. Her heart was racing and she broke away from him, gasping for breath. He let her go. She caught the flash of his victorious grin and then there was a snap as he broke the tie securing her wimple, tugging the garment off her head. Pleasure flared in his eyes. He boldly stroked her hair, sending a ripple of enjoyment through her.

"I will have you, Isabel, and you will find my bed pleasingly warm."

She braced her hand against his chest, but it felt as if she were trying to keep herself from clinging to him. "Nay…it is unwise—"

"It is…*sweet*."

He bent his head and captured her lips once more. This time the kiss was carnal. There was no other way to describe it. She shuddered with need, rooted deep in her belly, curling and twisting through her as he pressed her lips apart and boldly thrust his tongue into her mouth. For one wild moment, she thought she might burst. Sensation tightened to an almost painful tension inside her. It froze her breath in her chest until she felt as though the room were spinning. He boldly cupped her breast, massaging the tender globe and unleashing a burst of pleasure she'd never suspected herself capable of feeling.

"My bed will be a duty you will find to your liking. I swear you will be well satisfied," he promised darkly against her ear. Her nipple had risen into a tight nub. He teased it with his thumb until a soft sound of delight escaped her lips. Pleasure was spiking through her, teasing her skin and leaving gooseflesh. She was fascinated by it, surprised by her own body. "It will be my duty to ensure you find pleasure." His voice was harsh and edged with arrogance. His arms tightened for a moment before he released her. "We shall take vows tomorrow."

He turned and crossed to the door, leaving her feeling his departure far more deeply than she should have. Frustration gnawed on her, stunning her with just how much she enjoyed his touch.

She sank into her bed in confusion, her knees feeling weak as her lips tingled.

Tomorrow?

Her breasts felt swollen and eager for his touch.

Tomorrow was a very long time away.

She shook her head but the sensation persisted. Between her thighs, there was a throbbing that demanded surrender. Confusion swept through her in a thick cloud. How could she desire something she knew would bring her grief?

Was it Satan's trickery? As the church preached? She curled into a ball, trying to will the tide of cravings to subside, but his kiss replayed in her mind instead, her eyes slipping shut as another wave of need washed over her.

What she also thought of was the way she'd pulled him to her. As though he'd been too far away. She'd needed to be pressed against him, from shoulder to knees. It had been stronger than any urge she'd ever had.

She craved him.

*Wanton…lust…sinful…*all the words she knew to shame herself weren't working. Instead of feeling guilty all she felt was a sense of being trapped. It wasn't the wedding vows that would make her his possession, it would be her own weakness for him.

Christ help her, for her defenses were already crumbling.

Three

WHISPERS WOKE HER.

Opening her eyes took more effort than it should have. Isabel allowed herself to linger for a moment, hoping whoever was near might leave her in peace. She felt in desperate need of privacy.

"Do you think he ravished her?"

"Is she dead, maybe?"

"He's so large a man, little wonder she's senseless. A member like that would force the breath from a woman…"

Her eyes flew open. "Naught of the sort happened."

There were gasps, but what made her sit up was the soft *hmph* she heard. Mildred was looking at her with doubt, and the young maid standing beside her noticed it, her eyes widening with alarm.

"He did not have me," Isabel defended herself as she got to her feet. Her words fell on deaf ears. The maid was already hurrying from the chamber, eager to tell her tale.

"Mildred," Isabel beseeched. "Forbid them to gossip. Please."

"It will be truth soon enough. That man has his mind set." Mildred pegged her with a long, steady look before her lips rose into a smile of approval. "This will be a far better match for you, my lamb."

She turned and made her way through the door. Isabel found herself battling a second urge to sink down into her bed.

But she squared her shoulders. She wasn't going to accept fate's odd sense of humor so easily. Ramon needed to be gone. If he wasn't near, she would forget him and his appeal.

She was just going to have to ensure that he had a reason to forget about her.

❧

Supper was the last meal of the day. It was not the largest but it was the only time the inhabitants of Thistle Keep allowed themselves to linger at the trestle tables in the great hall. The sun had set, so work would have to wait until dawn. The scent of roasted meat filled the hall, along with bread and stewed vegetables. Once again, Isabel was sitting at the common tables. Ramon stared at her, enjoying the way the lady fought not to look at him.

"More rabbit, milord?" He paid the serving girl no attention at all. She leaned over in front of Ramon, holding a platter out and making sure he had a clear view down the front of her open robes—a generous amount of cleavage for his enjoyment. A long lock of her flaxen hair teased his cheek. She sent him a saucy look full of passion.

The collar of his tunic suddenly felt tighter.

Ramon locked gazes with her. "My captain will be more appreciative of your efforts, madam. I am to wed on the morrow."

Ambrose choked but controlled himself when the maid gave him her full attention. She brushed right up against him as she served him, a soft, husky sound rising from her lips before she straightened and went on her way.

"Ale...*milord*?"

Ramon jerked as a second maid pressed up to his side. This one had dark hair and rolled her lips in when their gazes met. She traced the handle of the pitcher she held. Up...down...and up again.

His collar was definitely too tight.

His squire bumped into her, holding Ramon's goblet out in front of her. She tipped the pitcher up but shot Ramon an invitation when she was finished.

"Methinks your bride is less settled than you are when it comes to taking vows on the morrow." Ambrose was trying to contain his mirth, leaving his face looking pinched while his eyes sparkled.

Ramon jerked his attention back to Isabel. He caught only a flash of her satisfied expression before she turned away and gave him nothing but the back of her wimple to look at.

He was going to have every wimple in the keep burned on the morrow.

"Then best I go and see to her contentment."

Ramon pressed his hands flat on the tabletop to rise. Ambrose reached for his forearm. "Be considerate and sit a while longer. I have no plans to wed and would happily enjoy the efforts being put forth."

Ambrose cast a long look toward the side of the hall where the passageway opened up, allowing food to be brought in from the kitchens. There were three more women lined up, waiting to serve the high table.

"So kind of Richard to take the men away for so long…" Ambrose muttered softly. "I admit, I have never seen this advantage to Holy Crusades. We should have retired years ago."

The women were rosy-cheeked with excitement as he sent sly, hopeful smiles toward them. Each appeared freshly bathed, their hair brushed and hanging free, tempting him to feel it. They giggled as they mounted the stairs to climb to the raised platform the high table was placed on.

Ramon looked back at Isabel. She was ignoring him. But her companion was watching the high table, astonishment on her face. Her lips were moving as she sent a stern look at her young mistress. Isabel shook her head and squared her shoulders.

Ramon held out his hand for his goblet. His squire tripped as he tried to perform his duties, too busy watching the women serving the table.

"Vixen," he growled softly. He took a long sip from his goblet and nodded.

Aye, vixen it was.

❧

"You are playing a dangerous game," Mildred warned.

"Ramon de Segrave needs to be on his way. I am simply helping him notice that I am nothing exceptional."

Isabel laid her over robe aside and turned so Mildred could loosen the ties in the back of her under robe.

Mildred humphed as she tugged the knot loose. "He will demand what he wants from you, sure enough. Or did you not learn that when he tossed you over his saddle this morning?"

"What I learned was that I should not be changing my mind when it comes to wedding him. Such would be a distraction."

"Oh aye. A man like that is surely a distraction, on that I agree."

Mildred lifted the under robe away. Isabel released the tie on her wimple, sighing as she tugged the thing off her head.

"You detest that wimple," Mildred scolded. "Yet you wear it now because of Ramon. Would it not be simpler to enjoy what you may from the man? You adore children. I recall how disappointed you were when you bled."

"I shall not wed him."

Mildred pressed her lips into a disapproving line. "Stubbornness is a form of pride and that is a sin. You were not unmoved by his touch. I saw the proof with my own eyes. He stirred your passions."

"Passion is a form of lust and that is also a sin," she argued.

Mildred surprised her by offering her nothing but a gentle smile. "I forget you are yet young."

"What do you mean by that?" Mildred shook her head and headed toward the door. "Mildred? I do not understand."

"I know you do not, my lamb. But 'tis for Ramon de Segrave to teach you in this matter."

"I wish no lessons from him. Our life is good. There is no need to change."

"Are you saying you'd rather not make improvements until you are desperate for them?" Mildred shook her head disapprovingly. "Careful. Fate has a cruel side to her nature."

"Can I not simply be grateful for what I have, without longing for more?"

Mildred didn't hear her. Or if she did, she paid Isabel's argument no mind. The door closed, leaving Isabel with only a single candle for company.

The chamber was suddenly darker than she recalled. Larger maybe…colder…

Enough.

She chided herself. There was no reason to feel lonely. Her bed had always been a sanctuary, the one place Bechard was certain not to bother her. When he'd wanted to use her, he'd summoned her to his chamber.

She shuddered with disgust and climbed into the bed. The bedding was newly washed and smelled like sunshine. The candle was a beeswax one, gently lending the sweet scent of honey to the night air.

Perfect.

Yes, perfect, and she would make sure that she focused her thoughts on what was most important.

She was happy in her life. Content beyond measure. She reached for her comb and began to work the tangles from her hair.

But the door opened and the comb slipped from her fingers. Ramon de Segrave strode boldly into the chamber.

"Are you insane?" She'd meant to sound demanding, but her voice was too high.

Ramon lifted one eyebrow in a lazy manner, as if to convey that his appearance in her bedchamber wasn't alarming.

"Does your tone mean you doubt my honor, lady? You seemed quite willing to test me this evening. I am here to prove myself worthy."

Her chemise suddenly felt nearly transparent as opposed to simply thin. She fought the urge to cross her hands over her breasts. The baron's squire walked across the chamber and placed his master's goblet on the table.

"Appearing in my bedchamber is not proving yourself, my lord."

The baron sat down and his squire immediately set to work removing the spurs that were tied to each boot.

"How else will you know for certain that I did not partake of the generous feast you laid before me at supper?"

Her cheeks stung. "I trust my people to speak the truth." She was stammering. Ramon's squire looked at her curiously.

"Mind your gaze, Alfred," Ramon corrected the youth.

The youth turned his attention back to his master.

"As I told you this morning, Isabel, bring your needs to me, for I fully intend to bring mine to you."

The spurs made a soft chink when they were set on the tabletop next to the goblet. The boy then began removing one boot. Isabel blinked rapidly, but the sight of the man sitting in her bedchamber remained.

"Very well. You have assured me that you are—"

He tilted his head to one side and fixed her with

a stare that was unrelenting. "Willing to rise to any challenge you give me?"

Ramon let his gaze slide down her length. Behind the sheer, worn fabric of her chemise, her nipples drew tight.

"Be assured that when you challenge me, I will rise to the occasion." His voice deepened, becoming sensuous. Her cheeks heated but she couldn't make herself look away. The promise glittering in his eyes stoked something inside her.

The squire removed the second boot and set them neatly next to one another near the chair. The baron stood and the boy unhooked his sword belt.

Isabel stood and shook off her fascination with him. "This is my chamber. Leave."

He offered her only a soft grunt while his squire took his sword from him. Isabel nearly choked, for no knight went anywhere without his sword. The boy laid the weapon on the table within reach of the bed.

"There are chambers that my husband used on the north side of the tower," she insisted.

The squire climbed up onto a stool and began to pull his master's over tunic off.

"Yes, Ambrose and my captains are making use of those chambers. The expansion of this fortification will include more chambers."

"Since it seems you are intent, I shall sleep elsewhere."

The baron suddenly sent his squire away with a flick of his fingers and stepped into her path. The boy was halfway to the door before Isabel realized she would soon be alone with Ramon.

"Wait—" Her hand flew up to cover her lips when

the boy turned, a stunned look on his face. He didn't stop moving, and continued on through the doorway while she sucked in a gasp of horror.

"Do not ever countermand my orders to my squire. My training is what will keep them alive."

She shook her head. "I know…I didn't think before I spoke." She suddenly recalled exactly why she had been so brazen as to interfere between a knight and his squire. "Yet it is your own fault. You have no right to shock me in such a fashion."

Determination glittered in his eyes, and she recalled the look very well from when he had stood up in the bathhouse. She should have combed her hair before the nightmare had arrived.

"What shocks you, lady?" He crossed his arms over his chest. "A knight of honor may share a bed with a widow so long as his sword is placed down the center of it." He reached over and lifted his sword in one sure motion and placed it on the surface of the bed.

"That is acceptable within the chivalric code." Triumph flickered in his eyes as his lips curled into a victory smile.

The man was attempting to outmaneuver her.

Isabel tried to resist admitting that Ramon de Segrave was very good at forming strategy.

Far too good.

"I will sleep elsewhere." She kept her tone low, to hide the emotions that were roaring through her. She struggled to remain poised and calm so the beast wouldn't know how much he needled her.

"There is not a foot of space anywhere in this keep not being used by my knights."

"But—"

He turned and picked his goblet back up. "I have spoken."

Isabel lost her patience. "Indeed you have, Lord de Segrave, but that does not mean I shall meekly obey you. One of the reasons I have declined to wed you is that I have no desire to be submissive."

"Ahh…" He chuckled. "I have noticed you play the game of meekness when it suits you and only when you have something to gain from doing so."

She felt her breath lodged in her throat. "That is insulting of you to say," she sputtered at last.

He watched her over the rim of his goblet, his eyes full of some emotion that looked very much like enjoyment. "I mean it as a compliment, Isabel. I enjoy the vixen in you." He used her name deliberately, drawing it out in his deep voice. His gaze traveled over her hair. "You are too young for a widow's wimple."

"Yet I am a widow, and your eyes are too bold by far." Her hands settled on her hips. "A true knight does not leer at a lady."

One of his dark eyebrows rose. "Ah…but a lady does not look at a man's form, even if he stands in front of her." He set the goblet aside. "Yet you looked, and I daresay you were pleased at the sight."

"You dare too much." He was also too correct for her comfort. "It seems you have honor only when it suits your purpose."

His eyes flashed with warning. Isabel stepped back, but it was too late.

"As I warned you, question my honor and I shall be happy to show you how I deal with a vixen."

"I am not a vixen," she said. "Go back to the hall if that is the sort of entertainment you seek."

She stopped, but he remained in place, watching her from beneath lowered brows. "To the women you set upon me?"

The judgment in his tone was impossible to hide from. What she had done was questionable at best. Less than honorable at worst. But she wasn't repentant. She squared off with him.

"It was no worse than you hauling me across your saddle for the entertainment of all."

"It was," he agreed.

His expression should have filled her with foreboding. Instead she discovered herself pleased to have landed a blow worthy of gaining an admission from him.

Isabel lifted her chin, victory warming her. "If you seek some sort of apology, you shall not hear it. You had no right to treat me as you did, or to kiss me."

A warning flashed in his eyes. "What I seek is the ability to keep you from retiring after delivering your last blow. When you start a competition with me, be prepared for me to battle until the bitter end." He closed the distance between them once more and she winced as she heard each soft footfall. "And you enjoy my kisses."

It was on the tip of her tongue to deny his statement but the glitter in his eyes warned her against it. He wanted a fight with her, for it would lead to passion. She drew in a deep breath and searched her mind for logical arguments. She was far too conscious of the bed so close behind her.

You want to stroke his skin again…

"I have nothing to assure me the king in fact blessed you with permission to marry me."

He chuckled. She retreated from the look that entered his eyes; a shiver shot down her back from the unmistakable glitter of anticipation in those dark orbs.

"If you fail to respect my honor as a knight by doubting my word—"

"I did not say I doubted your honor," she interrupted. Mildred would have been horrified.

"You accused me of not telling the truth about the king's blessing upon our match." His eyes flashed with unmistakable challenge. "Vixen."

He loomed over her, closing the last pace between them. Her heart was suddenly beating faster and harder. Her breathing deepened, drawing in the scent of his skin. A strange awareness of him flooded her. She noticed the scent of his skin and heard the slight rasp of his breath. Every one of her senses was keener and more attuned to him, her skin feeling more sensitive, as though the most delicate touch might startle her.

Anticipation was driving her mad.

"With you, there is part of me that enjoys dispensing with chivalry." His eyes darkened and slid down the length of her body. She gasped and sensation twisted through her while he lingered over her curves.

Part of her enjoyed the look on his face. There was no way to ignore the fact that she liked him appreciating her form. It was something no polished words might truly convey.

Excitement ignited inside her.

But she could never admit it.

Never indulge it.

Unless she wanted to accept everything that came with it. It would be nothing sort of complete surrender.

"The chivalric code maintains civilized behavior." She didn't care for how disappointed she sounded. Or wounded.

He chuckled again, low and deep, and the sound triggered a new wave of emotion that washed down her body. This time she felt it rippling across her skin, and she stood frozen in place as he reached out to stroke the side of her face.

"Yet you sound so…torn."

She jerked; it was overwhelming and she couldn't remain still. Isabel drew in a stiff breath and stepped back only to collide with the bed.

"I am. Yet I am also resolved." She tried to make her tone smooth, but it betrayed her with a high pitch.

"I disagree, Isabel." He stepped toward her and she felt his heat radiating out from his body. "I would test your resolve to remain uninterested in sharing a marriage bed with me."

"It is merely lust. When you depart, it will subside." She shouldn't have said such a thing; it wasn't a topic any lady discussed, but her mind wasn't working properly. In truth, she felt more like the vixen he called her. A creature responding to her instincts instead of logic.

And he was once more someone she had a great deal in common with. Formality was slipping away so easily, making it feel so natural to speak her mind with him.

To share her secrets.

"Lust has its place in passion." His tone was pure temptation. Ramon lifted his hand once more, this time cupping the entire side of her face. She shivered, her body responding instantly to his touch. "And passion was clearly missing in your last union, which makes it difficult for you to trust my word. I am happy to prove my worth."

His hand smoothed along her jawline and down the length of her neck. She wanted to let her eyes shut and be immersed in the sensation.

"Such would be…sinful."

She tried to hide how much she was enjoying it.

How much she wanted to rise to his bait.

He leaned down and his breath teased against her ear. "I am being truthful. Isn't that more honorable than any words I was taught to speak because of chivalry? Shall I rattle on about how virtuous you are when in fact I am consumed by how much I enjoy your spirit? Which pleases you more?"

She shivered, blushing and enjoying his praise. She had never been the fairest. Every maid she'd set on him at supper was more comely. Yet when he pulled back, his gaze was full of desire for her.

His hand glided over her collarbone and onto her chest. Sensation raced downward and she felt her breasts tingling with anticipation. Her flesh was eagerly clamoring for his hand to proceed downward, begging for a caress. Behind the thin fabric of her under robe, her nipples drew into hard peaks that raised the fabric.

"Ah…" He groaned softly against her ear. "Unmistakable proof that your body is pleased."

"It must be…wrong…somehow…" But she was suddenly unsure as to why it mattered at all.

He moved his hand back up, smoothing along her neck, and disappointment coursed through her. Her breast craved his touch and her nipple ached from being denied.

He cupped her chin and raised her face.

"Your honesty pleases me, Isabel. More than any polite, simpering reply every could."

His lips pressed against the side of her neck, drawing a cry from her lips. She wasn't sure what the sound meant, only that she was powerless to contain it. Her mind was struggling to sort all of her thoughts into logical order and failing miserably. Impulses began to rule her. She lifted her hands to push against his chest, only to discover she liked the way he felt. She spread her fingers over the hard ridges of muscle that lay beneath the single layer of his tunic.

His lips pressed a trail of kisses along her neck, and she lifted her head so he might continue. Pleasure bloomed under each kiss, her legs quivering with delight. Her nipples hardened even more and she leaned toward him, seeking out his embrace.

He cupped her cheeks and this time, when his mouth found hers, she was eager for his kiss, her lips parting beneath the pressure from his and returning the motions. She expected him to take what she surrendered and enjoy his victory immediately. But he lingered over her mouth, tasting her lips with delicate motions, in no hurry to raise her chemise.

Yet she felt impatience brewing deep in her belly.

The tip of his tongue swept along her lower lip,

sending sweet delight through her. His hands glided down her neck, unleashing gooseflesh as they traveled to her collarbone and then down onto her chest. The breath froze in her lungs as her breasts tingled with excitement. Once again, he didn't rush but smoothed his open palms over her shoulders in small circles before beginning to trace a path down toward her more delicate flesh. Isabel discovered her back arching, lifting her chest up so her breasts might receive what they craved.

Ramon didn't disappoint her. He brushed his thumbs across the puckered peaks of her nipples in a touch that was almost too soft to feel.

A sigh surfaced from her chest, and he took advantage of her open mouth, his tongue gently probing inside until he touched her own. At the same time his hands closed around her breasts, cupping each tender globe gently. A jolt went through her, traveling down to her belly where it twisted and turned so violently she recoiled.

It was too much.

She pushed at him, shoving him back so that their kiss was broken. Her senses cleared enough for her to slip along the smooth surface of the wall, and she heard him snarl when he ended up facing the gray stones instead of her.

"I prefer…" Her lungs labored to draw in breath to supply her racing heart. "I prefer the Code of Chivalry between us in place of this…savageness."

Ramon muttered something profane. His voice was edged with the same disappointment that was racing through her. It was sharp and harsh, making her want to flinch. Confusion flooded her. She had always been relieved to be free from her husband's embrace.

"There was nothing savage between us." His eyes narrowed but she didn't lower her chin.

"Savage in the way that it prevents me from controlling my response. Your touch unleashes a wildness in me. I cannot control it." She was confessing, pleading with him to not exploit her weakness.

His face flushed but his eyes narrowed with satisfaction. It was a frank, male sort of pleasure, one that made her feel like she'd witnessed some sort of secret that life had hidden from her until now.

It was fascinating and so very tempting. She teetered on the edge of reason, ready to deny her doubts and embrace the churning storm his touch unleashed.

He reached for her but she put her hand into his, blocking his advance. It was a feeble attempt to hold back someone as powerful as he was, but he drew in a stiff breath and stopped.

His lips lifted for a moment into a grin that transformed his face into something very charming indeed.

"I will earn your trust."

Heat surfaced in her cheeks and the reaction irritated her. How could she blush now when the man had been handling her breasts but a moment past?

Because he touched your tender feelings with his words...

Such was more terrifying than having the man claim her body, for her feelings were the only thing she might keep for herself.

"Dawn will arrive early, with a great many tasks," she said.

She turned her back on him but discovered that

resisting the urge to look over her shoulder at him was almost too strong to ignore. Isabel forced herself to walk away from him and not check to see what he was about. They would observe the rules of chivalry; she demanded that of herself. The alternative was too uncertain to contemplate.

His sword still lay in the center of her bed. She shuddered at the sight of it but forced herself to reach for the bedding and lift it so she might lie down. She tried hard not to look at him. She kept her eyes on the canopy that stretched over the top of the bed to keep the heat inside.

She strained to hear him approaching the bed, flinching when she detected a single soft step. A soft chuckle followed.

"What worries you, lady?"

What indeed?

Heat was still curling through her.

The bed shook and the ropes groaned as he sat down.

"That is obvious, my lord. I have never had a man in this chamber."

The sword between them moved toward her because the baron took up more than half the bed. He pulled the bedding up and over his shoulders, and the sword slid onto her chest.

"It is obvious, I agree. Yet we will not become more familiar to one another if we are separated by stone walls."

She lost the resolve to keep her attention from him, turning her head and smacking her chin on the pommel of his sword. He moved quickly, lifting the weapon up and away from her before she finished sucking in a harsh breath.

"Sleeping with a sword between us sounds all well and good until we must actually do it." He sat up and sheathed the sword before leaning it against the wall near his pillow. "In a bed this small."

Isabel held the bedding against her body, grateful to have something to hide her hard, pebbled nipples.

"This bed is quite sufficient for my needs."

He turned to her and the ropes groaned ominously. He placed his elbow against the bed and cradled his head in his hand. Heat licked its way down her body, making the thick coverlet too warm. He was far too attractive.

"Sufficient?" His eyes narrowed as he considered her lips once again. The delicate skin tingled with the memory of how much she had enjoyed his kiss. "Ah…but I would see that you find this bed pleasing instead of merely sufficient. Dare I suggest you find true ecstasy? Whereas you have always settled for merely sufficient?"

She laughed. Scoffed, really. The sound resulted from memories of her husband's boasting whenever he had decided to partake of his marital privileges.

The baron frowned, his eyes opening wider. Isabel sobered and discovered her eyelashes fluttering to conceal her emotions from his keen gaze.

"I'll bid you a restful sleep, Lord de Segrave."

She closed her eyes but jerked them wide again when she felt his fingers gliding softly across her cheek. She quivered, becoming irritated by how much she enjoyed his touch, unable to stop the soft sigh that escaped her lips.

The sound pleased him. She saw it in his eyes.

"There can be much pleasure between a man and wife. Your husband was a selfish man for not demonstrating such to you." His tone was soft and serious, tempting her.

Lust truly was a destructive force.

She had to resist its pull.

Because it would lead her to hell…on earth. Only courting was sweet, and so vastly different from what marriage would allow Ramon to demand of her.

That reality of marriage would be a bitter duty. She knew it well. Somehow, she had to ignore her emotions, which were willing to lead her astray.

❧

Jacques Raeburn sat on his horse, watching Ramon de Segrave's men. They were camped in perfect position to defend themselves, but there was no sign of Ramon's tent. His banner was not flying anywhere in the camp, which meant he'd taken possession of a bedchamber.

"We are not riding up to the keep, my lord?" Jacques's lieutenant asked.

Jacques Raeburn shook his head.

A woman left alone was easy prey for a man. How irritating that the king had made it possible for Ramon to make it to Thistle Keep ahead of him.

It was his duty to marry Isabel and regain the land his brother had left her. Jacques felt his mood darkening as he thought about being saddled with a wife who had failed to give his brother an heir.

That didn't matter to him. His father had

commanded him to wed her, and he had to see the duty done. He also had to keep her alive long enough to avoid suspicion when he did rid himself of her. At least he might enjoy her during their marriage.

"We will find a suitable place to occupy before I have the lady brought to me."

"By force, my lord?"

Jacques nodded stiffly. "If necessary, but with restraint. I need to woo her into wedding me."

His lieutenant looked unsure. "If she is brought by force, how will you achieve such a goal?"

Jacques grinned and the expression changed his face completely. He was a handsome man. It was one of the reasons he had been sent to serve Richard, instead of his brother. His father had hoped Jacques might attract an heiress in Europe with his comely features.

Instead he found himself back in England with the task of reclaiming the wife who had failed to breed a grandson for his father. He'd have to secure her and let time soften her resolve. Time was growing short, and it was apparent that Ramon de Segrave was intent on having Thistle Keep.

Jacques refused to allow that to happen and he would do whatever it took to prevent it.

Four

"CHRIST'S WOUNDS!" MILDRED SWORE LOUD ENOUGH to wake the dead.

The sun was just warming the horizon. Isabel opened her eyes, feeling as though she'd slept little.

Ramon sat up with a snarl. He yanked his sword from its sheath with a roar as he turned on Mildred.

"No!" Isabel threw herself down the length of the bed, stumbling onto her feet and flattening herself in front of Mildred. "'Tis only my nurse."

Mildred froze, staring wide-eyed at the baron.

Ramon blinked to clear sleep from his mind before he grunted, "'Tis not a wise thing to surprise a man so newly returned from the Crusade."

The door burst open, and Ambrose stood there in only his shirt with a sword in his hand.

"'Tis only her nurse," Ramon growled.

Ambrose swept the chamber twice before he lowered his weapon. Beyond his wide shoulders, Isabel could see the chamber on the other side of the keep. Two women watched from the doorway, holding a length of bedding to cover themselves. One gasped and scurried back into the chamber.

"The service at Thistle Keep is quite unmatched," Ambrose murmured with a satisfied grin. He aimed an amused look toward Ramon before turning and making his way back to the other chamber. They heard a pair of giggles before the door shut.

"Church is going to be crowded this morn," Mildred muttered.

"Not on my account," Isabel replied. "I have no special blessings to seek."

Ramon gave her a hard look but said nothing. Soon his squire arrived and Mildred was gathering up Isabel's under robe. Isabel should have been pleased that Ramon was holding his tongue, but all it did was stir up a feeling that she had never had for Bechard. Her husband hadn't cared who was present when he berated her.

Ramon was different. The idea stuck in her thoughts as she finished dressing and headed out of the chamber.

She chuckled softly, her cheeks turning red. She gathered up a fist full of her robes and ran. She arrived out of breath at the morning service but at least no one questioned her about those red cheeks.

&

Her morning meal wasn't even half finished when Isabel found herself blushing again.

The hall was full of hushed whispers and quick glances toward her and Ramon.

She hurried through the last spoonfuls of her porridge and rose.

"You have a fine appetite this morning, Lady Isabel," Ramon called from the high table, his voice deep and full, echoing off the hall's stone walls.

She bit her lip, trying to quell the urge to turn and look at Ramon. But everyone in the hall was looking at her, their eyes bright with curiosity. She turned and smiled sweetly but determinedly.

"Yes. The day holds many challenges. I intend to be fortified."

Ramon curled his fingers around his goblet. "It does indeed. I enjoy challenges and women with the strength to meet them."

"That is a solid truth," Ambrose agreed with a wolfish grin. "Know you this lady. I have seen this man outlast every opponent he has chosen to pit himself against."

Isabel raised her eyebrow. "A common enough claim from men, yet so often disputed by women."

Ambrose's lips twitched, his chest shaking with amusement. But it was the look in Ramon's eyes that stole her breath. For a moment, she indulged in it. The look made her shiver, sensation moving down her body in response to his dark stare.

Everyone was watching her, enjoying the double meaning in their words. She wanted to lift her chin and let Ramon know that he was going to be disappointed, but the way her heart was still racing made her bite her lip. She looked back at him, locking gazes once more, and feeling her belly twist.

Challenge?

Oh aye. It is going to be a challenge to deny the burly knight.

Yet she was up to it.

She turned with a swirl of her robes and ended up facing the priest who stood in the arched doorway, his hands tucked into the wide openings of his sleeves. The inhabitants of Thistle Keep suddenly looked down at their bowls, their expressions becoming bland as their whispers died.

Hell on Earth.

Exactly as she'd known it would be.

❧

Ramon chuckled.

"That must be the first time I've known you to be amused by a priest taking interest in your affairs," Ambrose mocked.

Ramon took another swallow from his goblet. "Better mine than yours, my friend. You owe me gratitude for diverting him. He has a great amount of zeal for his calling and his flock."

Ambrose lifted his goblet in a salute. "Many thanks."

"Of course, once I wed, the priest will have no reason to direct his interest toward me."

Ambrose grinned. "I will do my best to keep the man amused." The maid serving him smothered a giggle as she tossed him a saucy look. Ambrose growled softy. "My very, very best," he muttered.

❧

Griffin was eager for a morning hunt.

Isabel lifted him, glaring at the sun because it was far later in the morning than usual for taking Griffin out.

But she forbade herself to linger over her discontent.

The air was losing its crispness and the grass was growing high. The fields were full of sprouting crops. In the distance, she heard the geese calling to each other. She moved toward them, lifting her forearm and letting Griffin fly free. He let out a screech as he took to the air, climbing quickly. He stretched out his wings, the longer feathers at the tips flared out, and began to circle once he'd reached a good height. Isabel shaded her eyes to keep him in sight.

Isabel moved around the strings marking the nests, careful to give the mothers enough space. There were a few warning honks from birds sitting on eggs, but Isabel moved away on slow, controlled steps.

Griffin flew down and popped back up with a rat. Isabel raised her arm but he screeched at her and flew to a tree to enjoy his prize.

Griffin was too hungry to wait. It was Ramon's fault for making her late.

She frowned. Once Griffin's appetite was sated, he wouldn't be eager to hunt.

You are simply cross because you don't want to return to the keep.

Well, yes. The man was testing her resolve. The best way to maintain her desire to remain unwed would be to avoid contact with him. She looked out over the fields. The breeze was carrying the scent of fresh growth and turned earth. The little bits of string marking the nests filled her with happiness because spring was upon them. The first days of summer would arrive with the goslings. There would be new fruits and the sight of the fields ripening to make everyone at Thistle Keep feel content.

She was a good mistress and didn't need a master.

There was nothing to fear.

But the sound of hooves approaching made her turn with a frown. Her time was finished.

The knights bearing down on her didn't look like Ramon's. Isabel studied them for a long moment, trying to decide what it was that made her belly twist with apprehension.

It was the leers on their faces.

They were leaning low over the necks of their horses, urging the beasts faster…

They were intent on running her to the ground.

She turned and grabbed her robes.

"Too late, my lady!"

The pounding was so loud it shook the ground beneath her feet. Her heart raced but the horses were much faster. She turned and ran toward the marsh, hoping the horses would shy away from the murky water. Geese reared up, beating the air with their powerful wings to defend their nests.

The horses screeched but charged in after her.

"You are just the prize I've been seeking!"

Someone grabbed the back of her robes and her hair. He yanked her off her feet, dragging her onto the back of the horse. Pain exploded in her side as she was dropped in place in front of the knight.

"Let's claim our reward!" her captor declared to his companions.

Isabel turned her head, trying to see through the tangle of her hair. She was heaving, trying to catch her breath, as the knight wheeled his horse around and headed out of the marshes.

A gander chased them, biting at the legs of the horse. She caught a glimpse of its mate, frantically trying to salvage her nest, which was torn to pieces.

Isabel snarled, fighting her way up. "Put me—"

A hard blow sent her back down, blackness washing over her in a thick wave.

❧

"She's rousing, milord."

The voice was far away. Isabel's head ached and all she wanted to do was drift back into sleep. It was so tempting. There was no pain in the dark embrace of slumber.

But someone tossed cold water into her face.

When she opened her eyes, there was a dark-eyed woman leaning over her, an empty cup in her hand.

"As I said, she is roused."

The woman turned and moved away. Isabel stared at her, wondering if she was still locked in a dream. She was in a tent and lying on a bed that was covered in soft silk and an abundance of pillows. The woman's eyes were outlined in something black. They were also slightly almond-shaped, making her look sensuous. Her skin was a warm honey color and her fingernails were long.

Isabel shook her head but the sight of the tent and the strange woman remained.

The woman had long hair that flowed down her back in a curtain of dark satin. She wore only a robe that fluttered as she moved and looked like it was made of silk.

"You never fail to satisfy me, Rauxana."

The woman stopped near a man who was washing his hands in a bowl near the door of the tent. She lifted a pitcher and poured water over his hands. Setting it aside, she picked up a length of linen for him.

"Serving you is my reason for life."

He smiled at her, reaching out to cup her face. Isabel pushed herself up and brushed her hair from her face as the man leaned toward the woman and kissed her deeply.

They didn't care that she was present. No shame at all. The kiss was deep and passionate. The woman pressed toward the man, moving her body against his as she boldly stroked him from chest to groin, her hand closing around his length.

"Later," he announced as he broke away from her.

"As you wish," she purred. "I shall prepare myself for you, master."

She disappeared between the flaps of the tent opening, leaving Isabel facing her captor.

"Why did you send your men to abduct me?"

"I intend to wed you, Isabel of Camoys."

Isabel stood up, the bed suddenly burning her. The man watched her, grinning.

"And this is the manner in which you choose to begin a courtship?"

He moved to where a chair rested on a beautiful Persian carpet. He sat down, settling himself in it before looking back at her.

"I am Baron Jacques Raeburn. Bechard was my brother."

"I am sorry. The fever took him quickly," Isabel said quietly.

"Perhaps because you did naught to save him."

She drew in a stiff breath, a tingle of fear teasing her nape. He was a baron, the highest law in the kingdom with the king away. "There are witnesses to assure you I did everything possible."

Jacques tilted his head to one side and contemplated her. He was far more pleasing to the eye than Ramon, but she found him repulsive.

"I don't really care if you smothered Bechard with your tits. You seem to have a nice, plump set of them." She gaped. Jacques snickered at her horror. "But the fact that my dear brother is dead leaves me suffering my father's demands to retrieve our property." His gaze lowered to her breasts. "He ordered me to wed you, fuck you, and plant a Raeburn babe in your belly."

"You are being overly blunt, sir." She squared her shoulders and glared at him.

"Because I said *fuck*?" He spread his legs apart and rubbed the bulge his tunic was covering. "Or *tits*?"

"Both." Her tone was sharp. There was no way she'd show the brute any fear.

He smiled wide and pushed out of the chair. Fear twisted through her belly but she stood in place. Jacques slowly circled her, leering at her. When he passed behind her, it took every ounce of control she had to stay still. She would not let him see her unsettled. Couldn't. A panicked animal was very soon slain.

"I plan to enjoy…both," he muttered next to her ear.

She jumped and turned to face him. "You shall not. Although you have kidnapped me, I will not be taking vows with you."

But she was in his tent. She refused to ponder the thought. Refused to consider how dire her circumstances were.

He crossed his arms over his chest and pointed behind her at the opening of the tent. "Do you know what is out there?"

"Your camp."

"And my men. Many, many men," he confirmed with an amused expression. "They are hardened men who enjoy spoils."

"This is England," she interrupted. "I suggest you make your way to richer lands if you seek plunder."

Jacques shrugged. "A country without a king is a fine place to plunder. You'll wed me and obey me or I'll let them enjoy you until you accept your place. I don't really need an heir from you. If you throw a bastard, it will be useful. I'll keep it around for a few years, inherit Thistle Keep, and bury it beside your body when it gets too old to be controlled. Perhaps I'll bury it first and let you anticipate what day will be your last."

Horror gagged her. Sick pleasure shimmered in his eyes.

"You have until tomorrow to decide which fate you prefer. I'll have to send for a priest, since the one on your land will likely refuse to perform the ceremony under the circumstances."

"As if any man of God would wed me to you with my body broken from your men."

"Oh, there are men of God who will bind us in holy matrimony." His face brightened with insane enjoyment. "Priests who see women as temptresses, descendants of Eve who must be controlled else they entice men to sin. I rode with a few of them on the Crusade. They never left a single infidel alive, be it woman or child."

"That is horrible!"

He laughed. "Such is life, lady. Resign yourself to your fate or I will make sure you accept my will. Truly, I care not which method you choose."

His gaze lowered to her breasts and he smacked his lips before heading toward the door and leaving her.

❧

She was so foolish.

How could she think Ramon hell on earth?

Well, you know better now.

She did, but the knowledge gave her no solace. Chastising herself surely wouldn't save her.

Nor would Ramon, for he didn't even know that she was gone.

Which was her fault as well. He had warned her.

So she would have to help herself. Hadn't that been what she craved? For a moment, regret tore through her, ripping aside her pride and leaving her facing the harsh reality.

Men were not kind because fate was not kind.

Women became calculating because it was their only resource. Their wiles, their wits, were their own weapons.

Rauxana came to mind.

"Serving you is my reason for life."

Whether or not the exotic-looking woman meant what she said, there was one thing Isabel knew for certain: Jacques had believed Rauxana. Isabel had seen it in his eyes. The pure male satisfaction as Rauxana rubbed against him that last time. In truth, it was debatable who exactly was the master. When Rauxana flashed a look to him from beneath her dark eyelashes, Isabel thought the girl was the one in control of the man who believed himself her master.

So was Rauxana a sorceress? Or some other word that Isabel had only heard in half whispers? The way she stroked Jacques made it clear that she knew how to touch a man. And it had clearly beguiled him. Enchanted him.

She was treading on dangerous ground, for the church warned against such wild abandonment.

The sound of men talking came through the canvas tent walls.

Isabel squared her shoulders. She would contemplate anything that might free her.

And what will you do when you are back at Thistle Keep with Ramon?

For a moment, a wicked idea of stroking Ramon filled her thoughts. Would his eyes glitter with as much satisfaction?

She shouldn't have these thoughts, but it was better than weeping over her plight.

Anything was better than pitying herself.

༄

Isabel was not at the evening service.

Ramon scanned the congregation twice before striding across the aisle to where the women stood.

"Where is your mistress?" the priest hissed at him. Ramon lifted his hand and the man fell silent.

Ramon glared at Mildred. The old woman's eyes widened with alarm. "I've naught seen her since this morn. I thought she was hunting…in the marshes… She is never this late." Horror edged her words and she looked around again, frantic to catch sight of Isabel.

"My apologies, Father, but your mistress is missing. The ungodly have no respect for the evening mass, so I must beg your forgiveness," Ramon said.

There was a hush in the church, as everyone waited to see what the priest would make of Ramon interrupting the Lord's supper.

"Go with God," the priest said as he made the sign of the cross in the air over Ramon.

Ramon took a moment to acknowledge the priest by bending to one knee before he rose and headed out of the sanctuary. His men followed him, their boots stamping against the stone floor and echoing through the church.

"We've precious time to track her before the light is gone," Ambrose observed.

A hawk cried out and swooped low across the yard before perching on the roof of the mews. It let out another cry before fluffing its feathers. The ends of leather securing its band trailed below it in the fading light.

Ramon growled. His men knew the sound well. But this time, he felt something deeper. Something unfamiliar in his rage.

This time, it was far more…personal.

❧

Rauxana reappeared near sunset.

She wore a different robe now, one that was buttoned

up the front and slit up the sides to her hips. When she moved, her bare legs flashed.

She laughed, low and sultry. "You should see your face. Scandalized by the sight of my legs. Christian women are so boring, so timid. Yet my master must obey his father and take you for his wife." She glided over to a small table and poured what looked like water into a goblet.

"You cannot drink that," Isabel warned, but the other woman paid her no mind. She took a long sip from her goblet before glancing at Isabel with a satisfied look on her face.

"Water is what the body needs." She set the goblet down and looked around her. "Only the ignorant do not know such a thing. In the desert, the body dies without water. Give a man wine and he will still perish beneath the sun. Only water gives life. But I will admit that in this place, it is hard to find pure water."

"Drinking water brings fever. My husband died of such."

Rauxana shrugged. "Fermented drink is forbidden. Besides, your wells are too close to your privies. Your women empty their household pots into the streets. Your people do not bathe. Never have I smelled such a stench in this land. Little wonder there is fever. At least you do not stink." Her eyes narrowed. "I'd have to scrub you if you did. You'll not bring fleas into the master's bed."

"I do not have fleas," Isabel scoffed.

Rauxana peered at her intently for a long moment, clearly judging the matter for herself. For all her submissive behavior when Jacques was present, she was not meek. She finally gave a graceful shrug before making a slow path across the tent, as though making sure Isabel had time to admire her. Her hips swayed in a slow, sultry motion. Isabel sat on the far side of the tent. Rauxana smiled at her before she crawled up onto the bed and lay across the foot of it. She opened her robe, letting Isabel see several inches of her body. She stretched her arms above her head and then laid her head back while she watched the door.

"The master will be here soon," she purred.

It had to be a sin, the way Rauxana was so eagerly anticipating sharing intimacies.

But…Isabel was fascinated.

Rauxana wasn't preparing for her duties with prayer and courage. Her lips were set into a contented little smile and her expression was full of expectation.

Not of a duty that must be shouldered.

But in anticipation of pleasure.

Isabel blinked, not sure if she was seeing this correctly.

Rauxana suddenly laughed, shifting and rolling up to look at Isabel. "Why are you Christian women so brittle?" She shook her head. "You are no virgin, yet you are shocked by the welcome I would give my master."

"Why do you call him your master?"

Rauxana looked surprised. "Because he owns me," she said without hesitation. "If he had not bought me, I might have ended up in a brothel or an overcrowded harem where I would have to worry about being poisoned by the master's older wives as I fought my way to his bed and a position as his favorite." She suddenly sat up, her hand closing around the bedding like a claw and narrowed her eyes. "Do not think to take my place in his bed. I am his favorite. You are a duty." Rauxana glared at her. "Cross me and I will poison you."

She would, too. Rauxana's eyes were bright with determination.

"There are no slaves in England," Isabel said. "Such is against the law."

Rauxana slowly shook her head. "I saw the master buy me. Nothing you can say will undo this. I must live the life fate has given me. Or else I am a shameless creature. There is no place in paradise for such."

Isabel softened her tone. "Just as you did not wish to be one more among many, I do not wish to be a duty. Help me escape and there will be no need to worry about me taking your place."

Rauxana's eyes brightened for a moment before she shook her head. "I would never displease the master. He must obey his father."

Isabel fought the urge to jerk on her bindings again. She couldn't panic. She needed her wits. "You could be his wife if I were gone."

Rauxana slowly smiled. "I will be. When I please him enough, he will grant me permission to have his child." Determination edged her tone. "When I give him a son, I will be his wife."

She lay back down, stretching herself out like an offering.

For a long moment, Isabel battled self-pity again. Outside the tent wall, the men were getting drunk. She could hear their voices rising. Cracks of laughter split the darkness as the camp followers came out to earn their keep. Horror gagged her. She fought it but there was no way to defeat it. She looked around, her attention settling on a knife.

Maybe…with the cover of darkness, she might slip away.

The tent flaps opened, letting a gust of night air inside. The wooden poles creaked slightly as the flaps settled back into place.

"My pet," he drawled as he took a moment to acknowledge Rauxana. She moved her legs and thrust her chest forward so that the robe slid down to bare one of her breasts. It was crowned with a dark nipple.

"And my duty." Jacques turned to look at Isabel. "The priest will not be here until tomorrow. Perhaps you can learn something tonight about pleasing me."

He reached out and grabbed her wrist. She jumped but his hand was so big his fingers closed around her fragile limb. He tugged her toward the large chair and quickly tied her to the frame of it with a length of rabbit skin. He secured her wrists behind her, leaving her leaning against the side of the chair.

When he stood back up, he smirked, satisfied. "Tomorrow…I'm going to fuck you. With or without the church's blessing."

He turned and moved toward the bed. "I certainly don't have a blessing for you, my pet…"

Isabel should have looked away.

But she couldn't.

It was her shame that made her look at the couple on the bed. The shame of knowing that when her husband took his last breath, she had felt relieved. It was by far the most horrible thing she'd ever done.

Rauxana rose to her knees and let her robe slip down her arms to puddle around her like liquid fire.

Something else drove Isabel to keep watching—the dark memories that haunted her sleep. Those intensely clear recollections of being beneath her husband. The pain, the helplessness.

There was no such horror on Rauxana's face. She smiled invitingly as she undid Jacques's belt. She moved slowly, sliding her fingers along his body. Baring him little by little until they were both in naught but skin.

Then she kissed him. Not on the lips, but everywhere else. She trailed her lips across his chest, looking like she was savoring the taste of him.

"Suckle me…"

Jacques sounded pained. He pressed her head toward his member and she trailed kisses down its length as well.

"Suckle me!" he demanded.

Rauxana looked past him to where Isabel was watching. Power and triumph glittered in her eyes. For a moment, all of her true feelings were displayed on her face. She stroked his member with a single hand before sending Isabel a hard, promising glare.

Isabel couldn't have looked away if a priest was standing in front of her. Surely this was something that Mildred had told her ladies didn't need to know about.

Why?

It surely looked more pleasurable than what she'd experienced as a wife.

Or what Ramon made you feel with his touch?

Aye. There was no other way to answer but to admit the truth.

"That's it…more…" Jacques was working his member in and out of Rauxana's mouth, his backside flexing as he labored. "I'm going to let you suckle me before I fuck my wife…" His breathing was labored. "And when my seed is ready…I'll pump it deep inside her…and have you suck me hard again…"

He gasped, grunting before pulling free of her mouth. "But tonight…you'll ride me to the finish."

Jacques climbed onto the bed. For a moment, Rauxana faced her. Hate simmered in her eyes before Jacques flopped onto his back and demanded, "Mount me! Show my wife how to ride a man."

Isabel looked away at last, unable to bear the controlling nature that she recalled so well in her husband. The bed was rocking, groaning as the couple on it fucked. Isabel didn't cringe over the harsh word. It was appropriate.

"You'll be my pet…and my wife can swell with child…yes…*YES*…"

Jacques was yelling, his voice strained before he gave one final yell and the bed ropes stopped groaning.

Not long after, the soft sound of his snoring filled the tent. There was a creak from the bed ropes and a soft sound of fabric rustling. Isabel looked up to see Rauxana closing her robe. She moved across the tent on silent feet. She pinched out one candle and then another, until there was nothing but darkness.

And then she came toward Isabel.

There was only a hint of light coming from the fires burning on the other side of the tent walls.

A touch of crimson and yellow that flickered and danced off the blade of a knife. Isabel was happy to see the blade, for it promised her something other than what Jacques had.

"I will be his wife," Rauxana whispered.

She knelt in front of Isabel and lifted her hand with the knife in it. Isabel wasn't afraid, only regretful for the night she'd refused Ramon. It was an opportunity lost now. Just as her life was about to be snuffed out. Life was suddenly such a precious thing. Something she hadn't truly appreciated.

She had never enjoyed being a woman.

Rauxana slipped the blade between the chair and the strip of rabbit skin, jerking it up and snapping the binding. Isabel fell away from the chair. Rauxana grasped her arm and cut through the length that held Isabel's wrists together. Isabel was half sprawled on the ground but all she could do was look at the severed bindings in shock.

"Go, and do not betray me if you are captured." Rauxana pressed the knife into Isabel's hand.

"I swear I will not."

Rauxana moved back toward the bed. She shrugged from her robe and climbed silently onto the bed. There was only one groan from the bed ropes as she resumed her place beside Jacques.

Her master.

Yours as well, if you do not make good use of this opportunity…

Isabel watched the tent walls for a moment, deciding where men were talking. There were two men in front. Every now and then, there was a clinking of rolling dice. She headed toward the darker back of the tent and plunged the knife into the canvas. It popped and she froze, listening for any change around her. Jacques continued to snore and the men talking in front of the flaps kept rolling their dice.

Easing the knife down through the fabric felt as though it took too long. It also sounded loud. But the fabric parted, granting her freedom.

Isabel forced herself to be still. She had only one chance and mustn't waste it. She watched the camp for a few moments, all the time listening to Jacques snore behind her. There were tents all over and more men sleeping on the ground. A pair of people walked through the sleeping men. One of them wore longer garments and smothered a giggle with her hand. A man sleeping on the ground sat up.

"A whore…just what I was dreaming of."

The woman went to him and held out her hand. He dug in his tunic and brought something out that pleased her. She gathered up her robes and joined him on the ground.

Isabel looked at her robes. She stood and they settled around her ankles.

One chance…naught but a single opportunity to escape.

She slashed at the fabric of her robes, cringing at the waste. But she had to look like a man. Or at least a youth. She gathered the bottom of her robes and draped it over her head like a woodsman's hood. In the dark, no one would see it for what it was.

She kept the knife grasped in her hand and eased through the slit. She didn't dare make it any wider for fear it would be noticed. The canvas parted enough for her to pass and she crouched low next to the tent for a moment. The couple was busy when she stood up and started walking toward the woods. A couple of men rolled toward her and watched her in the dark. Most of them were taking the opportunity to sleep. But those posted on watch saw her.

Demons roam the woods at night...

She shook her head and kept her pace steady.

They roam the darkness, seeking souls to feast on...

She resisted the pull of fireside tales. They were just tales. Superstitions. Naught else.

But her heart was still pounding in her chest when she reached the border between the camp and the shadows of the forest. No one went out in the dark of night.

Well, you must, or suffer being Jacques's chattel.

She was sure to like being Jacques's wife less than a demon's meal.

She moved into the forest, forcing herself to take another step and another and another.

Every step felt like an eternity. Each breath seemed like it was surely going to be her last, because her lungs were freezing. Even her hearing was playing tricks on her. She jerked toward sounds, unable to identify them. Her skin crawled as though there were spiders on her, but when she brushed them aside, there was naught.

Don't be a child.

Exactly. She was a woman and one who ran her own estate. She could walk through the forest, walk to freedom.

Indeed, she would.

"Cry out and it will be the last sound you ever make, lad."

A sword slashed out in front of her, stopping just shy of her throat. She gasped, but flattened her hand over her mouth to stifle the sound. There was a hard grunt in response.

"Who's your master, boy? What man commands that army?"

She heard a whistle, one that might be mistaken for an owl, if one didn't know raptors well. Isabel did. She turned her face toward the sound as the men next to her chuckled.

"Know your way around the forest, do you?"

"I know birds," she muttered. "And I am no lad."

Whoever had been approaching pushed the sword away from her. Even in the dark, she knew Ramon.

"Isabel?"

She nodded, her powers of speech suddenly rendered unusable. Her lips were moving but no sound came out. Every muscle she had suddenly shook, her knees knocking and weakening.

"I-I—" she stammered, trying to force the lump in her throat down. Everything was fine now. There was no reason for her to be trembling.

Yet she was. Greatly so.

Ramon reached out and cupped her chin. "Isabel?"

She nodded and held up the knife. "I used this…to cut the back of Jacques's tent…"

"Jacques Raeburn?" Ramon demanded softly, his tone deadly.

She nodded. "He was Bechard's brother."

"So he planned to steal an heiress."

He whistled, and shapes moved in the night. Ambrose appeared, his normally easygoing expression gone. In its place was a hard, cold look that indicated war. Ramon looked back toward the camp.

"Since we have the lady, we may rid this world of pestilence," Ramon said firmly.

She felt sick with dread. No one had ever spilled blood on her behalf, but what truly horrified her was Ramon facing Jacques. Ramon had honor, where Jacques would likely use that trait against him.

She ignored her horror so she could speak. "He is a baron. You cannot challenge him. You'll face judgment from the other barons if you do."

Her announcement was met with smothered words of profanity. Ramon reached for her wrist but stopped when he felt the rabbit skin still tied around it.

"Baron or not, he deserves death, and I can challenge him for setting his men on you. Yet I need to make sure you are away from here first."

He wanted blood. She heard it in his tone. Felt it radiating from him.

Maybe that was what she craved. Vengeance. Retribution. She had to resist the urge to long for those things, for that was how bitter family feuds began. So close to the Welsh border, she had seen the suffering such blood feuds brought.

It could bring Ramon death. Even the most valiant knight fell in battle.

She could not bear such.

She walked and tried to make her steps light. At the edge of the woods, she smelled the horses.

Ramon mounted and reached down for her. Ambrose was already lifting her up before she realized their intent.

She craved his embrace and it brought her more solace, more comfort than she had ever believed possible.

So she'd be content and not seek vengeance. She'd find a way to make him see the sense in leaving Jacques be.

⊰✦⊱

"Thanks be to Christ and all his angels!" Mildred was fluttering around them when they made it back to Thistle Keep. The hall was still lit; those who should have been sleeping on its floor were wide awake. They muttered their thanks but Ramon kept her moving toward the stairs and up to her chamber.

"You disobeyed me, lady."

She turned and faced him as he sent the door closed and propped his hands on his hips.

"It was not my intention. Truly, I took Griffin to hunt as I always do. If I do not, the rats will…will take the goose eggs."

Ramon pulled his gauntlets off and tossed them on the table. But he nodded once and fought to rein in his temper. "You should have taken an escort."

He was right. She knew it but still felt as though her life was crumbling. Ramon snorted at the look on her face.

"Do you dare to tell me I am wrong?" he demanded softly. "That my words have no merit?"

He pointed at the polished tin on the wall. "Look at the way your face is darkened and the bindings still on your wrists. Dare to tell me there was not valid reason for me to tell you to stay near the keep or travel with an escort."

"I do not mean to say…" Her teeth were chattering as though she was freezing, but the chamber was pleasantly warm. She tried to tug the rabbit skin strips from one wrist, but her fingers were shaking too badly to grasp them.

Ramon muttered something and swept her off her feet. His body was warm and his scent teased her senses again, bringing her peace. He carried her to the bed and settled her there. He pulled the bedding up to her chin and smoothed it in place before pulling his hand back and hooking it onto his belt. The look on his face was sculpted from stone, but what shamed her was the concern in his eyes.

"You were right," she admitted softly. "Honestly, I meant no rebellion against you by taking Griffin out this morning. 'Tis my habit to do so every day. To protect the nests. The feathers are how we pay the taxes. We'd not have enough food without them."

He drew in a deep breath, fighting his temper, and settled for working the rabbit skin strips loose from one wrist and then the other.

"I have never lived in a world where I must fear walking on my own land," she offered. "I am not sure I wish to."

"You have simply blinded yourself to the dangers."

She stiffened. "Even if I am guilty of such, is it not better than living like a frightened mouse? I had to step up and run Thistle Keep."

He drew in a deep breath. "Aye, and you rose to the challenge well. Yet it is time for both of us to change." The bed ropes groaned as he sat beside her. "I cannot recall living anywhere but by my king's side on the Crusade. Yet I am here, in a place where I might consider having a family instead of only a king's demands to serve."

For a moment, he almost looked as uncertain as she felt. It was there in his dark eyes, a flicker of need, a need for understanding. A need to not be alone.

She knew that feeling well.

"I am glad you are here, and I do not want you to go seeking vengeance."

His expression tightened. "As a baron, I am the only one who can challenge Jacques."

"And yet, as a baron, you are duty bound to take your grievance to the barons' council for judgment," she reminded him. "Or risk breaking the law you are sworn to uphold."

"The barons do not meet until next spring." He smoothed the hair away from her bruised face. "Far too much mercy for that dog."

"And yet, if you go after him, you lower yourself to his level."

"That is harsh of you to say, Isabel." His tone was sharp and his eyes hardening. She could see him tightening his resolve, making his decision.

"I will not be the only one saying it," she argued. "You know I am correct. There are barons who are friends of the Raeburn family. They will try to discredit you in the hope a baron's title will become vacant for another of their kin. You must wait until the council meets. Besides, he did not gain what he sought. Is that not the most important fact?"

His eyes narrowed, warning her that he was going to shred her argument.

She leaned forward and pressed her lips against his. It was a tender touch, innocent but seeking. Hooking her hands onto his shoulders, she pulled him closer and opened her mouth as he tried to pull away.

She held him, kissing him with all the desperation brewing inside her to keep him from his destruction.

There was a soft pressure and the slide of his mouth against hers as he gave in. She tilted her head so that their lips fit together more perfectly. He cradled her head, taking control of the kiss.

It wasn't the hot, searing kiss he had pressed on her the night before. This was something else entirely. It was sanctuary. A safe haven from the evil trying to tear at her. He closed his arms around her, taking command of the kiss but not changing the tone. It continued as a seeking touch, an exploration, a tasting.

She slid down into his embrace, content to be pressed against his chest as she surrendered to the darkness. The sound of his heart was more comforting than anything she had ever heard.

❧

Ambrose was waiting up.

Ramon knew that he as well as his men would be. The hall was silent for so many filling it. They watched him as he climbed to the high table and turned to look at them.

"Seek your beds. Our duty is finished for the night."

There were frowns but also nods of obedience. The hall filled with the echoes of footsteps as his men departed.

Ambrose was not so easily dismissed. "You plan to allow that cur to see dawn?"

"The lady is recovered."

"You are no more satisfied with that than I am," Ambrose said curtly.

Ramon nodded. "Yet Richard warned me that it would be a greater challenge not to draw my sword. I see what he meant now. I will bring the matter before the barons' council."

"Piss on that," Ambrose declared.

"Yet it is the law, and what are men without law but beasts?"

Ambrose closed his mouth, defiance flickering in his eyes. Ramon felt the same but forced himself to climb back up to the chamber Isabel was sleeping in.

Solace came in the form of her sweet scent in the air, the soft sound of her breath, and the warmth from her body as he slid back into the bed with her.

It was solace, and yet his thirst for vengeance raged.

But his need for her was greater. He would be content that she was correct. Jacques had a powerful family. They would do everything they could to unseat Ramon if he gave them even a bit of incentive. The law was clear. Barons ruled over barons. To fight another baron was to risk losing his title and right to his army.

But most importantly, he would lose his ability to protect Thistle Keep.

So he would wait.

❧

Jacques roared and his men jumped. They knew from bitter experience that he would happily make someone pay for his displeasure if possible.

His squire was the unfortunate one today. He backhanded the youth, sending him rolling. The boy gained his feet quickly, wiping away a trickle of blood with his sleeve.

"You left a knife in my tent and she is gone!"

The squire offered no excuse. The men watching judged him wise, for Jacques wasn't known for his tolerance.

"Find a way into their confidence."

The squire blinked. "My lord?"

"Take off my colors."

His men stiffened.

"If you ever want to wear them again, get yourself taken in at Thistle Keep. I want to know everything Ramon de Segrave is doing. Everything my bride-to-be is doing."

Five

RAMON WAS GONE IN THE MORNING.

Of course, it was because she'd slept long past sunrise. Isabel yawned and fought the urge to close her eyes again. She was weary, embarrassingly so, considering how long she had been in bed. Still, waking up wasn't simple. Her belly rumbled and she fought her way past the clouds of fatigue pressing her down. With a soft moan, she rolled over and sat up.

The moment she did, her eyes widened as pain went shooting through her. It raced along her side and through her belly, and a groan got past her lips before she clamped her mouth shut.

Being handled roughly did not agree with her, it seemed.

As if it would agree with anyone…

She shuddered; moving across more than just her skin, it felt as though it were soul deep. Her mouth went dry at the memory of Jacques's eyes when he'd looked at her.

The man was a demon.

No, she wouldn't give him that sort of hold

over her. He was just a man. A bad one, but flesh nonetheless.

She shrugged into her over robe and combed out her hair. A sense of urgency was making her clumsy and the comb clattered to the stone floor.

There was a rap on the door before the small window set into it slid open.

"I will send your nurse up, lady."

Isabel jumped but the man wasn't looking into the chamber. She caught only a glimpse of the back of his head before the window slid back into place.

There was someone guarding her door?

It prickled her pride. Yet, at the same time, she would be lying if she didn't admit that knowing the man was there calmed her.

She snorted as she picked up the comb.

She would not turn into a mouse, frightened of the world because of some misfortune. It was hardly the first time fate had delivered a blow that sent her reeling.

"Look at you…" Mildred said as she entered the chamber. "You should be in bed…what with the ordeal you've been through."

"I have wasted enough daylight today," Isabel said firmly. "Yet I am glad to have you here to tie my laces."

She turned around so Mildred could secure her over gown, but her nurse was moving to the large chest sitting against the wall.

"You'll be wanting something finer for your wedding."

Mildred fit one of the large keys hanging from her

girdle into the lock on the chest. It groaned when she turned it; the chest hadn't been opened for a long time.

"I do not need any finery. There is not going to be a wedding." Isabel wasn't certain she thought about the words before they crossed her lips. A shudder shook her again and she was very sure that she wanted nothing to do with being bound to a man in the eyes of the church.

"I would like to know the reason," Mildred declared as she turned and propped her hands on her hips.

"As would I."

Awareness rippled through her as Ramon's voice filled the chamber. His tone was low and tightly controlled. She turned to face him as he lifted his hand and gestured Mildred toward the door.

"Your mistress and I have important matters to discuss."

Mildred started toward the door with a firm expression of agreement on her face.

"Wait... I need to be laced."

"You slept in my embrace, Isabel. I am well aware of your body."

She sucked in a harsh, shocked breath. She looked back at Mildred, beseeching her to remain, but her nurse paused in the doorway and sent her a stern look.

"'Tis best you come to an agreement," Mildred said with a clear tone of expectation. She turned and the man guarding the door shut it.

"That was harshly spoken," Isabel reprimanded. "More so than necessary, I think."

"Not so if you intend to persist in your stubborn desire not to wed."

Ramon was standing near the door. The sight of him sent a curl of heat through her belly.

Sweet Mother of Christ! What would it take to end her lusting for the man?

Her cheeks burned scarlet when she answered her own question.

Ramon's dark gaze narrowed. "You blush for me, Isabel."

"I know," she conceded. She turned and walked away from him, feeling him too keenly.

He followed her, his steps slow and measured. "And you sought my embrace for solace and comfort." He stepped to the side, blocking her path when she tried to go around him. "And I enjoyed having you against me."

Her breath froze, her heart hammered inside her chest. His dark eyes were lit with determination and it stroked something inside her that felt very much like enjoyment. She had never felt so desired by a man before.

"Jacques Raeburn bought himself a baron's title. He will not be content with your escape. Voice your objections to our match. We must come to an agreement." The glint in his eyes was a warning one. He was not in the mood to be bested by her.

"He bought it?" She shook her head with distaste.

"Aye." Ramon's tone matched hers. "His men are brutal and often more like villains than Crusaders. But Richard cannot Crusade without gold. There are a great many sins that can be forgiven when money is being provided to keep the Crusades going. Thistle Keep is the next prize Jacques plans to add to his coffers. Why will you not wed me?"

"I have had a belly full of being a possession. A wife is the property of her husband. I would simply stay…free." She should have been more cautious and held her tongue but with Ramon, self-control seemed nearly impossible. His eyes narrowed and guilt chewed on her. "You are right to think me harsh. Yet I cannot reconcile myself to wedding."

He closed the remaining distance between them. "You are drawn to me."

She shifted, overwhelmed by the way he saw through her. Her cheeks stung once more and her lips tingled with anticipation.

Drawn?…she craved him.

He chuckled and stroked one scarlet cheek. "There is but one way for this passion to cool, Isabel. I would wed you first. So neither of us need feel shamed by our passions."

"You honor me…" But she shifted away, feeling trapped.

"Yet you do not trust me not to turn mean once the vows are consummated." He wasn't asking her. She turned and discovered him watching her with a knowing look on his face.

"I know you feel it an insult for me to think such a thing, yet would you have me lie to you? I am being herded into this by fate and unkind circumstance."

She was being bold and probably foolish for voicing her emotions. He was still strong, both in body and in the army he commanded. Many would advise her to make the best of her position.

To do so would allow her to indulge her cravings for him.

But to what end?

She honestly didn't know.

"I would have you trust me," Ramon said.

A memory surfaced.

"Do you trust me not to cuckold you as your first wife did?" she asked. "Or shall your man be posted to guard over me?"

Ramon drew in a sharp breath. "You are combining two issues to make your point. My man is posted because you disobeyed me and left the keep without an escort. Argue against the need and I will tell you to look at the scabs around your wrists."

She looked down, unable to avoid looking at the dried blood on her wrists. Dark bruises decorated her forearms as well. She pressed her lips into a hard line of frustration.

"I have known you for only a short time. Why must you press me for vows? Can we not…court?"

"We are past the age of courting," Ramon grunted. "I fight to keep my hands from you, more so because I see desire in your eyes to touch me back. I have never faltered, yet you test my devotion to not take you to my bed until our union is blessed."

That wasn't what she'd expected to hear.

"You look surprised," he said.

"I am," she answered.

"You doubt your own appeal?"

She shook her head. "I am surprised how differently your admission makes me feel than Jacques's."

Like night and day.

One made her flesh crawl, the other set her heart racing.

His lips twitched into a wolfish grin. He leaned forward and hooked his arm around her, pulling her into his embrace in a swift motion that left her breathless. She flattened her hands against his chest, feeling his hardened flesh. The faint vibration of his heartbeat teased her fingertips.

She didn't want to resist. "You test me, it's true, and I find it most pleasing."

His expression became one of wonder. For a moment, it was as though she were seeing something that he hid from everyone else. It felt…intimate. Like a part of himself that he never showed because he couldn't appear needy.

She wanted to kiss him, the way Rauxana had kissed Jacques.

Ramon leaned down to press his lips against hers, cupping her nape, but Isabel smoothed her hands down his chest, stunning him. He hesitated for a moment, watching her. Something stirred inside her, a sensation she wasn't sure she understood.

But she liked it.

She stroked her way back to the center of his chest, shivering as her fingertips registered how hard his body was beneath his tunic. Ramon closed his eyes to slits, a rumble escaping his lips.

This time, the sensation was strong and it filled her with confidence. She smoothed her hand up to where his tunic ended and she was able to stroke his bare skin. He stiffened but lifted his chin so that she might trail her fingers along the firm column of his throat. His skin was smooth, and beneath it more firm muscle.

A pulse began to throb between her thighs, but this

time she welcomed it because it only added to the passion sweeping her into something she craved.

Might it be ecstasy?

She didn't know what that was, but she couldn't stop. Wouldn't stop.

She pressed herself up against him, shuddering at the hard contact. She refused to let her lower back curl away from completing the embrace. The contact was jarring, a soft sound rising from her as she discovered the hard shape of his member pressing against her belly.

It didn't leave her cold.

Not sure when she had closed her eyes, she opened them to discover Ramon watching her. His dark eyes glittered with passion but it didn't make her cringe. There was something else there, a need that somehow set them on equal footing.

Of course, such a thing was not possible, but she didn't want to think rationally. No, she didn't want to think; in fact, she was going to ensure that she didn't have to.

"Kiss me, Ramon."

His lips parted in a satisfied grin before he tilted his head and leaned forward.

But he didn't give her what she'd asked for. He pressed a kiss against her jawline, then another and another. All of them soft, slow motions that twisted her insides. Impatience was welling up from that knot of need burning in her belly. She moved, rotating her hips as Rauxana had done.

She gasped as pleasure shot through her. Ramon lifted his head and studied her face.

"I would like to know the reason behind your new

boldness, Isabel…" His gaze lowered to her mouth. "But I have not the discipline to listen to explanations just now."

His grip tightened on her nape and he completed the kiss this time. The kiss was hard, but excitement leaped inside her. She mimicked his motions, taking his lead. He pressed her mouth open, growling when their tongues met for the first time. She shuddered but moved onto her toes so that she might kiss him hard in return. There was a desperation clawing at her, filling her with demands that were born from some instinct she hadn't realized she possessed.

It was sinful, but that only increased the enjoyment. She wanted to fling herself into the churning sensation and let it wring her until…until…something burst.

Ramon suddenly set her back, gripping her biceps and lifting her off her feet so that he could move her away from him.

"Enough." His tone was clipped and harsh. "As I said, you test me to break my personal vows. I would honor you, Isabel, above all others."

Isabel withdrew from him, the sting of rejection burning away some of her intoxication. But the look on his face fascinated her. She would never have thought him a man who struggled to maintain control. Yet in that moment, she clearly witnessed a conflict warring within him.

He craved her as much as she did him.

The knowledge was balm for the sting and fuel for the brazenness brewing inside her. "'Tis not enough," she argued. "You promised me ecstasy."

He cupped her shoulder firmly and turned her around. A moment later, he was threading the laces through the eyelets on the back of her over robe. The fabric groaned because he tugged on the laces so hard.

"We will wed first."

Isabel turned to find Ramon trying to convince himself as well as her.

"Now, Isabel." He held out his hand.

But she went cold. All of the confidence and boldness froze as she recalled the words of the law. Everything, even her body, would become his.

"I cannot." She choked on the words.

He ground out a curse. "Would you have me dishonor you?"

She tried to look away, but he stepped closer and pressed her back against the wall.

"Would you have me raise your robes and satisfy myself between your thighs without a care for your honor?" he growled. "You want it. You want me inside you."

"I do," she whispered, feeling like the admission scorched her lips because it was so sinful.

"Wed me," he demanded.

"I will become chattel again." Misery was twisting through her because she could see no resolution. "It is not the same for you. A few days is enough time for you to know if I raise your passions, but it is not truly enough time for trust to grow. Admit you have no true trust in me. Not yet. We barely know each other."

"Aye, true trust takes more time to grow." Ramon drew back, hooking his hands into his sword belt. His expression was tight, his dark eyes stormy. "I suppose I will win none of your favor if I say you should be content with the place the law says is yours in a marriage, either."

Surprise flared through her. "You…agree?"

He drew in a deep breath and exhaled. "Nay, for I would have the blessing of the church so I may claim you. Yet I understand your argument."

"Understand?" she asked incredulously. "Men and women do not understand one another. We are as different as the sun and moon."

His lips twitched, rising into a small grin that banished some of the sternness from his visage.

"Aye. Yet you are not alone in feeling the weight of injustice on your shoulders." He nodded. "I see Jacques Raeburn flying a baron's pennant, the same honor I earned. I do not care to know it was my king who belittled what he bestowed on me by selling that same honor to another. Yet to my king, I am as duty bound as a wife is to her husband. I must take what he gives without complaint. My questions must be confined to private conversations with those I confide in."

Her eyes widened. "I had never thought to hear a man say such."

"I'm not sure I would have ever voiced such a personal complaint even to Ambrose. Yet with you, I discover myself at ease."

She nodded, feeling some of the walls pressing in on her retracting. "I wouldn't have told Mildred how I felt about taking a woman's place. It would have been…well—"

"Too personal?" he questioned.

"Aye."

Which left her looking into his eyes once more and feeling like they had a unique understanding.

Ramon reached out and cupped her chin. "Let us not be too demanding of the world, but content in knowing we have passion between us and an…ease when in private. It is far more than many have. Come with me to the church door. I would not act dishonorably toward you." His lips curved with hunger. "And your touch makes me forget my good intentions."

It was far more than any husband had to promise. "I am…torn."

It was the kindest reply she could make. He deserved more from her, had earned it. Guilt slammed into her with the force of a winter storm.

"I have known you but a few days." She was pleading, but not entirely sure with whom. Herself or him? "I would not have you think me fickle."

He suddenly grinned at her. "I think many things of you, and most of them make me want to haul you to the church over my shoulder so that I may get down to the business of immersing myself in your sweet flesh. You are not fickle, merely…wise. Yet I know what it is I crave, and the knowledge is nearly undoing me."

He moved toward her, pinning her against the wall and kissing her until she was breathless. Her heart was hammering as he boldly cupped one of her breasts, stroking her beaded nipple with his thumb. She arched toward him, pressing her flesh into his hand.

"And you crave what I've promised you." He pulled back. It felt as though he were ripped from her.

"I will satisfy you, Isabel. Yet I crave trust from you almost as much. You wish to be courted? Then prepare to have yourself held under siege until you surrender to temptation. Such is the only sort of engagement I know how to conduct."

He left her sagging against the wall, his challenge ringing in her ears.

And passion burning in her belly.

Never before had she realized that an honorable knight might be so hated a creature.

For in that moment, she loathed the chivalric code.

❧

"I would have thought you'd be at church," Ambrose remarked.

"I would like nothing else."

Men were hauling stone into the courtyard. Sweat glistened on their brows as they stripped down to under tunics to move the heavy load. Larger foundation stones had been dragged up with teams of horses, one at a time, to form the foundation of what would become a second keep. A wall would be built between them the following season.

Ambrose took a long look at Ramon before he chuckled. "The lady proves herself resistant to your charms?"

"Tread carefully, Ambrose." Ramon closed his hand into a fist and sent it into his opposite palm. "I could use a good fight."

"Aye, I see the need for release burning in you sure enough."

Ramon popped his knuckles.

Ambrose threw his head back and laughed. "And to

think…the lady is such a dainty thing to look upon…
Yet she has you by the balls."

"The day may come when retribution is mine, and
I shall recall quite clearly how much amusement you
are enjoying at my expense."

Ambrose turned and flattened his hand over his
chest. "Unlike you, my friend, my heart has room for
many, many, and even many more lovelies. God has
not made a single lady who can satisfy me."

"You may hope so, for when you face her, you will
wish you had not tempted the Creator to test you."

Ambrose threw his arms wide. "I await all temptations!"

Two women nearby giggled. Ambrose looked at
them and curled his arm so that his bicep bulged. They
smiled, their expressions turning carnal.

Ramon turned away. He wanted something different. No one was more surprised than he was, but
Isabel's scent was clinging to him, stirring his cock,
and no other woman would satisfy him.

So he would just have to make sure the lady suffered
as greatly as he. He would have her, but conceded that
trust needed time to grow. So he would give her until
sunset before pressing her again.

His cock throbbed, proving it was going to be a
very long day.

❧

Ramon was watching her.

Isabel snorted. Nearly everyone at Thistle Keep was
eyeing her, yet it was the baron's dark gaze that she
noticed. She could feel it.

When she crossed the yard, he watched her.

She suddenly realized her hips were swaying as Rauxana's had.

By supper, she was on edge, exhausted by the way her body heated and cooled. She fled to her chamber and brushed out her hair before Ramon finished his meal. At last sleep claimed her, granting her a shred of mercy.

But it was only a small reprieve. She woke a few hours later, darkness close around her. She still felt Ramon near her. His scent and the sound of his even breathing touched her senses. She tried to fall back to sleep but her mind refused. She was awake, unable to quiet her thoughts.

"You suffer needlessly, Isabel." Ramon lifted his head and rolled toward her. The window shutters were still open, allowing the moonlight to glitter off his eyes.

"I am simply—"

"Aroused," he interrupted. "Something you need not suffer."

He leaned down and smothered her protest beneath his lips.

In truth, she didn't have any words of protest in her. There was only need and craving, and Ramon was what she hungered for. The night seemed like a cloak, shielding them from everything except one another.

She reached for him, opening her mouth to let him deepen the kiss. He teased her lower lip with a longer sweep of his tongue before seeking hers. She arched toward him, the carnal nature of the kiss snapping through her. It broke through the last of her

inhibitions, and she purred when she encountered his
swollen member.

Thick and long.

It was hard against her belly as he pressed her down
onto her back and trailed his kisses down her neck.

She remembered what it looked like.

But now, the image was a welcome one. Her passage was needy. She rolled toward him, pressing her
body to his. For a moment, the connection pleased
her, sending a rush of enjoyment through her, but it
wasn't enough. She yearned for a deeper connection.

Ramon didn't disappoint. He ran his hands down
her, boldly cupping her breasts through the thin, worn
fabric of the chemise. She groaned and opened her
eyes, surprised to hear such a carnal sound coming
from her own lips.

Ramon chuckled. "Sinful or not, I enjoy hearing such things from you." He lifted his head for a
moment, capturing her gaze. "And knowing my touch
is responsible."

He was still holding her breast, massaging the tender
globe. Pleasure surged through her. She arched, unable to
remain still. Somehow, she'd never noticed how sensitive
her skin truly was or how much she wanted to be stroked.

Ramon stroked her, his hands unleashing a delight
that left her breathless. From her breasts and down
across her belly and farther still, until he cupped the
mound of her sex.

She cried out, unable to contain the swirling mass
of sensation he was stirring inside her. She was alive
with impulses. To move, to stretch toward him, to
seek…something.

"Aye…anything but cold," he said.

She opened her eyes, trying to focus on his words, but her thoughts were clouded, her lips dry and unwilling to form a reply.

Ramon didn't let her. He pressed a kiss against her lips and boldly thrust his tongue inside her mouth. She writhed, reaching for him and twisting her fingers into his hair. He wasn't close enough. She needed to be… something.

Instinct offered the answer. She thrust her hips toward him and sighed when she felt the hard shape of his member.

But he pressed her back, rubbing her belly with one large hand before venturing lower again. He tugged her chemise up, baring her naked body. The touch of the night air was blissful relief from the heat blistering her. A moment later, his fingers stroked her sex, sending a jolt of sensation through her passage.

She broke away from his kiss but he pressed her down on her back with the weight of his body.

"I will show you ecstasy, Isabel…"

She licked her dry lips, shocked by the fact that he was touching her in so forbidden a place, but gasping because it felt so very good. Somehow, she'd never truly understood the meaning of the word *delight*, because what his fingers were sending through her flesh was more enjoyable than anything she had ever experienced.

He dipped his fingers between the folds of her flesh and growled. "Your body welcomes me…"

When he drew his fingers back to the top of her slit, they were moist. She shuddered, clawing at the bedding, needing release.

But she had no idea how to gain it.

"Show me." Her voice was raspy and almost unrecognizable. He looked at her and the breath froze in her chest as she saw the look in his eyes.

It was a savageness, but a welcome one. A burning need that existed only between them. He bared his teeth at her and plunged his fingers into her sex.

"As you demand…"

She cried out, losing the will to keep her eyes open. The only thing that mattered was the motion of his fingers. In and out. He worked two of them against the troubling point hidden at the top of her sex, drawing more of her juices from the opening to her passage as he went.

"Yes…" It wasn't really a word, but more of a sound. She twisted and strained toward him, her thighs clamping around his forearm. Everything was spinning, sweat dotting her brow in spite of the coolness of the night. Her heart beat frantically inside her chest, like a bird trying to escape a cage.

Yet it wasn't enough, not just yet. She lifted her hips, and her hands twisted in the bedding as her entire body was tightening beneath Ramon's fingers. Every thrust sent a new bolt of pleasure through her, and her only thought was to gain another and another and another, until she burst.

She shuddered, caught in a moment of pure rapture. The intensity held her like a vise, squeezing the breath from her as she moaned with delight. It twisted through her, burning away the hunger and dropping her back into reality, with the rich glow of satisfaction warming her. She couldn't move, except to drag in deep, hard breaths to feed her burning lungs.

Ramon pressed a tender kiss against her temple, his scent filling her senses and bringing her another measure of satisfaction. It was bliss, like she'd never expected to feel.

He withdrew from her and lowered her chemise. The bed rocked as he settled back to lie beside her. The moments moved by, seeming long and drawn out as slumber tried to pull her down into its embrace.

But she resisted, needled by the fact that she had given nothing in return. She rolled toward him.

"Sleep, Isabel." He turned his head to look at her in the dark. "I know you want to now." She did, but his expression was tight once more.

He craves what he just gave you...

Of course he did. She rolled her lips in and moistened them, because she realized that she wanted to please him. She moved onto her side, shifting her legs so that her thigh brushed his.

"Yet you are unsatisfied..."

He rose and pressed her back, cupping her shoulder with a firm grip before he buried his face in the nest of her hair and inhaled.

"Aye," he confessed, his breath warming her neck.

He settled onto his back, the bed ropes groaning. "You are not the only one who wishes to maintain their sense of what they are. I am a knight. You are a lady I wish to wed. I will not dishonor you."

He turned his head and reached out to stroke her jaw with one finger. She shivered. "When I lie with you, it will be as your husband."

He drew in a stiff breath and settled, sounding as though he was pressing his back into the mattress.

"Yet now you know what ecstasy is and that nothing but lying with me will truly satisfy you." There was a hint of smugness in his tone, but what rang in her ears was the warning.

She very much feared she was going to learn exactly what he meant.

Six

RAMON WAS WAITING FOR HER.

She had never desired to have a man dependent on her will, for such would be vain, but Isabel was giddy knowing so powerful a man was willing to wait for her to decide to wed him.

Of course, he was also inflicting a very devious sort of torment on her because he refused to bring her to ecstasy now. The memory of that release drove her nearly insane when the man withdrew from her after kissing her breathless each night.

She had dark rings around her eyes from the hours of sleeplessness her frustrations had brought her. The days grew longer, but her longings didn't diminish.

"Lady."

It was a full fortnight later when Ramon's squire found her working in the stillroom. The youth looked taller than he had the first time she'd seen him, if that were possible. He was lanky but there was a faint growth of beard on his face.

He lowered himself. "My lord would have you

attend him." The squire straightened and stood with his arm outstretched toward the yard.

It was early afternoon. Ramon had spent every hour supervising the training of his men and the construction of the new keep.

Isabel dusted her hands on her apron, removed it, and hung it on a hook set into the wall. She smiled when she reached the steps of the keep, tipping her head back to enjoy the warmth of the sun on her cheeks. Only at the end of the summer would the keep's stone warm completely through.

"My lady?" the squire inquired.

Isabel opened her eyes and lifted the front of her robes to descend the steps to the yard. It was two hundred feet to where the ground had been cleared for the new keep. Ramon stood atop the foundation. Isabel froze again, stunned by the sight of him and what he'd accomplished. He looked majestic, a portrait of strength and control. He had accomplished a lot in a mere two weeks. The new keep's foundation was five feet higher than Thistle Keep's foundation.

Ramon turned and offered her his hand. "Come, Isabel. See what we can create together."

She took his hand and climbed onto the structure. She gasped at the expanse of stone. The foundation was twenty feet wider than Thistle Keep's. Already, two feet of the walls were in place.

"This hall will be large enough for all our people."

"And it could not have been built without both of our resources." She marveled at the way the stones were fitted so well together. There were vats of fresh mortar, which smelled of lye. Ramon's men helped carry the heavy stones up the steps, where the master masons were waiting with the tools to make certain the stone was placed level.

"Aye," Ramon answered her. "Together, we are strong."

His grip tightened. She turned and caught his gaze. "There will be a new chamber in this tower for you."

"My chamber is sufficient."

"It will be our chamber, Isabel. A place where only the two of us have ever been."

Something moved through her and she realized it was happiness.

When had she stopped being happy?

Ramon reached out and stroked her chin. "Tell me your thoughts."

Did she dare?

She suddenly felt bold. "I enjoy having you here."

His eyes narrowed with pleasure. He maintained his firm expression, but he hooked his hand into his belt, and she saw his knuckles turn white.

"Wed me."

His tone was short but she heard the passion. Or maybe she felt it. Honestly, she wasn't sure she had ever completely cooled.

"I am considering it."

He groaned. "I am not a man practiced in the arts of courtship. Be merciful. Two weeks feels like an eternity."

She was suddenly giddy again. Full of an excitement that warmed her cheeks and made it impossible not to smile. "I have never been courted, either. Yet—" She opened her arms wide and pointed at the new foundation. "I admit your efforts warm my heart."

"Isabel—"

An impulse to toy with him was burning brightly in her. His greater size suddenly something she need not fear.

So that was trust.

Isabel lowered herself slowly and gracefully. "You impress me well, my lord. I cannot wait to see what else you shall do to soften my will."

A promise flickered in his eyes. "Be assured there will not be so many eyes on us when that moment arrives." His gaze lowered to her lips and set off a need that pulsed deep inside her belly.

Her cheeks warmed, but this time she welcomed the surge of passion. It awakened a soft throbbing between her thighs that she enjoyed. "Be careful, for that is a game both may play."

He groaned softly but his eyes snapped with determination. "A challenge to the finish? Be sure, I am your man, madam."

"Perhaps you shall be," she simpered.

It was an astonishing admission to make, for she had always considered the action to be immature. With Ramon, it was a dangerous game that twisted her insides with excitement.

Ramon watched her as she left. She felt his gaze on her as though they were connected in some spiritual way. She looked back over her shoulder before she made it into Thistle Keep and watched his lips twitch into a small curve before he smoothed his expression and turned back to supervising.

He was a sight, so powerful and very welcome. She watched him command the men bringing up another large stone. They strained as they worked together to lift it into position. The grand mason held out a building square and made sure it was level. They pounded the stone into position, removing the mortar that squeezed out at the seams.

"When are you going to wed that man?" Mildred asked sternly.

"Perhaps by summer's end." Isabel looked at her. "Perhaps I will make him wait until Michaelmas."

Mildred humphed and propped her hands on her hips disapprovingly, but her eyes sparkled with mischief. "At least you stopped wearing those wimples. Time enough for those when your hair turns gray." Mildred's face crinkled as she smiled. "And still time enough for babes! It looks as though you will enjoy making them."

"Mildred!" Isabel admonished.

Mildred waved her off, and Isabel found herself smiling as well.

She just might enjoy being wed to Ramon de Segrave.

But there was no way she would tell him so just yet. After all, she shouldn't waste her only chance to be courted.

❧

Mildred and Isabel climbed up to the doorway of the keep and disappeared inside. Neither noticed the young man watching them. He slowly ran a sharpening stone along the edge of a stone chisel. There were several others waiting to be worked on as soon as he finished, and a mason came to take the one he'd straightened the edge on. It was slow, grudging work, but he was fortunate to have been welcomed into the yard at all, since no one knew him. Only Ramon's desire to see the new keep built quickly had allowed him to mingle with the inhabitants of Thistle Keep.

He remained at his post, his fingers aching by sunset from the labor. But when the bell was rung at sunset, he didn't follow the rest of the workers into the hall for supper. He slipped into the darkness and farther away through the forest.

Jacques was busy enjoying a supper that tempted the youth, the scent drifting up to tease his nostrils and make his mouth water.

"So you managed it," Jacques remarked as he bit into a piece of rabbit and pulled a chunk of meat free. He chewed it before continuing. "I am pleasantly surprised. What do you have to tell me?"

"The lady is not yet wed."

Jacques dropped the meat. "Good."

"But she told her nurse that she is considering wedding by the end of the summer. The Baron de Segrave courts her gently, with a patient hand."

"Ramon always was soft with women," Jacques declared. "He's had the time to starve her into submission if that priest insists on a willing bride."

He wiped his mouth on his sleeve. "Still, his softness will be my opportunity." He was lost for a moment in contemplation before his gaze landed on the youth again. "Return."

Jacques ripped a section of bread from what lay before him and cut a section of rabbit free with a long dagger. He tossed it to the youth. "There will be silver for you after I secure the heiress. Until then, keep your ears open."

The youth lowered himself as he cradled the food. His belly knotted with hunger and his hands shook as he clutched the meal.

This was the best he could hope for. His mother had been a whore, and his only bit of luck had come from actually being born, considering his mother had taken more than one potion to rid herself of him.

He was strong. That was his blessing.

He had to make his own way and didn't dare spare a thought for the lady of Thistle Keep. Everyone had a master. It was simply the way life was. She'd settle in just as he had, for nobles were set above them all by God.

No one argued against God's will.

❧

"Where are you going?" Ambrose asked.

Ramon lifted an eyebrow at Ambrose. "To share the company of someone fairer than you."

Ambrose sniffed and covered his chest with a hand. "I'm wounded, my lord…deeply." A woman shifted behind him, doing a poor job of stifling her laughter. "Aww…April…come to me."

The woman walked up the steps of the platform that the high table sat on. Several of the candles had already been pinched out to save them, leaving the hall in semi-darkness that felt as though it were conducive to seduction. The way the serving woman looked at Ambrose made it clear she was receptive to being seduced.

"I see how deeply wounded you are." Ramon pushed his chair back and rose. "Do enjoy drowning your sorrows, my friend."

"I shall," Ambrose assured him. "But…April has something for us both."

April was perched on Ambrose's thigh, his arm anchoring her against his body. Ambrose lifted a pottery jar with a thin neck that was sealed with a length of hemp rope and tar.

"Honey mead…a courting necessity."

"The cook didn't want to part with it," April said. "I had to convince her and it wasn't easy, even with the silver penny you gave me."

Ambrose smiled at her. "I'll have to show you how grateful I am."

"The cook is worried what the lady will say if she knows it's missing."

Ambrose hugged April close and looked over her shoulder at Ramon. "I think the lady might enjoy the way she discovers it missing."

Ramon picked up one jug and grinned. "She just might."

"She'd better, for you owe me a ha'penny."

April nuzzled Ambrose's neck. His friend was closing his eyes, looking pleased.

"Well then, best you come along with me now," Ramon insisted. "I wouldn't want the debt to linger."

April straightened and started to move off Ambrose's thigh. He clamped her back against his body and tucked his thumb beneath his forefinger, offering Ramon the "fig" insult.

Ramon laughed but performed a slow reverence to

Ambrose in gratitude before he turned and carried the honey mead toward the stairs.

❧

Isabel stubbed her toe when she took the candle back to the hearth to relight it. She hopped twice and dropped the candle. She jumped out of the way to keep the flame from touching her chemise.

"I see the wisdom of not having rushes on the floor."

She looked up, the candle casting only a tiny amount of light from where it lay on the stone floor. Ramon closed the door behind him, his squire nowhere in sight.

The candle sputtered and she scooped it up before it died. Ramon set the jar on the table. She fit the candle into its holder and gaped at the jar.

"How did you pry that from the cook's storeroom?"

He grinned at her. "I am courting you, Isabel. The secrets of my cunning will not be revealed." He used a knife to cut through the tar sealing on the top of the jar and pulled the rope stopper free. "Besides, I would be forced to confess that Ambrose is the one who managed the feat."

She laughed softly. "Your captain knows the art of seduction well."

Ramon poured a measure of the mead into a cup and offered it to her. She climbed onto the bed and sat next to him before accepting it.

"Ambrose also knows what the pillory feels like," he said.

The mead was strong and sweet. She savored it

as she shared a look over the rim of the cup with Ramon. "I might be bound to join him before the summer is finished."

Ramon swirled his mead in his cup and inhaled the scent. "What sinful secrets could you possibly have, dear Lady of Camoys? Dare I hope they concern me?"

"You can be certain they do."

Ramon's eyes narrowed with enjoyment. "In that case, this mead was worth every bit of grief Ambrose will extract from me."

"I'm not going to wed you just yet," she informed him as she drained her cup.

Ramon finished off his mead and poured her another measure before serving himself. "Greedy for more attention?"

She nodded, her lips curved into a mischievous smile. He contemplated her for a long moment over the rim of his cup. "On the morrow…"

"Yes?"

Ramon took a slow sip of his mead, letting his thought lie unfinished between them.

"Ramon?"

He chuckled darkly and raised his cup to her. "You will have to wait to discover my plans." He set his cup down and captured the back of her head. "Linger in anticipation, for I will have you and you will be had very, very happily."

He pressed a kiss against her lips. It stoked the hunger inside her, and she reached for him.

Summer was suddenly far too long a season.

But she'd not tell him her thoughts until the morning. She could wait that long.

But not much longer.

❧

Isabel heard screams in her sleep.

She rolled over, trying to decide if it was a nightmare, but Ramon roared as he left the bed.

"To arms!" He pulled the window shutter open and yelled to his men. "To arms!"

The door flew open as Ambrose strode into the chamber and joined Ramon at the window. Yellow and orange light lit the night in a nightmarish scene.

"Raeburn?" Ambrose asked as he studied the view.

"I would bet my horse on it," Ramon growled. His squire skidded to a halt and scrambled to dress his master. Isabel sat up and pulled the bedding to her chin. Beyond the window, the flames rose higher, brightening the midnight sky. Screams came with the breeze as the sound of men and horses from the yard joined it.

Mildred was panting when she arrived in the bedchamber, wearing only an under robe and her hair swinging in a long braid behind her.

"Come, my lady, there's people needing stitching..."

Everyone hurried but it wasn't quick enough. Each screech made Isabel cringe. She couldn't get into her clothing fast enough. The scent of smoke grew thick, nauseating her as she finally got her boots laced.

"Bar the door behind me, Isabel."

She turned in horror, her lips moving but no words coming out.

"Do it!" Ramon ordered her softly. He was once more the man she'd watched ride up to Thistle Keep: his armor in place, his face only visible because his visor was raised. "And let no one in that is not me or has my head with them."

Her belly knotted, threatening to send up the remains of her supper. She gasped and fought for composure. She should not distract him with pitiful emotions. She must stand tall and steady.

His head…

"Isabel?"

"Yes. I will bar the keep." No words had ever felt more difficult to get past her lips.

Ramon nodded once, firm and resigned to his duty. There was a clank and shift of armor in the hallway as Ambrose appeared. Ramon turned away from her and something inside her felt as though it tore.

She lunged after him, unable to bear the separation.

"And…I shall pray for you."

Mildred reached out to stop her, grabbing her clothing. The fabric strained as Ramon looked back at her. His dark gaze looked her up and down, a flare of enjoyment in his eyes. His lips curved, his expression softening until another scream shattered the moment. Hard, cold reality returned. But Ramon nodded again, this time gently. More appreciative.

"My lady…there is great need…" Mildred stammered, unsettled by the sounds coming through the window.

Isabel gathered her composure and straightened her shoulders. "Aye. And we shall see to it."

The sounds of men in armor filled the keep as Ramon and Ambrose descended to the bottom floor. Their squires followed and the few torches left burning through the night flickered off their armor. A steady line of villagers were fighting their way toward the keep, carrying the wounded with them.

The hall filled with the sound of weeping and the scent of blood. The sound of Ramon and his men marching decreased. The maids looked on with wide eyes as children huddled in corners, their faces wet with tears. Everyone waited on her word. She watched the last of the villagers make their way inside.

In the distance, the first sounds of battle rose: the cries of men charging forward with courage and the sound of swords connecting.

It might very well be the sound of Ramon dying.

"Bar the door," Isabel commanded. She didn't have time to wallow in her personal fears and neither did anyone else. "Stoke up the fire. Boil water and bring in the stores…"

With something to do, her people started to move.

"Stop crying. If you've no skill to share, set yourself to praying for the men riding out to defend us."

Children wiped their faces on their sleeves before they fell to their knees and folded their hands.

Isabel had only a moment for a silent prayer before someone pushed her healing basket into her arms. Those lying on the tables looked to her, their faces full of pain and their eyes filled with desperation. She fought back the sickness making her belly roil and squared her shoulders.

Water hissed as it was poured into the kettles, heat touching her cheeks as the fires were stoked and the bellows worked to push air into the coals. The sound of the doors being closed sent a chill through her heart. The hard lowering of the bar sounded like the top of a coffin closing. She prayed that it wasn't Ramon's. But she couldn't ignore the possibility.

❧

"Damned bastards have fled to the high ground." Ambrose gestured with his sword. The light of the fires shimmered off the blood on the blade.

Ramon looked up, but the night hid Jacques.

"The bastard won't even face you." Ambrose spat on the ground.

"He craves only the prize." Ramon looked around the village. A dozen homes were smoldering ruins now, the hen houses emptied, and milk cows missing from their pens. "Which he has for the moment."

Ramon dismounted and walked over to a fallen man. He kicked the body, turning it over, but he kept his sword ready, in case this was an ambush.

The body flopped over, revealing a slit throat. Ramon noticed the Raeburn crest on the man's tunic. "Raeburn is usually not satisfied with livestock."

He didn't care for the sense of foreboding brewing inside him. It churned and grew as he turned and looked toward the high ground that was still shrouded in darkness.

"It's trickery," he decided. "Mount up! We ride for the keep!"

His men responded instantly. Horses snorted and armor shifted as they regained the saddle and turned their horses toward Thistle Keep. Only a dozen men were left behind to guard the village and help put out the fires.

Ramon kept his errant thoughts at bay as he covered the ground back to Thistle Keep. He couldn't lose his sense of command.

But he worried that Isabel had been headstrong

and not barred the keep. He admired her spirit, but she was too naive to understand the sort of man Raeburn was. Trickery came easily to him, as did riding through a village with swords slashing to ensure that Isabel would have reason to open the doors of her keep to the wounded.

He prayed that he wouldn't be too late. Jacques wouldn't make the mistake of allowing her the opportunity to escape a second time.

Thistle Keep was set on the high ground, and the cleared yard around it allowed the moonlight to illuminate it. A man hobbled up to the steps, dragging one limp leg up the steps as he groaned with the effort. He fell against the door and pounded on it with his fist.

"Shelter…mercy, lady!"

His cries were pitiful, the moonlight shimmering off a wet patch in his tunic. The metallic scent of blood drifted on the night air.

The tiny window opened, giving the man hope.

"Mercy!"

There was a groan as the bar moved. Ramon urged his stallion faster as he raised his sword.

"Hold the door! Hold the door!" Ramon yelled.

Flattened against the sides of the keep, Jacques's men waited to push in the doors. The man looked back, surprised as Ramon and his knight bore down on him. He turned his head and let out a terrified sound as he realized he was surrounded.

The men cried out, raising their swords to meet the oncoming charge. Ramon veered off, riding behind the storerooms, and found what he sought.

"Jacques Raeburn!" he roared as he raised his sword high in challenge.

Jacques was with his captains, his helmet adorned with a gold baron's coronet. There was no honorable way to refuse the challenge, and his captains were guiding their mounts away as Ramon leaned into the charge.

Their swords met with a loud clang. Ramon used his knees to control his horse as he lifted his sword high and swung it around toward his enemy.

"Preying on peasants again?" he demanded as Jacques ducked and avoided the slice of the blade. "Dismount and face me!"

"Play the chivalrous fool if you like, Segrave!" Jacques replied. "Make an easy target of yourself and I'll present your head to my bride as a wedding gift!"

"Isabel will not be yours!"

Ramon guided his horse around for another pass but Jacques was retreating, his stallion gaining ground as it was allowed to run.

There was a thunder of hooves as Ramon gave chase and his men followed. But Jacques made the forest, the trees swallowing him and his men. The ample leaves blocked out the moonlight.

Ramon pulled up with a vicious curse.

"Agreed," Ambrose said next to him. "That bastard has planned his game well."

"Not well enough to claim victory."

The knowledge brought little comfort. Ramon knew that the man would be back. He turned his mount around and swept the yard before dismounting.

"Rest while you can," he advised his men. "You

may be certain this fight is not finished. Post a watch and keep your eyes open! Or risk waking with your throats slit."

He climbed the steps, reaching down to hook the peasant man's arm and haul him to his feet. The man shivered, barely able to stay on his feet.

Ramon pounded on the door. "Open the doors. We have vanquished the raiders for now."

The small window opened. Ramon pushed his visor up and there was a muffled cry of joy from within. He heard the groan of the bar being lifted away by thick chains. The doors creaked as they were opened.

Relief didn't sweep through him until he spied Isabel. When it did, it nearly buckled his knees.

⁓

Her insides quivered.

It had naught to do with the blood surrounding her. But everything to do with the knight returning to her.

And Ramon was coming back to her.

It was there in his dark gaze, the fierce light of determination as he swept the hall until he found her. She stared back, drinking in the sight of him. She straightened, rising from the patient she tended, drawn to Ramon.

Her champion.

His captains crowded around him, drawing his attention. She looked back to the man she tended but felt relief surging through her.

And gratitude.

Without Ramon, they'd have been lost.

God help them. The sun rose, but her belly was

knotted as she looked out at the burned shells of homes lost to the raid. She walked toward the cemetery with the rest of the people of Thistle Keep to bury those who hadn't been spared. The newly turned earth nauseated her. Father Gabriel intoned prayers in Latin. Widows wept and orphaned children stood looking bewildered beside the graves of their parents.

Isabel tended to the duty of finding them homes, finally taking one boy to the church, because with so many men recently departed for the Crusade, there was no home that could take another mouth to feed. Even though service to the church was honorable, her heart ached for the choices she was depriving the boy of. He sucked on his thumb, looking to her with hopeful brown eyes. One young monk offered him a hand.

Isabel nodded and stood outside the doors of the church. The little boy looked at the monk and finally reached up to grasp his hand. The monk's sackcloth barely fluttered as he led the boy through the church toward the corridors only those devoted to the holy order walked.

It was the only way to ensure he did not starve. But her heart was heavy as she walked back to Thistle Keep. The lack of sleep was wearing on everyone. No stone was being hauled today, as the men needed to preserve their strength in case of another raid.

Ramon appeared on the steps, still in his armor with his sword hanging from his waist. It was late afternoon, the sun beginning to set.

But night did not offer the restful respite everyone needed. It was full of threats, and a shiver went down her back as she looked at Ramon and saw his determination.

"Isabel." His tone was grave. His expression tightened in distaste before he moved down the steps, with his captains and men following him. He stopped in front of her and hooked his hands into his belt. Sensation prickled on her nape as she faced him.

"Jacques sees you as a prize."

She swallowed the lump trying to form in her throat. She'd be damned if she was going to let Jacques frighten her. He was to be detested.

"I know it."

Ramon eyed her. "You will accept escort from my men."

Two of them left their lord and walked to stand behind her.

She shook her head but Ramon continued without mercy. "From the moment you leave your chamber, lady, until you retire for the night."

Ambrose was watching her from beneath hooded eyes, his carefree expression gone. In fact, it felt as though they were all different people than they had been just the night before. Playfulness seemed as lost as childhood to them all.

"Do not be difficult, Isabel," Ramon implored her. "I do not wish to be unkind, but Jacques Raeburn will not stop until there is no longer a prize to be had."

Ramon's gaze was hard. It sickened her to see it, but what horrified her was the grim resignation in his face. The same resignation was lodged in her chest.

"We will track him down," Ramon promised in a deadly tone.

He didn't have to.

That knowledge flared through her. Ramon owed her naught. If he departed for his own land with his knights, she could not label him a blackguard. But he took care of his people, and he was building a keep on her land even though she had refused to wed him.

What scared her was the certainty in his eyes that he would find and fight Jacques.

She couldn't bear his death.

"Do not engage him," she pleaded. "I will stay with the escort. Raeburn will tire of waiting and seek a new prize. A simpler one to claim."

"I know him, Isabel." Ramon spoke gravely. "He will not tire easily. There will be more blood spilled before he accepts defeat. I will not allow him to do this to your people, Isabel. It is my duty and that of my knights. But he knows such of my character and is likely counting on it."

"Yet this is not your fight—"

He made a slashing motion with his hand. "I know Raeburn. He will not stop unless he is forced to. He will raze every field before giving up on his quest. You think I can turn my back?"

"No. That is not your nature."

Every field.

It was too horrifying to consider and yet she had to face reality. She looked past Ramon, to where the smoke lingered in the air, darkening the summer sky. She recalled too clearly the newly filled graves and the faces of those who lost their loved ones.

She'd failed them. Failed them by indulging herself in a game of flirtation. Girls might enjoy such things, but she was the lady of the keep. She had her duty to think of. Her people to safeguard through her alliances.

"Then let us deny Raeburn his prize." Isabel drew herself up. "I will wed you."

Ramon's lips twitched just a fraction. There was a glitter of appreciation in his dark eyes that she drank in. He offered her his hand and she took it to the soft sound of his men's approval.

"To the church."

She expected Ramon to sound victorious, but instead she heard happiness.

And it was a very sweet sound.

⁓

Father Gabriel was a man sworn to dedication and piety, but he smiled brightly as he performed the wedding. There was also a very arrogant lift of his chin that Isabel admitted the man was allowed. Or at least it was in keeping with his holy vows because she was at last bending to his demands that she wed.

You are more interested in Ramon's demands...

It was a solid truth but one that didn't shame her. Someone had woven her a crown of greens, and the people of Thistle Keep were crowded around them with hastily scrubbed faces shining in the evening sun.

She wasn't sure she'd ever lived a day so full of extremes.

She prayed never to do so again, but she did not lament. The priest raised his hand and made the sign of the cross.

"You are married," he pronounced in a clear, unfaltering voice. "You may bestow the kiss of peace upon your bride."

Ramon tightened his grip on her hands and leaned forward. She squeezed his fingers back. Doubt tried to quell her happy mood, but she ignored it.

There was no certainty in life except death.

His kiss was light and quick. Her people let out a cheer as his men roared with approval and banged on their mail shirts with their swords.

At last her return to the keep was a journey of hope. Their supper was simple, but Ramon led her to the high table where more greens were laid out in celebration. In spite of their exhaustion, there was a festive air in the hall. A few musicians lent their skill to the moment, playing tunes that had the younger women dancing once they had eaten. Children laughed, making the most of the unexpected festivities.

In jest, they pulled and tugged on her robes, leaving Ramon watching over the rim of his drinking bowl. He lifted it in a toast as the women laughed at him. The children chanted as they circled Isabel, but their mothers broke in and dragged her toward the stairs before the dance was finished, intent on taking her to her bedchamber.

She giggled and slapped a hand over her mouth as she heard herself.

"Well, 'tis right good it is to hear you happy," Mildred remarked as she unlaced Isabel's over robe. There were still four other women in the room and they happily pulled the loosened garment up and over her head. They were witnesses, there to testify that she was healthy and not marked by either disease or Satan.

"Aye. Glad I am."

"A blessing," one woman remarked.

"We'll certainly sleep sounder this night," another added.

Isabel was wide awake. Excitement was prickling along her limbs, warming her as two of the women raised the bedding for her. She crawled into the bed and found it odd to lie on her back. Her cheeks turned scarlet as the women all sent her amused, knowing looks.

"A fine bridegroom you have to look forward to," someone stated boldly. "I hear he's built well beneath his tunic…"

Isabel gasped, but the line between peasant and lady seemed to be missing tonight. There was no polite phrasing, no modest flutters of eyelashes as the experienced women held their tongues in her presence. They were taking delight in their teasing. Yet they were not the only ones.

There was a crashing sound on the stairs and a snarl before the door was pushed in and Ambrose shoved Ramon forward as the two fought like two bears. More of Ramon's captains joined the fray as the women lined up in front of the bed.

"We're getting him ready for you, lady!" Ambrose informed her with a wolfish grin. "Just one more tunic…"

"The risk is yours, Ambrose…" Ramon growled and rotated his arms in huge circles to loosen up his shoulders. "Try me if you dare."

Ambrose squared off with his master, the rules missing between them as well.

"That will suffice. Have done with your games." Mildred's tone was full of authority. Her age allowed her to take command of the scene. She'd propped her hands on her hips and stood facing the men. They offered her only a few more snickers before they straightened in deference to her and lowered themselves.

She pointed Ramon's men toward the open door. They wickedly grinned at Ramon on their way out. Isabel felt her heart accelerating. Anticipation rippled through her, awakening every yearning Ramon had ever inspired in her. Her skin became ultrasensitive, her breasts heavy beneath the thin fabric of her chemise. She craved to be bare and pressed against Ramon.

What she craved would be hers. She smiled shyly at him. He straightened and his lips curved as he caught sight of her between the women.

"Good night, goodwives," he dismissed them.

There was a soft scoff from one that drew a suspicious look from Isabel.

"Good night to you, my lord," Mildred answered. She lowered herself modestly before she pointed at the door. "You will sleep with your captains."

"The hell I will," Ramon bit back. He snapped his mouth shut when he heard how harsh his words were. "Forgive me. Yet I intend to pass the night with my bride."

He gave her a hard look that made her shake her head. "I know not what this is about."

Mildred smiled gently, the way she might if she were addressing a child. Isabel cringed, for she knew that smile well. She was certain she was not going to like what Mildred was about to say.

Not at all.

"My lady has not bled since her abduction."

Ramon drew back, obviously surprised. "Does she bleed now?"

Isabel shook her head, mortified. She had forgotten how little privacy a wife enjoyed.

Ramon's eyes narrowed, his body drawing tense. "Then what is the issue you raise, good nurse?"

"There will be doubt cast upon your issue if you do not wait to consummate this union until she has bled."

Ramon's complexion darkened and he sent a hard look toward Isabel, his fists tightening. "Did Raeburn—"

"Nay," Isabel protested. She shook her head, shuddering at the idea of Jacques's touch. "He did not."

Ramon relaxed.

"There will still be rumors," Mildred insisted. The other women nodded. "So you will wait until there is no longer any reason to cast doubt."

Another woman entered the room, carrying several lengths of wool that the women standing in front of her took. They shook out the wool and bedded down along the edges of the chamber.

"Mildred," Isabel implored.

But Mildred shook her head and came around the bed. She climbed right into it and settled back against the pillows.

Ramon was fighting to maintain his temper. He looked at the women and Mildred before stepping over one and scooping Isabel up. She gasped as he settled her against his chest with a satisfied grunt.

"We shall only follow you, my lord." Ramon was halfway to the chamber door when Mildred issued her warning. Isabel cringed, her fingers tightening on the neckline of his tunic. "You know my thinking is sound, even if you have no liking for it."

Isabel sighed. "She is correct."

Ramon softly growled next to her ear. "Do not deny me."

She cupped his face and turned him so that their lips were only a breath apart. "I am not. Circumstances are." He nuzzled her temple. "Never have I been so tempted to curse God and his direction for me."

"Agreed."

He grunted and his arms tightened around her for a long moment before he turned and deposited her back in the bed.

"As you say, good nurse." His tone was tight as he nodded.

He strode through the doorway and across to the chamber Ambrose occupied. He laid his fist on the wooden panel of the door a single time before pushing it inward.

"I need a bed, since I have been turned out of my lady's."

There was a gasp and Ambrose lifted his tousled head from the bedding.

"You will have to find another bed, madam," Ramon said before he pulled back the bedding for the woman.

"The hell you say," Ambrose argued.

"The hell my wife's nurse says," Ramon said as he helped Ambrose's bedmate out and took her place. "By all means, try your luck with the woman. It seems I have none."

Mildred cleared her throat and wiggled against the pillows as Ambrose eyed her across the passageway.

"Why are we not on the Crusade again?"

The displaced maid stood for a long moment before she gathered up her clothing and exited the chamber. Her bare feet made soft sounds against the floor as she descended the stairs.

Isabel envied the girl, for at least she did not have everyone concerned about her. Being a lady was often more trouble than being a nun.

"I thought you wanted me to wed," she groused quietly.

Mildred nodded and opened her eyes. "Are you regretting your heated emotions toward the baron now, my lamb?"

Isabel pouted but it gained her no more attention from Mildred than it had when she was young. "I cannot help that the man makes me forget all reason."

Mildred cackled with amusement, her eyes disappearing into the folds of her face.

Isabel grumbled, "It is not like you to be so unkind, Mildred."

"Only knowledgeable." Mildred laid a kind hand on Isabel's forearm. "When age steals away your years, you will understand why I told you not to reject your opportunity to be a wife again."

"I have wed him. You are the one between us now."

"And you will thank me when your belly rises and no one whispers when you pass by as to the origins of the child. Perhaps you think such rumors will die with the passing of years? They will not. When time comes for your offspring to wed, they will stalk you like specters, for there are always those who try to profit from the misfortunes of others." Mildred's voice held

a firm resolve that Isabel recognized as unmovable.
There was also a ring of truth too loud to ignore.

But she cared for it not at all.

Not at all.

❦

Jacques snarled. His young squire didn't flinch. He'd
learned years ago to stand true in place or suffer worse
for being a coward.

"Let Ramon have her. I will find another heiress."

Jacques nodded and reached for a portion of meat,
but his expression remained troubled as he chewed.
Finally he cursed.

He sat back in his chair and considered the youth.
"Return to Thistle Keep. I may yet need to know
what is happening there."

The youth lowered himself and left. Jacques toyed
with his dagger, spinning it as its point dug into
the tabletop.

Aye, he might need to know what was happening
if his father did not agree with allowing Isabel to keep
the land. It was Raeburn land, and a Raeburn never
lost land.

He wouldn't be the first son to break that tradition.

At least she was beginning to interest him with
her cleverness. Of course, she'd be conquered if he
wanted it so. She was merely a woman and made for a
man's use, but it was always more interesting when he
encountered a female who made the chase entertaining. He grinned, his member stirring. He would draw
out breaking her to savor the experience.

He called out for his scribe. The man carried

a small desk with him as he lowered himself and entered the tent.

"A letter to my father."

The man nodded silently, arranging a smooth sheet of paper in front of him and removing the fitted leather top from his clay ink well. He lifted his quill and sharpened it with a small knife before he dipped it and waited.

Seven

Mildred was right.

Isabel tried to clear her mind and let that single thought sink in. It slid right off and she huffed. Mildred was very knowledgeable.

She pressed her hands together and attempted to concentrate on her prayer. She ended up opening her eyes.

Mildred was driving her insane.

Isabel left when the service was finished but two women trailed her. Seven days had never felt so long. She went to the mews, seeking out Griffin.

"I thought your nurse agreed with your wedding."

Isabel looked up to find Ambrose leaning against one of the walls in the mews. Griffin bristled but settled back down.

"She does."

"Yet she stops the consummation?"

Isabel held out her gloved hand for Griffin. "Forgive me, sir, but I shall not discuss so personal a matter with you."

Ambrose crossed his arms over his chest as he

leaned back against the wall. His blond hair had a curl to it, giving him a boyish flair, but one look into his blue eyes and she knew he was no boy. There was hard muscle beneath the sleeves of his tunic and broad shoulders to attest to the hours of training he did with his sword. The man was a knight, and a proven one at that. Deep in his eyes was a knowledge of things she couldn't possibly fathom that would make her shiver if she looked too closely.

"It is the talk of the manor, madam."

"Of course it is."

She gave him a withering look. He groaned and straightened. "I would have my bed back. Tell me what your nurse likes, the way to her heart."

Isabel laughed. "Mildred is past the age of wooing, Sir Ambrose."

He grinned, full of mischief. "No woman ever is. It is simply a matter of the right methods of persuasion."

His tone was confident. It stirred a hint of mischief in her, which was a welcome improvement over the frustrations of the past week.

"You are a rogue."

He spread his arms wide and bent slightly at his lean waist. But when he straightened he sighed. "Yet I will admit that your nurse has proven resistant to my charm. Which leaves me the option of stuffing her into an arrow sack as a means of achieving my goal."

"Do not," Isabel scolded, but found him looking at her with a teasing glint in his eyes. "She adores quail eggs."

His face brightened, intent flashing through his eyes. "Excuse me, lady, I have my own hunt to embark on."

He left the mews before Mildred emerged from the shadows.

"Selling my secrets, are you?"

Isabel carried Griffin toward the doorway. "Merely ensuring you enjoy the attentions being given to you." She fluttered her eyelashes. "You shouldn't waste opportunities. A wise person recently offered me the same advice."

Mildred humphed, but there was a small smile decorating her lips, proving she was amused.

"You might have told him you have started to bleed."

Isabel fluttered her eyelashes. "And deny you the pleasure of being the object of his attention?"

Mildred narrowed her eyes and shook a bony finger at Isabel. "Inside this time-ravaged body is the girl I was. Setting that man on me is unkind, for I know he has no true appetite for me, and he is a fine sight."

"Hmmm…" Isabel offered her nurse an innocent look. "Since you have ensured his bed is not as… warm…as he would like it to be, perhaps he might—"

"Have done!" Mildred tossed her apron up to cover her face. "When did you become such a wicked child?"

When indeed.

"I believe it was about the time Ramon de Segrave marched his men up to my keep and you advised me to enjoy it."

Mildred chuckled. "Agreed, although you did not admit it at the time."

"Was it so great a sin to want to be courted?"

Mildred cackled and shook her head. "Not that any man would agree with me."

Isabel stepped into the morning sun and scanned the yard. Ramon was overseeing the training of his men. He'd stripped down to only his under tunic. Sweat glistened on the sides of his face, wetting his hair as he demonstrated how to swing his sword: up high, and then in a sweeping motion designed to cut a man from his collarbone through his chest and out his side.

Brutal. Savage. But coupled with devotion to honor, it was a combination she could not resist.

When had she become wicked?

When Ramon de Segrave kissed her!

⤫

"The lady is bathing."

Ramon growled. "Tormenting me now, Ambrose? A fine friend you are. Not only am I barred from my own wife, but you would let me know she is sitting in the bathhouse wearing naught but water."

Ambrose chuckled. "I believe this is the first time I have heard you whine."

Ramon popped his knuckles and sent his fist into his opposite palm. "I have a great deal of pent up frustration, Ambrose. Make a target of yourself and I will happily use you as a release."

"Hoping your sweet lady will come to nurse you?"

Ramon growled but stopped, contemplating having Isabel tending to him. "It may well be worth allowing you to land a few blows for a change."

Ambrose snorted. "Allow nothing."

Ramon bared his teeth at his captain.

Ambrose chuckled. "You are woefully ignorant of women's ways, my friend."

"And you are overly knowledgeable," Ramon answered. "Or so the priest keeps bending my ear with dire predictions for your soul if I do not curtail you. Why do you tell him all of your conquests?"

"Because I need to know what manner of amends I need to perform. Does not the man preach daily for sinners to come to him? I give him obedience and he goes to you," Ambrose shot back. "Yet..." He lifted a single finger into the air between them. "That is not the subject I came to discuss. However, if you do not want to know that your lady is preparing herself for you, I will be silent and say not another word. Personally I would not like to consummate my vows with the salt of a hard day's work on my brow, but perhaps—"

Ramon looked toward the bathhouse. There was no flurry of activity, just the last of the evening sun lighting up the thatch roofing. "How do you know she prepares?"

Ambrose's expression became sensual. "The look in her eyes, my friend."

Ramon glared at him suspiciously.

Ambrose shrugged. "And I heard from two of the maids that the lady began to bleed last week. You really should not underestimate the value of being in the confidence of scullery maids."

"Father Gabriel warns against it," Ramon offered dryly. "Quite passionately, for a man of the cloth."

Ambrose chuckled. "The man is jealous."

"He's a monk."

"A fact that does not prove me incorrect."

Ramon groaned. "He's going to make me build a pillory just so he can have you sentenced to it."

Ambrose shrugged again and pointed at the platform standing off to the left of the church door. "I rather prefer being on display."

"Exactly," Ramon agreed. "As soon as the good priest learns how much you are in favor of his punishment, he'll be hounding me to build a set of stocks."

Mildred came into view, guiding two maids toward the bathhouse. She fussed at them, opening the door because their arms were full. One had new garments and the other Isabel's silver comb. They caught him watching and erupted into giggles before disappearing inside.

"I am grateful." Ramon wiped his brow on his sleeve.

Ambrose lifted his eyebrows. "Yet you sound so cross. Have I displeased you, my lord?"

Ramon growled but the sound lacked any true menace. He was too busy controlling the rush of heat flooding him. The final tasks he'd intended to accomplish before the sun set diminished in importance.

In fact, they became completely insignificant. Ambrose chuckled, drawing his attention. Ramon glared at his friend but Ambrose only laughed harder. For once, Ramon didn't care. In fact, he didn't care about anything except the fact that Isabel might be his now.

His…

৵

"It's too late in the day to wash your hair." Isabel didn't bother to reply as Mildred scolded her. "Well, if that's the way it is, go stand by the fire and dry it before you take ill."

She'd never felt more alive.

Isabel moved toward the fire, but she wasn't cold. The water had been refreshing, cooling the heat that had been building inside her. She ran a comb through her hair, lifting a section of it so that it might be warmed by the fire.

She'd be a wife tonight.

And what of tomorrow?

She frowned, disliking the doubt surfacing to taint her joy. Could she not be simply happy?

Yet it was a valid question. Would Ramon remain devoted to her? Or would he consider her in her place and his plaything?

"Are you still troubled by the thought of being my wife?"

She turned slowly, thinking for a moment that she must have imagined Ramon's voice. He was all she thought of anymore, her dreams as full of him as her waking hours were.

This time he was real. She trembled, her body tightening as she looked at him. His hair glistened with water, wetting the collar of the tunic he wore. She slowly shook her head but tightened her grip on her comb as she became uncertain. Perhaps timid was a better word. Her knees felt weak as she tried to decide how she should proceed.

His eyes narrowed. "Then what thoughts trouble you so much your brow is furrowed, my lady?"

His tone was soft and enticing. He moved closer and her belly tightened. It was a thrilling sensation that left her a little breathless. She shifted away from the fire without truly thinking about it. She was simply responding, her thoughts scattering.

"Answer me." There was a hint of demand in his tone, but what drew her interest was the dash of need.

He was so formidable, so strong, her thoughts couldn't be something that he needed.

And still, his gaze was beseeching. She struggled to form her thoughts into words. "I do not know…how to proceed." She placed her comb down and took a deep, slow breath that did little to calm her racing heart. "It is too early to retire and yet…"

"I cannot wait either."

He stood in front of her, a single space between them. He reached out and stroked her cheek. "You are my undoing, Isabel. A force I have never felt…"

His breath brushed her cheek. A ripple of sensation moved across her skin. It broke through the indecision holding her back. She reached for him, for what she craved, tracing his collarbone with her fingertips before flattening her hands against his chest.

He groaned and she withdrew. But he pressed toward her, until her hands rested on his chest again.

"More," he rasped.

Her back hit the wall but he stood still, waiting for her to make the next move. An insane little twist of power went through her, stunning her with how intense it was to reach for the man she desired.

As Rauxana had…

Heat licked up her insides, setting off a throbbing at the top of her sex. She smoothed her hands over his chest, delighting in the feel of his body. He was hard in places where she was soft, and she realized that they were made to fit together. He groaned again, but this time she smiled, her eyelids feeling heavy as she leaned toward him.

"Touch me," she barely whispered. She expected him to chastise her for such boldness. Wives did not demand. Yet she wanted more than to submit.

He settled his hands on her hips. She felt each red-hot fingertip, but instead of burning her, they made her shudder with more need. He smoothed his hands along her sides, and then down and over the flare of her hips before slipping down to squeeze the backs of her thighs.

"I have dreamed of doing nothing else for the last three weeks."

He leaned down and buried his face in her hair. His breath teased her nape as he drew in a deep breath and slid his hands up her body to cup her breasts.

"I want to stroke you, Isabel…" He gathered each breast in his hands and held their weight, sending a jolt of pleasure through her. "Kiss every place that I've touched."

He leaned down and fastened his mouth around one hard nipple. She gasped, a thin cry filling the bathhouse as he swirled his tongue around the puckered point. The barrier of the thin fabric of her under tunic frustrated her.

Ramon lifted his head and locked gazes with her. "And have you do the same to me."

She stiffened, rolling her lower lip in and setting her teeth into it, as she stared into his dark gaze. He was waiting for her, and the idea sparked a boldness she never expected.

"As you wish," she said sweetly but huskily. She

leaned toward him, pressing her body against his from knee to breast. His member was hard against her belly, fanning the flames of desire licking the inside of her passage. She wanted him inside her and felt her body growing moist for him.

He threaded his hands into her hair and rested his forehead against hers. "You have enchanted me."

"It is only right, for you swept away my will with your kiss."

He tilted his head and pressed his lips against hers, scattering her thoughts. It was a tender touch at first, a gentle tasting that sent ripples of delight through her. She opened her mouth, needing more contact between them. She reached for him, gripping handfuls of his hair as he traced her lower lip with the tip of his tongue.

It was too much. She shuddered, her heart thumping madly. Her head felt as though it were spinning and she didn't care. But her knees wobbled, like they wouldn't hold her weight any longer. She wanted to sink down and just writhe against him.

He slid an arm around her waist, binding her against him as he deepened the kiss. Demanding more from her, which she eagerly gave. Their tongues met and stroked in a motion that was carnal and welcome.

Every other thought slipped away, leaving her nothing but the desire to sate herself on his hard flesh.

She rubbed against him, moving her hips in a motion that felt perfect.

But not perfect just yet.

She reached for his tunic, trying to tug it up. He pulled away from her, breaking the kiss, and glanced at her, his need turning his expression wild. For a moment, she stared, feeling pride rise inside her. Aye, she was glad she had driven him to the same desire. Be it sin or not, they would burn together.

"Forgive me, Isabel, for I cannot wait."

"I share the same failing," she confessed as she tugged on the fabric of his tunic again. It was stuck between them, and she felt desperate to have his skin pressed against hers.

"Tonight…I will prove my worth to you. But now, I must have you."

He pulled away from her, just a single inch, but it was enough for her to pull his tunic up. The evening air brushed against her thighs as he pulled her under robe all the way up to her waist. She sighed but gasped when he boldly pressed his knee between her thighs.

He froze, stroking her jaw and raising her face to meet his. A question flickered in his eyes, concern that disrupted the pleasure flowing through her.

She lifted her knee and locked her leg around his hips as she had spied a maid or two doing in the passageways when they thought no one was about. His member slipped between her thighs, stroking across the folds of her sex and sending a bolt of sensation through her.

"Sweet mercy," she gasped, on the edge of ecstasy.

"Aye, sweet indeed."

He reached between them and stroked her folds. She shuddered, leaning back against his arm, unable to stop straining toward him. Sweat was beading on her forehead, her breath coming in tiny pants as she thrust toward him, the motion as necessary as drawing breath.

She was wet, her body flowing with enough fluid to coat his fingers. He slipped the wet digit into her, parting her folds with delicate motions.

"Claim me," she begged, certain that madness was going to claim her if she didn't find release.

"You'll be too tight." He drew his fingers up her slit to the point that was throbbing. "Take your ease."

He rubbed the little button at the top of her sex and leaned against her, keeping her thighs raised as he rubbed harder. She wanted to resist, wanted more, wanted to be filled, but there was no way to control herself. She thrust toward him, riding his hand as ecstasy burst and shot up into her womb. It was blinding and overwhelming, spinning her around and around and around until it flung her away into a churning whirlwind of pleasure.

Ramon held her, his body her source of strength and solace. She'd never felt something so intimate with another soul and she clung to him.

Yet it was not enough. Her appetite was not sated, only ebbed. She lifted her head from where it had slumped onto his shoulder, seeking his dark gaze.

"I would be your wife." All lack of certainty was gone, leaving only firm determination. She lifted her leg higher, locking it around his hip as she clasped him around his hard shoulders.

"Aye," he growled. It was more of a sound than a word and fit the moment perfectly. Just as his body felt perfect against her own. She'd never realized how compatible men and women were, or at least never guessed that it could be so blissful.

He shifted, withdrawing his fingers and guiding

his member into her. It was hard but covered in soft skin that slipped easily into her wet folds. He nudged against her opening, reaching around to cup her bottom and lift her.

Her body accepted but strained as it was stretched. He hesitated when he felt the resistance.

"Thrust true," she demanded. "And be done quickly."

He shook his head, withdrawing from her. "It can be done with patience, Isabel."

Surprise flashed through her but she had no time to linger on it. He moved toward her again, pressing more of his length into her. She stiffened, her passage taking him as it stretched.

"I would not pain you," he whispered against her ear.

"Tight is not pain."

But it was discomfort. He withdrew, granting her a moment of reprieve that turned out to be more of a torment because she hungered for him so much. When he thrust forward again, she lifted her hips and pressed toward him.

"Be still," he bit out, strain tightening his tone.

"I did not promise to be that sort of wife." She smiled. "And you promised me a passionate marriage bed." She locked eyes with him. "I am hungry for it."

"Then you shall be satisfied," he vowed.

His powerful body moved with far more purpose. He withdrew and thrust into her, filling her completely. She gasped, a moment of discomfort drifting through her but he didn't allow her to linger in it. He was moving, thrusting with a steady rhythm that sent her back into the blaze of hunger and need that had burst into such a storm of ecstasy. It was deep this time, the pleasure more intense. Every motion of his hips pressed the breath from her, but she met him, desperate for another stroke. His hardness satisfied her in a way she didn't understand and didn't want to think about.

All she wanted was to keep moving, keep lifting for his thrusts, keep straining toward him until she shattered. She clawed at him as the pleasure twisted through her, wringing her until every last bit of breath was gone from her body. She didn't care. Couldn't care because her mind was numb as her flesh reigned supreme.

"Aye…as I promised, vixen," he growled next to her ear. "You will forget your last husband, for he was not truly a husband to you."

His hands cupped her bottom, tightening on it as he rode her with hard thrusts. His chest labored to draw in enough breath to feed his heart as it hammered against her breasts. She felt his member growing stiffer, swelling inside her before it burst. Ramon snarled, his body drawing tight as he pumped his seed into her, holding himself as deep inside her as he could while the hot spurts hit the mouth of her womb.

He relaxed, but kept her clasped against him as they both struggled to catch their breaths. She didn't want to start thinking again, would have preferred to simply fall asleep against his shoulder with the scent of his skin filling her senses.

She had never enjoyed a man's scent before.

"We both need another bath, now that I have acted impulsively and lost the battle to wait until tonight."

"I will not chastise you, 'Iusband." She let her legs lower but her knees still felt wobbly.

He cupped her chin and raised her face. His expression had lost all of its guardedness. For the first time, she saw the man beneath the baron, the one who doubted and sought approval. She stroked his neck, feeling shy but excited at the same time.

"You may yet change your mind, for I plan to be a very, very demanding husband."

There was a playful gleam in his eyes that delighted her. A soft giggle escaped her lips, horrifying her because she thought she was far past the age of giggling. One dark eyebrow rose and then he tickled her. She gasped, squealing as she tried to escape from his fingers.

"Fiend!" she accused as she bent over to duck beneath his arm.

Ramon scooped her up with an ease that left her breathless. He turned around, carried her to the tub, and deposited her in it.

"My under robe," she protested as the fabric instantly soaked up the water and lay against her skin, displaying her every curve.

"Mildred can fetch you another, since she is hovering outside the door."

There was a *hmph* before they heard Mildred's steps.

"She was…right." Isabel's cheeks burned scarlet.

Ramon laughed softly at her mortification. He reached into the tub, grasped her wet under robe, and pulled it from her. It came free with a wet slosh and he tossed it over the edge of the open window that they had just been pressed against.

Her cheeks burned brighter, but she smiled too, realizing that the sun had set. Leaving her nothing but the night to enjoy.

Demanding? Her husband might discover that she intended to be his match.

&

His master would want to know.

But Donald hesitated.

Thistle Hill was a fine place to live and they welcomed him. It was true he had to sleep in the stable, for he was not trusted yet with a place on the floor of the great hall. Yet in time there might be much more for him.

But not if they discovered he had served Jacques Raeburn.

He swallowed his distaste and slipped away into the forest again. That was the difficulty with life—there were pitiful few opportunities for someone like himself. His mother had sent him to work when he was six. Some might say she had hoped for a better life for him with Raeburn, but he often doubted if the real reason was that his mother wanted to be rid of him and didn't have it in her to drown him. He'd often wondered if maybe she'd actually felt some emotion for him.

He'd never know, because she'd dropped a kiss on his brow and told him to work hard for his new lord. He didn't really even remember her name now, only that she'd had a wicked temper in the mornings and he'd learned not to wake her.

He hadn't chosen Jacques Raeburn but God had set the man above him, so he made his way through the forest to the edge of his camp. The moment the inhabitants of Thistle Hill learned he had been a squire to Raeburn, they'd remove his head.

There was no way to be certain the information wouldn't come to light, so he had no choice but to make his way to his master's tent and wait. The master's cries came through the canvas walls, indicating to the boy that Jacques was enjoying his woman.

The flap didn't move until the moon was overhead in the sky. The boy rubbed his arms to warm them and lifted his feet in a march to keep the chill of the night away. His leggings were thin and worn and he worried that he'd have to suffer through the winter with nothing better.

"The master will see you, Donald."

The boy lowered his eyes as he walked past the master's woman. She smelled good. He couldn't help but notice that. He didn't dare look at her—the master was a jealous man.

"What have you to report?"

Donald raised his head and looked at his master. Jacques was wrapped in a fur-lined dressing robe. Donald stared longingly at the thick fur as he fought to keep his teeth from chattering.

"They've consummated their union."

Jacques's forehead furrowed. "Just now? Why the delay?"

"The lady's nurse, she insisted that they wait. Wait until the lady bled, so no one would say the babe was yours."

"You fool!" Jacques roared. "You should have returned to tell me so!"

Donald fought to stay in place as his master surged out of his chair and struck him across the mouth. Donald fell in a heap but got back up and faced his master.

Donald fell in a heap but got back up and faced his master.

Jacques cursed and sat back down. "This is what I get when I trust a whore's son like you to know what is important and what is not."

He took a sip from his drinking bowl and leveled a hard look at Donald. "Return."

"My lord?" Donald hadn't meant to question, but it slipped out.

"I said, return to Thistle Keep. I will await instruction from my father."

"Of course." Donald lowered himself and backed out of the tent. It made sense now. Even a man such as Raeburn took orders from a more important man than himself. No one but the king was without a master.

No one.

Eight

THE NEW KEEP WAS RISING RAPIDLY.

Ramon's men had built cranes: two men walked inside huge wheels to lift the weight of the stones. Father Gabriel was often watching the stones rise into the air to be set into the walls of the keep. Although he was a man of God, Isabel could see the desire flicking in his eyes for those cranes to be used to raise a new church.

In time.

The summer brought flowers to the marshes; Isabel was eager to enjoy them and felt as though her feet were so light, she might skip. The grass grew high, roads marked only by their worn dirt tracks. The geese would have their hatchlings now. The little chicks grew so rapidly. The marshes would be full of mothers mentoring their young on how to find food while the ganders returned to keeping company with their own gender.

She hummed a merry tune as she went into the mews. But her elation died when she discovered Griffin missing from the mews. She emerged to discover one of Ramon's men leaving with the merlin perched on his arm.

She found Ramon working on the tower and went to him. His men tried to stop her, making slashing motions as she entered the work area.

"Hold." Ramon lifted his arm into the air with his fist closed tight. The work came to a halt as every man looked to see what would cause such a disturbance.

"My lady, return to the keep."

The man who had tickled her was hidden behind the one who had ridden up to her keep and informed her they were to wed. There was no hint of weakness or even kindness, just purpose. He was in command of everything she considered hers.

"Why did your man take Griffin?" she asked.

"Because the hawk needs to hunt and you will not place yourself at risk by taking him to the marshes."

Ramon cupped her elbow and turned her around easily, driving home how much stronger he was. But she shook off his hold, stumbling at her effort.

"Are you to tell me my place now, sir?" She stood up straight when he reached out to steady her. "Is that to be the tone of this union?"

He made another motion with his hand toward the workmen and the work resumed. The wheels groaned as the men inside them strained to start them and the rope took up the weight of more stone. A steady scraping filled the air as masons spread mortar and hammered blocks into place.

"When it comes to your well-being, Isabel, you shall listen to me," he said.

"I have run Thistle Keep for many seasons."

Ramon planted himself between her and the work being done. "Yet together, we shall make it stronger."

"Only if I bend completely to your will, it seems." Her temper flared but she couldn't control it.

"You will not go to the marshes. On that matter, you shall bend."

"You promised me…"

"I have kept my word to you." His eyes flashed with his rising temper. "In the matter of moving you to ecstasy and ensuring our bed is not cold. My men bled to protect your land." He drew in a deep breath to soften his tone. "I never promised you the freedom to be foolish."

"Yet you claimed you understood my feeling on becoming chattel."

His expression softened, but only for a moment. "I treat you like a wife I value. Were I to allow you to roam the marshes, where Jacques's men might come upon you again, I would be a husband that wed you only for the gain of your holdings. That is true caring." There was truth in his words but she didn't want to hear it. Ramon's expression tightened. "I protect you, even if it must be from your own whims. Call me harsh if you like, but in truth, I prove my caring for you."

He left her standing in the yard. She wanted to run up to him and argue but turned around and fled back to the keep. Until she realized she was making herself a prisoner. She turned and looked out over the fields. They were rippling with crops that would soon start to turn golden brown as harvest time approached. The new keep was three stories high now, the stones she had paid to have cut for the last three years put to good use. Anyone looking at her land would say it was bursting with good fortune.

All she saw was the freedom she would be denied.

"Come inside and stop your fussing," Mildred said. Of course she was there.

Isabel turned and gave her a hard look. "Do not lecture me."

Mildred propped her hands on her hips. "You can be sure I will. At least until the sun sets and your husband can deal with you. But you like the way he takes you to task, sure enough."

She did.

A ripple of sensation went through her, stroking the hunger hidden in her flesh. She'd never guessed she had such a carnal nature. But she wanted to be more. More than just the vessel for her husband's seed.

She stomped back into the keep, cradling her injured pride.

She would be more.

Somehow.

❧

"I do not find it amusing, Ambrose," Ramon said.

Ambrose choked on his laughter. He leaned back against the stone wall of the passageway and said, "It is very amusing, my friend. Very, very much so!"

Ramon resisted the urge to pound on the barred door of Isabel's bedchamber again. His man stood outside the door at his post, staring down the stairwell instead of looking at Ramon as he tried to get his wife to lift the bar.

But the man's lips were white from being pressed

so tightly together. Ramon felt his temper straining. Ambrose wiped his eyes as he chuckled softly.

Ramon turned on him. "I wonder how long you will be amused, as I share your bed once more."

Ambrose frowned, straightening and looking at the closed door.

Ramon chuckled at the rising terror on his friend's face before he walked across the hallway and settled on his back in bed. Ambrose joined him and stared at the ceiling.

"Do I want to know if you are planning on taking your wife in hand?" Ambrose asked.

Ramon chuckled softly, menacingly. "Be very sure that I have no plans to accept defeat."

None whatsoever.

⤫

She was being stubborn.

Isabel found the bed impossible to stay in and left it. She paced across the chamber and back again. The stone was cool beneath her feet and she shivered. Which only made her long for Ramon even more.

How had she become dependent on the man in so short a time?

You are craven…

She was. And her husband used the weakness against her. So she would simply learn to be without him. She looked at the bar across the door and nodded.

Indeed. Ramon was not the only one who could impress his will upon another. She could as well.

She just wished it did not make her bed feel so lonely.

But wishes never came true. She knew that well.

❦

"Locked him out of her chamber…"

"She did not!"

Isabel forced her chin to stay level as she walked into the sanctuary the next morning. More than a few curious looks were cast her way before the service began. She stood through it, noticing no one was paying attention to the priest but to her and Ramon, who was standing on the other side of the aisle with his men.

Apprehension filled her as she said the final prayer. *Now you'll know what sort of man you've wed…*

Well, that would be good too. Knowing the truth. She turned and gaped as Ramon strode from the church without a backward glance.

"Look at you," Mildred admonished her in a hushed whisper. "Looking forlorn when you're the one who barred the door."

"I'll not be denied—"

"Hush." Mildred poked her in the ribs to get her moving. Everyone except for Ramon's men was still standing in the sanctuary, waiting for her to leave.

Isabel forced a serene expression onto her face and walked quickly from the church. The moment she cleared the arched doorways, the whispers started.

She would not be swayed.

She increased her pace and left Mildred behind. The tasks waiting for her were many and she devoted herself to them to keep her mind busy. She didn't want to think about the pleasure she'd denied herself the evening before, because it came at the cost of her freedom. Jacques wouldn't want her now that she was wed.

The day went by, the sounds of the building common now. When they stopped, she raised her head. The yard remained quiet, not a single groan from the cranes. She dusted her hands on her apron and went toward the doorway of the keep. The heat of the day was waning, a breeze blowing in with the coolness of night. The sun was on the horizon, the last rays turning the sky orange and scarlet.

The new tower was crimson, its stone lighter in color because it had yet to be weathered. She lifted a hand to shade her eyes as she looked up at it. A prickle of dread touched her nape at the silence. Everything was sitting where it had been left, not a single one of Ramon's men anywhere in sight. It was as if they had vanished.

She trembled, her belly knotted.

There was a soft step behind her. She whirled around, her robes rising up, and saw Ramon looming over her.

"What have we here?" he demanded. "A prize to claim, I think!"

He grabbed her hips and lifted her up, tossing her into the air and over his shoulder.

"Ramon!"

His men laughed from behind the keep, some of them roaring encouragement to their lord. She glanced quickly at their revelry before Ramon carried her down the steps and tossed her over the back of his horse.

"To camp, men!"

"What are you doing?" She wasn't sure if he even heard her demand because she was being bounced with every step the powerful stallion took. Her head ached and her hair worked free, whipping around her face.

Ramon made a wide circle of Thistle Keep, making sure everyone saw him before he headed to the camp his men lived in. She saw the canvas tent walls before he lifted her by her girdle and handed her down to a man. She sputtered and pushed her hair back to find herself facing Ambrose.

"My thanks," Ramon said as he hoisted her once more and left her hanging over his shoulder.

"Ramon..."

Her protest went unheeded as he pushed through the tent flaps and inside. He lowered her to her feet, but her relief was short-lived. She faced a high bar of steel with a set of chains on it and a thick collar. She shuddered.

"What are you doing?" She stepped away from the chains, fighting the urge to rub her neck because it felt as though the collar were locked around her throat. "What are you thinking you've proved?"

He flopped onto his back in the middle of the bed and contemplated her. "That I understand the way of warfare more than you. It would be simple to lock you in that."

"So I must accept your will," she demanded, not caring for how much truth there was in his statement. Beyond the flaps of his tent she heard his men. There was no escape.

He crossed his boots and his lips lifted into an arrogant grin. "At the moment, you must deal with my whims, and I assure you, lady wife, they are carnal in nature."

She crossed her arms over her chest. "I think I will not be joining you in that bed."

"I have already proven that I do not need a bed to enjoy your sweet flesh."

Excitement brewed inside her. She didn't want to feel a thing, but as was the way with her body when it came to Ramon, there was no controlling the rise of hunger.

"This is preposterous, Ramon. Let us return to the keep."

His face lost its teasing expression, becoming serious. "I think not."

"You cannot—"

"Yet there is naught to stop me."

A new sensation went through her, and this one hurt. It was centered in her heart and grew from the fear starting to tear into her.

Ramon sighed and rolled off the bed. He closed the distance between them and cupped her chin. "Frightening you brings me no pleasure."

She scoffed at him and backed away. "Yet you abduct me and show me your chains? Is this to show me your tender devotion?"

His eyes flashed with a warning. "Aye. Better you learn the fate Jacques would give you if he is given the opportunity."

There was a hard note in his voice. She didn't care for how it dredged up the guilt that began to needle her. "You cannot expect me to be happy about having to change the way I live." Frustration burned through her.

"Yet you were as eager for marriage as I was, Isabel."

He caught her around her waist with his arm, pulling her against him even as she struggled to avoid him.

She'd melt, she knew it.

She pressed her hands against his chest. "I cannot lose myself."

He stopped, pulling her close, but stroked his hand along the curve of her hip. It was such a simple touch, yet so tender, it sent a bolt of emotion through her heart.

"Do you think I fear your effect on me any less?"

She was stunned, locking gazes with him and finding something there that she'd never expected.

Uncertainty.

"Men do not—"

"In your case, I do," he growled. "I cannot stomach the idea of you placing yourself at risk." He pointed at the collar. "I had that put in here with the intention of making you feel the weight of it, yet I cannot bring myself to put it on you. That is how weak I am now. I cannot even deliver a stern lesson to you."

Jacques certainly wouldn't have cared how she felt.

Her wrists suddenly itched even though her wounds were long healed. She rubbed them, drawing Ramon's attention. He stalked back to her and folded her into an embrace.

"Take an escort with you if you must leave the keep."

"It is a waste of men."

His chest rumbled with a grunt.

"Of course you know such," Isabel said, disliking the facts. But there was no way to dismiss them. Guilt tore into her, shredding her reasons for being angry.

"I shouldn't have barred the door. I don't know why I did it...only that...I feared I was..."

Tears were trying to choke her. He stroked her back, slowly, soothingly.

She raised her head and found him watching her. "You feared you were losing yourself to me?"

He wasn't taunting her. She was surprised that he was sharing the moment with her.

"Aye." Her response was soft. "I simply can't stop comparing you to my last husband, even though I know you are nothing like him."

"I know the difficulty, for I fight the same battle." He stroked her cheek. "I think it is a good thing that you had all that stone cut, for I am done sleeping in that chamber you shared with your last husband."

"You cannot blame a chamber for the way I feel."

He scooped her up, cradling her against his chest as he carried her to the bed.

"Yet I can decide that it is best for both of us to start our life together someplace else."

"Such as your tent?"

He tossed her onto the bed. It was smaller and lower to the ground because it was made to be broken down for travel. The bed ropes groaned as it took her weight, her robes flipping up to expose her legs all the way to her thighs. Her instinct was to push the fabric down, but the way Ramon's attention was drawn to her uncovered legs made her quell the impulse.

"Seems an agreeable way, from where I stand."

A memory of Rauxana surfaced.

She shifted her legs, slowly drawing one along the

other, and watched Ramon's complexion darken. She was fascinated by the way he watched her, his gaze devoted to her every motion. But he looked up and caught her.

For a moment, she saw frustration flaring in his dark eyes. Something surged through her and she realized it was anticipation, but this time she directed it.

"I suppose such is only…fair…"

He frowned but she rolled over and rose to her knees. This gown didn't lace, but was held closed with a girdle. She opened it and tossed it aside.

"What game do you play, Isabel?"

She had started to pull her loosened over gown up, but stopped. "I was intent on trying my hand at seducing you, Husband. Unless you would prefer me…dull."

She flopped back onto the bed. The ropes groaned and her clothing settled over her. "Is this better?"

He captured her ankles and pulled her down the bed. As she moved, her clothing stayed where it was, and by the time he'd finished pulling, he'd bared her to the top of her thighs.

"Much better," he growled.

She twisted, uncertain, but he pushed her robes up until she felt the night air on her mons.

"Ramon…" Her voice was a ghost of a whisper as excitement flared inside her. "What…you cannot…"

"Oh, I can and plan to…" He boldly petted her mons, stroking the curls that crowned her sex. "Tonight, I am going to taste you."

Her eyes widened, but she wasn't sure if it was with horror or delight. She felt a crazy twist of need tunneling through her passage. Her clit throbbed and every inch of her sex suddenly felt more sensitive.

She shuddered when his breath hit her folds. She cried out and tried to twist away, but he pressed her down with one hand on her belly.

"I enjoy making you cry with pleasure," he muttered as he stroked her slit with a single finger, drawing her cream forward. "And knowing you find ecstasy beneath my touch."

He was smug, his tone arrogant, but hearing it only excited her more. It went against everything she thought she wanted, but she couldn't deny the way she felt.

He teased her again, stroking her folds as she twisted beneath his touch. Her eyes closed as sensation took over but she opened them wide when she felt his breath against her sex.

"You cannot mean to…"

"I most certainly do," he declared, then lapped her.

She cried out again, the contact between his tongue and her slit so intense she couldn't hold it inside. Something twisted inside her, wringing her. Every muscle tightened, but she didn't burst into climax.

He kept her on the edge as he teased her with long licks, each one hotter than the last. She writhed and twisted and strained, so close to release.

"Stop toying with me," she snarled, opening her eyes and giving him a hard look.

She gasped. His eyes were ablaze with pride and possession. He looked at her, studying her before lowering his head and fastening his mouth on the top of her mons. He pulled her flesh inside and worked his tongue against her pleasure point. She burst beneath the motion, straining against him as pleasure exploded inside her, racing up her passage and into her womb. She felt as if she were being burned from the inside out.

Nothing pleased her more.

She surrendered to it gladly, content to be tossed about on the waves of ecstasy. When it released her, she panted on the bed, too spent to move.

Ramon rose and fit his member against her spread sex. She lifted her heavy eyelids to watch him, mesmerized by his member—thick and rigid and swollen. She licked her lips, suddenly not completely satisfied.

His first thrust eased her hunger. She locked her thighs around him, rising to meet him. There was no room in her for thoughts, only impulses. They flowed like water as she moved with him, gasping as he rode her hard and fast.

Still, it wasn't fast enough.

Or hard enough.

"More," she demanded between gritted teeth.

"Aye," he rasped. "You shall have it."

His face tightened until it was savage, wild in its raw determination. He rode her hard, and just as she teetered on the edge she felt his member begin to give up its load. The hot spurt sent her spiraling into pleasure again, the walls of her passage gripping his flesh and pulling forth the last of his seed.

"Sweet Christ!" he growled, pumping his hips against her a few final times. He fell forward, catching his weight before landing on her. The bed rocked with a vicious groan from the ropes holding the mattress before he settled on his back next to her and pulled her close.

She shifted, uncertain. Ramon pushed her head onto his shoulder and locked his arm around her waist.

"I need you near, Isabel. Do not ask me to explain why, just know I crave it as much as I do riding you."

She craved it, too.

There was no logic to the idea, but she shifted and laid her head against his chest. The sound of his heart filled her with a strange sense of contentment. It was different than the satisfaction glowing inside her body. This was a satisfaction that warmed her heart.

She'd never felt anything like it.

∽

"Off in the military camp, were you?" Mildred teased when Isabel came back to the keep the next morning. "Well now, do not you know what becomes of women who walk among soldiers?"

Isabel blushed but smiled knowingly, which made Mildred blush as well. Mildred waved a hand in the air between them. "Do not say. I am too old a woman to be teased by the enjoyments of youth that I can no longer have. Yet you may tell me you are glad I urged you to wed."

"I am glad."

And she was.

But as the day wore on, she realized her husband instructed his men to watch her. She bristled, but finally accepted that she'd have to either suffer confinement or an escort. She'd rather have control and a say over the matter, so she marched across the yard until Ambrose stepped into her path.

"'Tis unsafe, lady."

"I seek you."

He angled his head and looked down at her from his greater height. "Aye?"

"The men watching me answer to you."

He offered her only a raised eyebrow. "I follow commands given for your safety, lady."

His stance warned her that he wasn't going to be sympathetic to her desires.

"Their time is wasted. Let us come to an agreement."

He hooked his hands into his belt. "Only if it does not compromise my word to your husband."

"I wish to fly Griffin in the mornings. Provide me with an escort, and I will stay inside the keep the rest of the day."

Ambrose contemplated her for a moment. "Your word?"

"Aye."

He lifted his hand and two of his men walked toward them. "On the morrow, you will gather an escort for the lady to go hawking. Today, your duties are finished."

They looked relieved and returned to the ranks of men training.

"Do not disappoint me, lady. I have begun to like you," Ambrose warned her.

"I keep my word."

And she would, because her shoulders already felt lighter. Ramon kept half of his men training while the other half built the new keep. The two men who had shadowed her were happily pulling on padded tunics so that they could join those practicing with swords.

The new keep was three stories high now. She tipped her head back and shaded her eyes to look at it.

"Making bargains with my men?" Ramon inquired.

"Doing my part to ensure we do not waste resources," she countered. "Yet you could have spoken to me before setting your men on me."

He looked down at her, reminding her of how much larger he was. She forgot such things from time to time.

That was trust.

The realization made her smile.

"When it comes to your protection, Isabel, there will be no discussion."

"And yet it is simple to have an agreement," she argued. "Ambrose shall provide me an escort in the mornings, and I have given my word to stay in the keep during the rest of the day."

"Does that please you?"

She nodded.

"Then I will allow it."

She bristled and his eyes narrowed.

"Have mercy, Isabel. I mean no offense with my words, but my life has been one of command. As has yours, which is why you take exception to my rules."

She laughed, a soft sound that she closed her lips against, trying to contain the sound because there were so many near. "We are both used to ruling."

"Aye." He pointed at the tower. "Our efforts combine well."

"Very well."

A calm settled over her and she realized it was more than peace. It was a sense of happiness.

One that was very welcome.

❧

Jacques growled at his scribe. The man's hands shook and he crumpled the edge of the letter he read.

"My apologies, my lord. But that is what your father has written."

"I know it is!" Jacques snarled. "Get out."

The man scrambled to collect his writing desk and stumbled through the tent on his way out.

Curse Ramon de Segrave!

But cursing the man wouldn't gain him what he needed. His father wanted the land and had charged him with recovering it.

So Isabel of Camoys would have to find herself a widow once again.

At least he would enjoy doing that part of his father's bidding.

Nine

Harvest time was a busy time.

Everyone at Thistle Keep raced to bring in the crops and store them for winter before anything spoiled. There were the cellars to be seen to and small beer to be brewed. There was barley and fruit to be stored, but every room was filled already. Isabel even handed off Griffin to her escort when the days began to shorten and there was too much to be lost by exercising him herself. Ramon sent his men to the fields to help bring in the oats, and then had them digging privies before the snow began to fall.

The autumn rain came but there was still much to do. By the time the last of the root vegetables were being brought in, the days were short and it was time to wear thicker clothing. During the long winter months, there would be sewing to do, while the villagers set their hands to making mail.

"My lady…"

Ramon's squire, Thomas, came into the kitchen in the early afternoon. "My lord would have you attend him."

Thomas was lanky but towered over her. She was sure he'd grown over the summer.

She dusted her hands and smoothed one over her hair before going to the yard. The sky was dark with gray clouds that promised a good downpour before the night was through. There was a chill in the air, too, but she found it soothing, for the kitchens had been overly warm with the brewing of cider.

Ramon was waiting for her, the yard quiet. His men stood or sat looking at the new tower. Ramon turned and offered her his hand.

"Are you ready to see our new home, Wife?"

Her breath caught. "It is finished?"

He nodded. "I would never have thought such a feat possible. But with the pile of cut stones you had—"

"And the addition of your men to build," she said as she reached him and placed her hand in his.

"The structure is finished but the kitchens still need work."

He led her up the steps and her heart skipped a beat.

"This will be the center tower for our castle, Isabel."

It was large and round, to make it difficult to attack. Just because they had no tall timber close by didn't mean someone couldn't bring in trebuchets. Once they were on top of the steps, she was able to see that Thistle Keep was aligned with the new building. It was a third of the size and people were spilling out of it to look at the new keep. Excitement lit their faces.

The doorway was huge. Isabel looked up to where the keystone was set into the arch to keep it in place. Ramon suddenly scooped her off her feet, to the delight of his men.

"Ramon," she admonished softly.

Her husband winked at her as he carried her inside for the first time. The first floor was a huge great hall. Half of it was already full of trestle tables, and she realized they were the ones Ramon had carried to the Holy Land and back; the remains of his Crusade camp.

He guided her toward the stairs, which were wider than the ones in Thistle Keep, and started up, working their way around the structure until they came to the second floor. Dust still floated in the air and there was a scent of fresh mortar. The only stirring of breeze came from the open windows. The stone was set solidly and would hold for generations.

The second floor was split into four chambers, all of them unfurnished but full of possibilities. Another flight of stairs and they reached the third floor. The stairs ended at a small landing in front of double doors.

"Our chamber," he announced as he opened one of the doors. Below them, they could hear the echo of footsteps and excited voices as people followed them inside. Children laughed as Ramon moved her inside the chamber.

"The lord's chamber," she said, in awe of its size.

"Our chamber."

She glanced at him, uncertain, but he returned her gaze with a steady confidence that warmed her heart.

"I have spent enough time in the company of my men. This will be our sanctuary."

It was sectioned off into two chambers. A wall with two arched doorways was set a third of the way into the room. The furniture from Ramon's tent was already inside: his chair and side table with his scribe's desk. Her own things were there as well. The chest where her few fine garments were stored was there, along with her silver comb and the small chest that had her silk ribbons in it.

The stone floor was swept clean, no fine carpet on it. That pleased her, for it meant Ramon was not a man who sat in comfort while his men wallowed in mud.

"This winter, I'll have a table made. So we might enjoy a private supper here if we wish."

He laughed at the surprise on her face.

"You needn't laugh, sir."

He chuckled. "And why not, Wife? Where is it written that a marriage must be all duty? Or that I may not enjoy my labors with you?" He turned his head toward the next chamber. "I have every intention of enjoying the bed I had made for us."

Beyond the wall was a bedchamber. Isabel gasped at the sight of the huge bed sitting in it.

"What is that?" The size of it astounded her.

"That will be the bed I ravish you in."

He scooped her up again and carried her to it. Her eyes widened when he followed her down onto it.

"You cannot mean now..."

He nuzzled her neck, pressing a hot kiss there that sent ripples of delight across her skin. "Have I not finished my work?"

He caught her hands and pressed a kiss against each one. "Should I not receive your tender touch as a reward?"

"A reward is given, not pinned down beneath you, Husband."

He offered her a hungry look. "My reward, so my rules."

She tapped a finger against his lips, heat moving through her and making her bold. "I am sorry to hear you do not have the strength to wait on my whim… I had thought I might…well, as you will not allow me my way, there is little point in telling you." Her tone become disappointed.

His complexion darkened. "Doubting me again…" He rolled off her and settled on his back in the middle of the huge bed. "I await your whims…vixen."

The word *vixen* shouldn't have pleased her but it did. She sat up and contemplated the huge man waiting for her to decide what she wanted to do with him. She'd never encountered such a situation. Women submitted to their husbands, after all.

Yet Rauxana hadn't.

Isabel thought of the way the exotic woman had looked when she drove Jacques mad, like it set fire to a bundle of ideas she had never been bold enough to admit having.

Isabel rose to her knees and traced her girdle with her finger. Ramon's attention followed her motion. She undid the closure and let it fall behind her. The fabric of her robes loosened, allowing her to tug it up and over her head. When it blocked her sight of Ramon, her breath stuck in her throat.

Was he waiting?

Anticipation twisted through her, setting off a hunger that she knew very well would only be sated by having him inside her.

But perhaps…she would be the one riding him tonight.

Her cheeks turned scarlet when she tossed her over robe aside. She boldly reached for her under robe and sent it onto the floor with a swift motion.

Slow down. Rauxana had moved slowly…

"Christ, you are a vision," Ramon growled, his expression tight as his gaze slid down her bare frame. He started to sit up.

"Wait." Her tone was soft but firm. He froze.

"I crave you, Isabel."

She drew in a deep breath and let it out before crawling across the bed to Ramon. He relaxed onto his back but his expression was strained.

"As I crave you… Yet, words are not always sufficient. You should allow me to…show you." She placed her hand on his thigh and stroked his leg… up…up…until she crossed over onto his body.

"Holy Mother," he exclaimed as her fingertips brushed his member.

His jaw tightened and his eyes slid closed. Her nipples beaded as excitement flared up inside her, but she controlled her own needs, intoxicated by the idea of driving him as insane as he so often did to her.

Was that arrogance? She didn't bloody care.

"I wonder if you will cry out as I do beneath your lips…"

He jerked, his eyes snapping open. "Nay—"

She cut him off as she grasped his member. It was hard and throbbing beneath the layers of his clothing.

"Nay?" she questioned softly, stroking his length up and down as his breathing became harsh. "I thought you craved your vixen."

She tossed his tunic up and grasped the top of his

leggings to pull them down. His member sprang up, swollen with desire. "A vixen does as she pleases with what she desires."

"Until she's caught," he warned, his tone promising.

"Oh well..." She rolled over onto her back, the amazing size of the bed allowing her space. "I suppose I shall just lie here and pray...since you desire submission."

He settled on his side and looked at her. "You are toying with me."

She rolled onto her side so that they were facing one another. Her belly was fluttering with nervousness, for she'd never been so brazen, but this was more fun than she'd ever had with a man. "Does not a vixen play?"

She was holding her breath, waiting to see what he'd make of her boldness.

He laughed and tore his tunic off. "Indeed." He moved off the bed and pushed his leggings down to his feet and stepped out of them. "Even if I am slightly bewildered to discover how much I enjoy the way we play together."

"It is...unique," she answered breathlessly. "I like it."

For a moment, she felt exposed. Their gazes locked and she witnessed the same need in his gaze.

"As do I, Isabel."

It took effort to remain still and not cover her bare breasts. His dark gaze devoured them but the reward was the desire glittering in those dark orbs. Her eyelashes fluttered as she realized how vain she was.

"You are beautiful. Do not think it a sin to enjoy the fact that I find you perfect."

He crawled onto the bed and lay on his back.

He gave her a challenging look that made her heart accelerate.

Did she dare?

Yes...

She shivered, but reached out and closed her fingers around his staff. He sucked in his breath, his face tightening with enjoyment. A surge of confidence filled her, driving up the level of boldness burning inside her. She wanted to drive him as insane as he had driven her.

She craved the same power she'd witnessed in Rauxana's eyes. Not for the sake of control, but because she wanted to be Ramon's match. At least while their chamber door was closed.

She trailed her fingers along his length, delighting in the silky smooth skin that covered his hard member.

"Your touch will be my undoing." His tone was harsh, but she heard the pleasure in it. That same twisting, burning enjoyment that she discovered beneath his lips.

She hoped he'd enjoy her touch as much as she had his.

She leaned down and pressed a soft kiss against his staff.

He snarled something profane.

She looked at him in shock; the expression on his face intrigued her. It was nearly savage.

She leaned down and licked his staff. Just a slow touch of her tongue to his skin. He jerked and she saw his hands claw at the bedding.

She recalled doing the same. It was empowering. And exciting. And more intimate than anything she'd ever experienced.

She licked him again, working her hand along his member as she licked the head. His breathing roughened, becoming harsh as she opened her mouth and took him completely inside. There she was free to use her tongue on the underside of his member, trying to mimic what he'd done to her.

He jerked and cursed again, his hips thrusting toward her mouth, driving his member inside.

"Enough!" he roared as he sat up and lifted her shoulders away from him.

"No, it is not." She pulled her legs up so that she was straddling him. "I will ride you this time."

His face tightened. She took advantage of his lapse and moved her body over his. She was shaking but refused to let uncertainty eat away at her resolve.

She needed to be his match.

Needed to be more than his to plow.

She lowered herself and felt his member pressing into her passage.

Just needed him.

And she was going to take him.

"Vixen," he accused softly. He cupped her hips and guided her down his length.

"Aye," she agreed before she rose and plunged back down.

Pleasure spiked through her, driving the breath from her body. She was rising again and then back down, the rhythm coming to her.

"You have me torn now."

Pleasure was building inside her with every rise and fall, making it hard to concentrate on his words. "You would rather I was on my back?"

He grinned at her. "I want to keep you in the saddle." His hands tightened on her hips, pushing her down. He groaned when she sheathed him completely. "But I also want to cup these…"

He reached up and filled his hands with her breasts. "These mouthwatering handfuls."

He curled up and captured one nipple between his lips. The contact was searing and sent a rush of urgency through her. She rode him faster, harder, gripping his hips as she felt herself nearing that peak again. He fell back, his lips curling as he thrust up to meet her downward plunges.

"That's it, my beauty…ride me to the finish…"

It wasn't even a question of whether or not she wanted to. She needed to.

It was the only thought in her mind. Completely controlling, gripping, and enchanting. She'd never needed anything as much as she needed the next thrust. Never craved anything more than the pleasure beginning to burst inside her. It consumed her, rising up from the motion of him filling her with his hard flesh. Erupting in a burst of pleasure so bright she cried out.

Ramon growled, holding her in place above him as he thrust up into her several more times and gained his own release. She was drawing a breath when she felt his seed beginning to fill her. The hot spurt sent another ripple of delight through her. The walls of her passage gripped his length, milking him of his seed, as she collapsed onto him, and nothing else mattered at all.

Nothing.

❦

"Wake and kiss me, Wife."

She rolled over, stretching, and felt as though she had never slept so deeply. The bedding started to slip down her body as she moved, and Ramon reached over and pulled it back up.

Her vision cleared and she realized Thomas was tending to his lord.

She grabbed the bedding and frowned at the amusement twinkling in her husband's eyes. He leaned down and kissed her pouting lips.

"I'm off to down a stag, now that this keep is finished." Her mouth started watering.

She smiled. "The meat will be welcome."

Only a noble or royal could down a stag. She sat up, careful to keep the bedding held up to her chin. A short snort came from the outer room.

"Ambrose St. Martin," she admonished softly.

Her husband's friend gave her an amused look before he turned his back on her. His mail shimmered in the early sunlight, and he stomped on the floor.

"Pull yourself from your bedchamber, Ramon! Even if I understand what tempts you to stay there, the day has begun."

Ramon sighed. He winked at her before walking across the chamber to join his friend. They left, and Mildred bustled into the chamber.

"What a fine keep!" her nurse exclaimed as she handed Isabel an under robe. "So much space. Mind you, it's already full because of the lord's men, but such a space nonetheless. He sent a third of his men to help cut more stone. By next season, we'll see the beginning of a true castle here."

Mildred wasn't the only one in a fine mood. Everyone seemed to be in good cheer. Isabel saw more smiles on her way down the stairs. There was even soft singing as the women went about their duties.

The harvest was still underway and the half-finished new kitchen was pressed into service. There was stewing and brewing to do. Isabel held back one of the large hearths, anticipating a stag to roast. The children started licking their lips with anticipation, for the only time they might have hoped for such a treat was at the harvest festival, still a month off. They sat on the steps of the keep, watching for Ramon and his men to return.

❧

"He is a baron, Lord Racburn." His men were always loyal, but only because Jacques made sure they were paid well. "And so long as he draws breath, we cannot claim the prize."

His man still didn't look appeased. The men behind him were frowning.

"When I wed that widow, there will be a new keep to man and more silver for the men loyal to me. As well as all those women to ease your cocks. We all know most of their husbands will never return from the Crusade," Jacques told them. "Why do you think I am here? Let Richard have his Crusade. There is plunder here for those of us wise enough to stay."

Grins appeared on his men's faces.

"But she must be a widow for me to claim her."

Jacques left his words between them. It didn't take long for his men to see the wisdom in his plan. They split into two groups and made their way through the woods. He joined them, enjoying the anticipation of driving his sword through Ramon de Segrave.

His father would not be disappointed.

~

The younger children settled on the steps of the keep as the sun sank low. They were giddy with excitement, watching the road for signs of the men and the possibility of a stag to roast.

"Riders!" the children cried out at last. They stood up, clapping with glee, their faces bright with excitement. But then their hands stopped, sending a chill down Isabel's back. She hurried out of the keep to see Ramon riding back into the yard. The scent of fresh blood filled the air, but there was no stag.

Horror shot through her. Time slowed as she searched each man for injury.

Ramon snarled as he slid off his stallion. His men were crowding around him and helping the other members of his party from their horses.

"Damned Raeburn ambushed us," Ambrose declared.

Ramon's men cursed, many of them spitting on the ground.

Ramon lifted his hand and bellowed, "Hold." His men stilled instantly. Isabel felt cold because her husband's fingers were red with blood.

His blood.

"There will be no vengeance," Ramon said clearly. He stood for just a moment before turning toward the keep. Mildred gasped beside her because his face was a ghostly white. Isabel bit her lip to contain her tears. She must stand firm.

He staggered toward her, finally accepting help from Ambrose when he found the first step impossible to climb. His leggings glistened with blood, the arrow still stuck in his thigh.

"Lady?" Ambrose implored her.

His tone snapped through the shock freezing her in place. "The kitchen," she directed, turning and shooing everyone out of their way. "Mildred?"

"I'm coming, child," Mildred responded as Ambrose helped Ramon through the new hall.

"And who thought it a bloody fine idea to make this keep so large?" Ramon groused.

"You did," Ambrose answered.

The women working in the kitchen shrieked when they arrived, scrambling to clear the long work table before Ramon made it to it. He snorted and refused to lie on the table. Instead he sat on the edge of the table and stretched out his leg.

"Damned bastard," he muttered as he grasped the arrow.

"Do not do that," Isabel warned. She covered his hand with hers. "It will tear your muscle if you pull it."

"Allow your lady to tend you, my lord," Mildred cautioned him. "I've taught her well."

"So long as this damned thing is out of my leg."

Mildred set a basket on the table. Isabel pulled a bound roll of linen from it and untied the knot holding it closed. When she unrolled it, several small knives were nestled into the pocket. She pulled one out and used it to cut the fabric of his legging away.

"Do it, lady…" Ramon said.

"I must have everything ready first…" she warned, rubbing a soothing hand along his leg. "Else you might lose too much blood."

She started shaking and forced herself to stop.

Mildred mixed boiling water with some powder she'd taken from the basket—willow bark for pain. Then she laid out a ground dust from mushrooms to stem the flow of blood.

Mildred pulled the pot from the fire and set it on the table. Another woman set a beeswax candle on the table and lit it, but there was no time to enjoy its sweet scent. Isabel took a long silver needle from the fabric and held it in the candle's flame. She threaded the needle when it had cooled and stuck it into the linen again.

She was trying to focus.

But it was hard.

She didn't have time to think about why it was affecting her so greatly; it was hardly the first wound she had tended.

She picked up a knife and held it in the flame. When the blade had been completely heated she turned to Ramon.

Her belly clenched.

Ambrose hooked his arm through Ramon's. Mildred tried to push a length of leather between Ramon's teeth, but he refused. He grinned at her, arrogant and as full of command as the first time she'd seen him.

"I trust your hand, Isabel."

Oh Christ...

She wasn't sure she did. Which didn't make any sense. She'd tended worse wounds, but the sight of his blood sent bile into her throat.

Enough! You are the lady of this keep...

She swallowed and looked at the arrow. Cutting it away was better than tearing it out. A cut could be sewn. She gripped the handle of the dagger and set to work. Sweat beaded on her forehead before she had the arrow free. Mildred handed her the mixture and she poured it on the wound.

Ramon sucked in a harsh breath but never moved.

"It will help prevent fever," she explained.

"Didn't your last husband die of fever?" Ambrose asked mockingly.

Isabel gave him a hard look. "He refused to take anything I made for him, placing his faith in divine intervention."

"Foolish," Mildred declared with a humph. "The Lord blessed us with a forest full of healing plants. Why would he do such a thing if we weren't allowed to use them? Do you tell the sword master not to forge the metal?" She looked into the basket with a knowledgeable eye and her lips settled into a satisfied smile.

Isabel began closing the wound, keeping her mind on the task of making sure her stitches were deep enough to hold. Time crept by, tormenting her with how slow it moved.

Stitching had never taken so long before!

When she finished, she wiped her brow and the sides of her face. She wrapped a long length of linen over the wound. Ambrose moved away and returned with a drinking bowl full of fresh hard cider.

Ramon took it with a grunt before he stood up. "You should rest."

Her husband started to argue but his leg refused to hold his weight. "Curse Raeburn for the coward he is." He ended up perched on the edge of the table again.

Isabel looked to him for an explanation but he lifted the cider to his lips and drew a deep swallow from it. She sent Ambrose a questioning look.

"Bastard loosed an arrow before crying attack. It was an ambush. The action of a coward," Ambrose answered her, his tone harsh with rage. "Let me ride out against him."

Ramon lowered the drinking bowl. "It's *my* leg."

Her mouth went dry and her hands began to tremble again.

His leg…so his right of vengeance.

❧

The harvest fair was drawing close, and all the inhabitants of the keep were getting excited. All except Isabel.

Children once again sat on the steps of the keep and watched the road; now they were waiting for merchants to arrive. The air was cool at night and rain fell more often. The last of the harvest was brought in and men climbed up on tall ladders to make sure the roofs were in good repair for the coming winter. The elders went down to the river in the early mornings, looking for signs of ice. The hay was stacked high in the fields to feed the livestock through the next season.

Isabel tried to focus on making sure the window shutters were in good repair and the other tasks a lady needed to oversee, like the making of soap. But her thoughts always returned to her husband's healing leg. He was walking around more now and she truly should have been more grateful for his recovery.

Instead she dreaded what he'd do when he was fit for battle again. She awoke to the sound of armor one morning and knew without a doubt that her fears were coming true.

Thomas was fitting on the shoulder pieces of her husband's armor with the use of a stool, so that he could be taller than Ramon. Isabel swallowed her distaste and rose from the bed.

The contentment that had settled over her shredded as she watched the squire finish his duties.

"Where do you go, my lord?"

He turned, his hair hidden beneath his mail hood. Thomas had his helmet in his hands. Ramon waved the squire toward the door.

Isabel came to the arched doorway in her under robe now that the youth was gone.

"What troubles you, Isabel?"

She bit her lower lip, trying to conceal her fears. "Can I not be curious?"

His dark eyes were sharp and keen, cutting into hers. "It is more than that."

She sighed. "Can you not be content with your recovery? Why must you give him another chance to kill you?"

Her voice trembled. She couldn't keep her emotions hidden.

A look crossed his face that she didn't recognize until his expression softened.

"You fear for me."

She felt exposed but couldn't argue. Not without lying. She looked at the floor. She heard him coming to her, his soft steps eating away at the dam she had her emotions held behind. She blinked rapidly, trying to keep from weeping.

It made no sense. Yet she could not deny what she felt.

Ramon cupped her chin, the scent of his skin filling her senses. She shuddered, so full of need for him, need that ran much deeper than passion. Her heart was involved now.

He lifted her chin until their eyes met again. His dark ones were so full of authority and strength, but it was the determination that cut her to the bone.

"Do you fear for me?" he asked softly.

"I would not have you risk yourself." It was a confession, one that was dug out of her soul.

"I am a knight; as such, danger is something I will not shrink away from." His tone was steady and strong, two of the qualities that she held most dear in him, but they also brought her worry.

"I question you riding out for vengeance."

His expression became guarded again. "And if the cause was just, would I not see worry in your eyes?"

She searched his eyes, trying to determine if he cared as much as she did. She wasn't sure she could bear it if he didn't.

"You would, yet I would keep my peace, for I know you would never turn coward."

He smiled slowly. "I never thought to find myself appreciating a woman's argument."

"Nor did I think I might worry over you risking your life." Yet she did.

He drew back. "It is a natural thing for a woman to become content when she is treated well."

"Are you not content?"

"Our union is very satisfying." His tone had a touch of heat in it. A flame that had been missing since his injury.

Still, that was lust and her passions had grown roots that went much deeper. "That is not the same thing."

She should have kept her lips closed. Shouldn't have empowered him in such a manner. Her tender feelings were on display now, the unreadable expression on his face wounding them.

"Men are not the same as women," he offered.

It was an attempt at kindness but she felt the sting of rejection. She stiffened and his expression hardened. His honor prevented him from lying to her, even to save her pain. She turned around, seeking escape, but the sight of the bed was her undoing. Two tears escaped her eyes.

She heard him let out a short breath before he moved, his steps closing in on her. She didn't have time to turn around before he wrapped his arms around her. His armor was hard, reminding her that she only touched the lust in him and not his heart.

"I do not ride out for vengeance, yet only to make arrangements for the harvest festival. I wear my armor because Jacques is a coward and I have no wish to spend the festival day nursing another wound."

She shuddered with relief and failed to keep him from feeling it. He rubbed her arms, his breath warm against her ear.

"I value your concern, Isabel."

But he didn't return it. She didn't have any right to wish for it. Love was something only the insane felt.

And still, when he'd left, she found herself weeping for the lack of response to her admission.

It seemed that her marriage still had its share of hurt.

Ten

Harvest festival was a time of joy.

Isabel tried to smile but the sides of her lips felt heavy.

You are asking for too much. Being greedy.

It was true, and yet she struggled to stop thinking about what Ramon had *not* said.

What she should be doing was concentrating on how warm her marriage bed was. No more dreading her husband's step outside her chamber door. The winter would be far more comfortable with Ramon sleeping beside her.

"Here now, you need to be wearing something finer than that today," Mildred said as she came into the chamber. She pulled one of the keys from her girdle and fit it into the lock on the chest. Two other maids had followed her and helped close the chest's lid. Its hinges squealed.

"The auburn one, I think," Mildred continued.

The maids lifted up the over robe and smiled approvingly. Isabel lifted her arms and the robe settled down, but got stuck at her bust line. She tugged on it but she was too large for the garment.

"It seems marriage agrees with you this time," Mildred observed before waving her hand at the maids to have them lift the over robe away. Mildred did not look for another robe. Instead, she eyed Isabel, inspecting her body for a long moment with a critical eye.

The maids came back with another robe that slid into place. It was a blue only one shade darker than her eyes. Once it was laced closed, Isabel decided that she would spend some of the winter making a new robe or two. Her breasts were larger, no doubt due to Ramon's attention to them.

The keep was almost empty. Everyone was on their way to the harvest festival. There would be feasting and entertainment. Music to dance to and other traveling entertainers to watch. Several little girls waited on the steps for her, holding a harvest garland made with stalks of barley and dried flowers. They giggled as they set it on her head and eagerly grasped her hand and robe to pull her across the yard toward the festival.

The music was inviting. Many of the monks went to the festival, enjoying the last of the fall weather. Some of their brethren would stay inside the church, refusing to take part in such a pagan display, but the brothers who did go smiled as they moved toward the vendors selling cheese and sweets.

People wore garlands made of scarlet leaves and berries. They danced in long columns that turned into huge circles as drums and flutes played merry tunes. The girls spun so fast that their robes rose up to their bare knees, and Ramon's men encouraged them with lusty cheers. The ground shook from so many feet pounding it in the same rhythm.

Perhaps it was a touch pagan.

Or at least carnal.

But it was exciting.

Two stags and a boar were roasting over open pits. The cook reached in to slice off the meat as it roasted and handed it out. On harvest festival day, the lord fed his people to thank them for their loyalty. People drank much cider and short beer, making the long hours to prepare it worthwhile. Little boys sat near the cook, rubbing and comparing their distended bellies before letting out loud belches in a competition to see who was loudest.

It was gluttony. An entire day devoted to naught but pleasure seeking. Girls let their hair loose, many linen caps left behind in the keep. Even the widows uncovered their heads and danced merrily.

Everyone was excited, the scent of the roasting meat bringing smiles to even the most forlorn faces.

Who knew what the winter might bring?

Isabel accepted a drinking bowl of cider but wrinkled her nose at the scent. Her stomach clenched and she set the drink aside quickly.

"No taste for cider, lady?" Ambrose asked.

"It seems not."

He grinned and picked up her discarded drinking bowl and poured the contents into his. "More for me!"

Isabel smiled and went off with the girls to see a man with two trained dogs. She danced with the other women, but by the afternoon, the single women left on the arms of Ramon's men. Most of the entertainers were finished and taking their turn to sample the meat now that they had earned what coin the locals were willing to part with.

Down the hill, though, the men were still celebrating loudly. A cheer rose, and another, and then a hard sound. Mildred tried to pull Isabel away but she looked toward the group of men and tried to decide what they were doing.

"It's no place for you, my lamb," Mildred warned.

She heard a roar. The men were all clustered around something, intent on watching.

Isabel walked in their direction, but Mildred blocked her path.

"They're fighting for sport. It's no place for a lady."

"Fighting?"

There was another cheer and the crowd parted as two men fell to the dirt where the spectators had been standing. They were locked in battle, their chests bare as they grunted and tried to tear each other apart with their hands.

And one of them was Ramon.

He staggered to his feet and lifted his arms high into the air as he roared with victory. Isabel put her hands on her hips, her temper flaring. He came full circle and ended up facing her. He stopped and his men looked up at her.

The moment they saw her they hooted. Their laughter increased until several men fell over from their amusement.

"Your wife is displeased!"

"Better soothe her temper else she'll turn you away!"

"A sour woman will leave your cock hard!"

"There is a field that is always in season to plow!"

Mildred pulled on Isabel's arm. Isabel finally tossed her head and turned her back on them.

They were drunk.

The men kept joking with one another. Isabel turned around in time to see her husband bearing down on her. He jumped onto the back of his stallion and rode toward her. She shrieked, backing up and grabbing the front of her robes to run, which delighted his men.

She only ran a short distance before he scooped her up. His men roared with approval.

"Put me down!"

"Not likely," he declared as he gathered her against his bare chest and leaned over the horse's neck. "I've a mind to ravish my vixen."

"You stink," she declared, teasing him.

He was sweaty and had the scent of the earth clinging to him, but there was something about the scent of his skin that pleased her. Her belly clenched with need, her passage feeling empty.

"If you want me bare, Wife…all you must do is ask." He dropped her to the ground and she realized they'd made it to the bathhouse. Her robes were settling when he tossed her into the air again and dropped her over his shoulder. The doorway was so low he had to duck to carry her through it.

"I will be happy to free my member for you."

When he put her on her feet again, she smelled the cider on his breath. There was a happy smile on his lips that she'd never seen before, as well as a swollen eye and dark spot appearing on his jaw.

"Do you think I'm impressed with your rough ways?"

He smiled wide enough to show her his teeth. "I think you are impressed when I move you to ecstasy."

"Enough." She put her hands on her hips. "I've no care for your rough entertainments."

She started to leave but he stopped her.

"Bathe me."

His tone was demanding and far too much like her last husband's to suit her. She took another step toward the door.

"Wife," he insisted. "Bathe me."

She turned around, seething, but she stopped because she'd been raised to obey such demands.

The look on his face wasn't one of arrogance. His dark eyes sparkled with enjoyment that touched the tenderness of her heart.

But when she looked at his face, her temper flared. His eye was swollen shut and his jaw had at least three bruises on it. When he grinned at her, there was blood in his teeth.

"Have you no more sense than a boy?" She stomped over to the trough and let the water flow into his tub. "Why do you put yourself at risk? Age will take your teeth soon enough."

"'Twas naught but good celebrating." He flexed his arms, the muscles bulging and sending a surge of heat through her.

"You were fighting," she corrected.

He shrugged. "I like to fight."

"You like to fight?" she demanded. "Well, sir, I liked to fly my hawk in the mornings, and it was you who told me to adjust to marriage and not place myself at risk. Shall I set my nurse to clinging to you so you will not brawl?"

He laughed so hard his eyes became glassy.

She was furious. Ramon grinned and watched her through his good eye. He walked over to the tub, dunked his head, and tossed it back so that water flew across the bathhouse.

"It pleases me to hear the concern in your voice."

"I am not concerned," she insisted as she lifted the kettle and poured the water into the tub. It hadn't truly boiled but she decided the brute deserved a cool bath.

"You are," he insisted as he tugged his tunic off and dropped it. There was a splash as he settled into the tub. "Admit it."

"Not unless you admit how foolish you have been behaving." Her neck was hot and her clothing felt too tight across her breasts.

"I'll admit to how much I crave your thighs wrapped around me."

She gasped and threw the square of linen she'd been ready to scrub his back with at him. "You are besotted."

"Of your sweet charms," he declared.

"Enough," she said. "Your squire can tend to you."

Her emotions were rolling in thick waves that made no sense; they simply overwhelmed her. She turned around, seeking the doorway, but there was a whoosh behind her, and then Ramon grabbed her.

"Stop!"

"You need cooling off more than I do, Wife!"

He dropped her into the tub as she shrieked. "My robes—"

"Now you may take them off." He reached behind her and jerked on her laces.

"Stop it, Ramon."

He didn't listen to her but kept at her laces. She tried to avoid him but instead spilled most of the water onto the floor. It splashed over the edge of the tub in huge waves as she tried to escape. Her husband was relentless, tugging and pulling on her garments until he was able to hold them up like a prize.

She sank down to her knees inside the tub to hide. "Have you no shame?"

"With you?" He stood firmly in front of her, naked, without flinching. "None. I confess it freely. You should as well, for you are quite brazen in my embrace."

She cupped a handful of water and threw it at him. "Knave."

He ignored her insult and his dark gaze lowered to her breasts. "I adore your tits."

She suddenly stiffened, the memory of Jacques using the same word. But at the same time the memory moved through her, stoking the horror of the event, tears flooded her eyes. There was no way to stop them. Big, fat, wet drops ran down her cheeks as she fought to swallow a sob.

Ramon's eyes widened.

He'd leave now for certain. No man ever dealt with a weeping woman. And that only made her cry more tears as she looked away, humiliated by her loss of control.

"Leave me," she muttered.

"Nay." He scooped her up and trapped her against his body. "Forgive me," he offered as he kissed her temple. "I have never had a woman who loved me."

She slipped free of his embrace. "I never said—"

Yet she did love him.

She knew it as the lie got stuck on her lips. She couldn't finish saying it because his expression made her want to weep again. It was so full of hope and need. Two things she'd never have suspected he craved.

"Oh...let me be."

He chuckled softly and captured her again. This time he wrapped her in a towel, trapping her arms against her body.

"I should not have worried you. Men fight. It has been the only way I have known. Forgive me." He buried his head in her hair and drew in a deep breath. "There is not a single other person I would have apologized to."

It wasn't an admission of love.

But it was a concession of caring.

That knowledge didn't soothe her bruised feelings much.

You are asking too much...

She was, but she couldn't stop. The hope was there inside her heart, nearly killing her with how bright it was burning. She feared it would consume her if he didn't love her in return.

What a different sort of torment her marriage was proving itself to be. Maybe it was true what the church said: There was no true happiness in this life. Only glimmers.

So she'd take the opportunities that came to her.

She shifted and stroked her hand down his chest, delighting in the feel of his hard body. He made a low sound of approval and cupped her breasts as she found the hard length of his swollen member.

She stroked it, trailing her fingers around its head and all the way to the sac where his seed was.

"You are truly a vixen, Isabel...fiery." He cupped her nape and held her steady as he kissed her. It was a hard kiss that set something loose inside her. All of her anger transformed into passion with just the touch of his mouth against hers.

Her thoughts scattered and she willingly let them go.

But Ramon pulled back and finished disrobing. He lifted his leg and climbed into the tub. "I do stink."

He was washing himself so quickly, water sloshing against the sides of the tub and splashing up as he hurried.

"Ramon," she admonished with a soft laugh.

He looked at her with an expression that hinted at the boy he'd once been. "Can I not be eager for your attention? Do you not find the compliment in my desire to please you?"

She laughed again, only this time it was a sultry sound. His expression changed, captivating her with the flare of excitement brightening his eyes. It set loose a confidence she didn't realize she had.

"Well now..." She moved toward him. "Since there is already water on the floor."

She lifted her leg and climbed right into the tub.

"Isabel," he groaned as he guided her down onto his length. "You are truly a prize to be envied."

She gasped as she took his length, pleasure shooting through her.

How was it possible to enjoy an act so much?

She didn't know and wasn't interested in contemplating an answer. A soft moan was all that escaped from her lips as she reached for his shoulders to steady herself.

"That's it, my beauty…take what you want."

"I will." She'd never sounded so demanding before, but she meant it. "I crave you, Ramon."

It was a dark confession. One that pleased her. She rose and pressed back down on him, her knees settling on each side of his hips. Water sloshed over the rim of the tub as she increased her pace.

"As I do you." His tone turned savage. She felt it as much as she heard it. Sensation tingled along her skin, raising goose bumps and tightening her nipples. "I must have you."

His expression tightened and there was a whoosh of water as he stood up, lifting her with him. He turned her and pressed her down onto her knees in the tub.

"I need to claim you." He pressed his member deep inside her from behind, locking her hips in place with his hands.

She gasped, holding on to the edge of the tub to steady herself. Each thrust drove more water onto the floor. But it also drove a shaft of pleasure through her. She was gasping, unable to draw in enough breath to keep pace with her heart. He was pounding into her, driving his member in and out with a savage rhythm.

"More," she demanded. *"More!"*

"You shall have it," he snarled next to her ear, driving faster and harder into her. He pulled her hips up, above the water level, as he stood so he could use his legs. She still braced her hands against the edge of the tub but pushed back into every thrust. She was straining toward him, every muscle drawing tight, passion burning away everything except the need to meet his thrusts.

His member was swelling, her body tightening around it. He growled, "Not...*yet!*"

She couldn't make a sound, ecstasy ripping through her. It was blinding. Bursting through her with the force of a thunder clap. She arched, feeling as if her spine might snap, but she didn't care. All that mattered was pressing herself against him, taking his length and holding it.

Ramon shouted her name as his seed spilled. It was hot and sent another ripple of satisfaction through her womb. They ended up kneeling again, Ramon draped along her back.

"You drop me to my knees," he muttered. "A place I do not mind so long as you are there with me."

There were several things she didn't mind at all, so long as he was with her.

Didn't mind them at all.

⌘

Ambrose had a black eye the next morning as well. He sat at the table as the maids came to tend to him. They clicked their tongues and put soothing compresses on him. He used the time to admire their cleavage. Ramon's lip was split, a dark scab sealing the wound. He passed Ambrose and the two smirked at each other. Their men who were filling the lower tables slapped the tabletops as they smiled.

Men...

Knights...

She was sick of it all.

In fact, her belly was twisting with nausea. Isabel looked away but her stomach refused to settle. Someone delivered a bowl of steaming porridge and the scent of it made her sick.

She shoved away from the table, running toward the garderobe as she fought the urge to retch. There was nothing in her stomach, but her body heaved all the same. By the time the fit had passed, she was shaking, and sweat darkened her hairline.

"Isabel?" Ramon asked softly.

She groaned. "You do not need to see me like this."

Her husband was not put off by her words. He cupped her shoulder and pulled her into the light. His dark gaze roamed over her face and noted the quiver in her lower lip.

"You are going back to bed." He scooped her up. "I will not lose you to fever."

"I am not hot."

She should have saved her breath. Ramon carried her through the hall and to the stairs. People dashed out of his path, his boots clacking on the stone floor. People rose from their seats, their eyes widening at the sight.

"Put me down," she pleaded.

He gave her a hard look. "I will not lose you."

His tone was strained and he carried her up to their chamber with a speed that accelerated his heartbeat. Ramon didn't notice it though. He didn't stop until he had her back in their bed. He yanked the bedding up to her chin and tucked it around her shoulders.

Only then did she see the worry in his dark eyes.

He brushed her forehead, smoothing her hair back with a tender touch.

"I will not lose you."

"Here, now." Mildred walked to the doorway with a huff. "There's no need to talk like that, my lord."

Ramon stood up. "Where is your basket?" he demanded. "She needs it."

"I do not," Isabel argued, pushing the bedding away and trying to swing her legs over the side of the bed. "I am not fevered."

Ramon hooked her knees and dropped her legs back in the bed. "You will rest, Isabel. Even if I must place a guard on you."

He turned his head around and glared at his squire, Thomas. "Fetch that basket."

"Aye, my lord," the youth responded instantly. He was a blur in the doorway before Mildred drew in enough breath to argue.

"There's naught in my basket for what ails my lady," Mildred said.

Ramon stiffened. "Then tell me what she needs. I will get it."

Mildred propped her hands on her hips. "Naught but time." She waved him away from the bed. "Get up now, my lady. Time enough for rest when the babe is born."

"Babe?" Ramon asked in a whisper.

Isabel started to rise but decided her knees were too weak at the moment.

"Aye." Mildred nodded. "I thought that might be the case when your robes no longer fit yesterday. It's the breasts that swell first." She turned and looked at Ramon. "Your seed has taken root. It's been two and a half months since you celebrated your wedding. More than enough time to be sure."

And she hadn't bled again.

Ramon smiled, his face lighting up until even his midnight-black eyes sparkled. He let out a roar and gathered her up against him. He swung her around several times before putting her down. There was a scuff of boot heels at the door of the chamber as his men responded. Ambrose pushed his way right through them, skidding to a stop when he saw the smile on his lord's face.

"We're to have a child!" Ramon announced. "Ring the bells!"

There was a scuffle on the stairs and a few moments later the bells in the church began to toll happily. Ramon captured her hand and pulled her toward the windows. The shutters were open, the scent of rain in the air. But people came out of the buildings, into the yard, and cheered.

He carried her down the stairs and out into the yard. Everyone forgot their chores and the everyday struggles to survive as musicians pulled out their instruments and filled the yard with melody.

❧

In the yard, Donald joined the celebration.

He didn't really have a choice. Everyone was dancing. Someone grabbed his hand and tugged him along. Truthfully, he didn't want to resist. He'd never been part of such happiness, and it felt good.

Better than good, even if he didn't know the exact

word for the feeling. But soon his belly knotted as he contemplated his duty.

Why did they sing songs about duty when it wasn't anything to be happy about? He was sworn to serve Jacques Raeburn, but all he wished to do was stay at Thistle Keep. Life was different here. Far different than any he had known.

Yet there was his sworn duty.

A man didn't have anything except his honor. Not truly. A title might be taken. Gold could be stolen or easily spent. Honor was all that remained, and he'd given his solemn word to Baron Raeburn.

God would know if he didn't keep his word and refuse him entrance into paradise. Such a sin could never be forgiven.

Donald's heart was heavy but he squared his shoulders and slipped away after dark. The way through the woods was familiar now. Even the twisted shadows no longer scared him into muttering prayers to protect him from evil. No demon had appeared in his many trips through the dark abyss he'd been warned about since childhood.

He only felt the touch of evil when he spied Raeburn's camp. There was a feeling of ungodliness here. Quite different from the sensation he had when he returned to Thistle Keep. Men were clustered around fires, the stench of unwashed bodies stronger than the smoke. Rotten carcasses lay on the edge of the forest from the animals they'd hunted. There wasn't a bare chin in sight.

There was also little order. Men used whores right in the open, grunting like beasts as they labored. Their chosen consorts were pitiful creatures, the lowest of the low: their faces darkened with soot from the fires, their robes filthy on the back from the number of times they had been pushed to the ground. They suffered in silence, accepting food with shaky hands and desperate looks, retreating into the darkness to eat like bitches.

Ungodliness, to be sure.

And yet it was his duty, his desire to refrain from sinning, that forced him to walk among them to the tent in the center of the camp where Jacques Raeburn's flags fluttered above the opening.

❧

Ramon did not go to bed that night.

Isabel woke only a few hours after she'd retired, but her husband was not at her side. The darkness felt colder and it had nothing to do with the approach of winter.

Or did it?

Was courting not the season of spring in a couple's lives?

Tears stung her eyes and she wiped them away.

You make no sense. Ramon has shown you more affection than anyone…

That was true.

It was humiliating the way her emotions wanted to drag her down to the pits of despair. She slipped a hand over her belly but there wasn't even a bulge yet. Just a tenderness and a little less of a waistline. Her breasts ached. That was for certain. Her chemise felt tight across them and she tugged on the fabric, trying to ease it away.

Many husbands didn't share a bed with their wives once there was a babe on the way. She knew it but resented it.

Actually, it stung. Her emotions felt too injured to lie still. She left the bed and went into the outer chamber to see if Ramon was at his desk.

He wasn't. The floor was cold against her feet, and the chamber felt unnaturally large.

Tears filled her eyes and she blinked them away.

Stop. It is not so late.

It truly wasn't. He might still be in the hall, enjoying the company of his fellow knights. She should leave him to them.

There was a step outside the doorway, before the door opened. She blinked, not sure if her thoughts had summoned him or if she was dreaming. All that mattered was that Ramon was there, his dark hair looking like liquid midnight.

So strong. Every inch of him was powerful, even his nature.

"You should be in bed, Wife."

She shrugged, moving back to let the shadows hide her as Thomas followed his master and began to help him disrobe. She crossed her arms over her breasts and they pressed against her chemise. Ramon watched her, and she was sure he noticed things she'd rather he didn't. At least tonight she was grateful for the way he seemed to know her so well.

"Good night, Thomas."

The squire lowered himself and made good use of his moment to retire. He slept on a cot just outside the doors before the stairs.

"You need your strength," Ramon said.

"I did sleep, but woke and you were not here." She bit her lower lip. "That is not to say that you should have been. Only—"

He picked her up and placed her in the bed before sitting on its edge and removing his leggings.

"My men insisted on toasting to our blessing...over and over." He rolled into the bed and pulled her close. "My head will be splitting in the morning."

She giggled and gasped at her own lack of control. Ramon chuckled and kissed her brow.

"I believe Ambrose enjoyed making sure I couldn't escape. Someday, fate is going to hand me the opportunity to even the score with him."

She smoothed her hands along his arms, shaking as she absorbed how real he was.

He shifted and lifted his head. "Why do you shake?"

She tried to ignore the question. It was bad enough that she was being a foolish chit.

He cupped her chin and lifted it. She sighed and opened her eyes. In the dark she could barely see his eyes, but she could feel his gaze on her.

"I am glad you are here."

"And?" He refused to let her leave things unsaid. "We will both have splitting heads in the morning if you insist on drawing out this conversation. For I can see that something concerns you deeply. I must know what it is."

She narrowed her eyes but not for long. It warmed her to know that he noticed her distress. Even if it meant he wouldn't stop until he found out what it was.

"I thought perhaps you did not intend to share a bed with me now that I have conceived." She felt guilty for saying it, and her words hung between them as she waited for him to speak.

"This is our chamber, Isabel. There will be no separate chambers."

"It is not to say that I would be unhappy—"

"That wounds me to hear."

He eyes widened. "Truly?" Her voice was barely a whisper but it felt as though the words were a reflection of her soul—that part of her that didn't obey what the world around her said was the way it should be.

"Many men—" she began.

"I conform to what many men in this world think I should on enough issues. On this one, I intend to do as I feel," Ramon interrupted her. He brushed her cheek before lying down and pulling her against him. "There is no place I would rather be. In truth, I need to have you beside me."

It was an admission. One she savored as she let the sound of his heart lure her into slumber.

It was enough.

Or at least, it would have to be.

Men did not love as women did.

⁓

Jacques was in a rage. He cursed and launched another attack on Donald, but the boy soon collapsed into an unconscious heap.

"Bastard!" he growled, before spitting on the unconscious boy.

He paced in a circle, his attention falling on Rauxana.

He growled at her but she stared straight at him, no fear in her eyes. "Get from my sight, woman. I need more than the ease from your body."

"I have the knowledge you need, my lord."

He took a huge swallow of wine and wiped his mouth across his sleeve. "Do not start thinking, Rauxana. It's your flesh I enjoy having near. I have no use for a woman who doesn't know her place. Keep to yours," he warned her viciously.

Rauxana didn't shrink away. She strode forward, far more confidently than she'd ever done before.

"I offer to share a woman's knowledge with my lord," she purred softly. "In the harem, it is always important to make sure your rivals do not become wives by birthing sons. My mother made sure I knew these things."

Jacques lifted his drinking bowl to his lips but stopped. "I bought you in the market. If you were more accomplished, you would never have been on the common slave block."

"Am I as tiresome as the other women you have taken to your bed?" she asked smoothly. "Or do you notice how many skills my mother made sure I was trained in, my lord? Uncommon skills."

He took a slow sip of his wine. "You don't bore me."

She smiled, taking praise from his meager comment. He didn't care for her becoming anything more than his plaything, but he wanted to know what else she might say. There was a gleam in her eyes that he'd never noticed before, and some women were crafty. Men might rule the world, but only a fool forgot how resourceful women could be. Or that they might turn deadly when a man was sleeping. He considered having her dragged from his tent. It might be safer, for it was clear she had more wit than he'd realized. But there was also confidence simmering in her eyes and he wanted to know if it was bluster or fact.

"What do you know of value to me?"

"My mother was not without enemies. One of them stole me away to punish her for making her lose her babe and chance of becoming a wife." Rauxana lifted her hand and opened it to show him a small leather pouch. It was waxed, to hold liquid, and tied tightly. "But she lost her babe all the same. This will see it done."

She moved across the tent, her robe flowing in tiny ripples like a water siren from a fable. A sensation swept through him that he'd enjoyed before, but today he wondered if he shouldn't keep his guard up with her.

She lifted his hand, placed the pouch into it, and closed his fingers around it before kissing the back of his fingers. When she looked at him, her eyes held no remorse, only adoration.

"Where did you get the ingredients for this?" he asked. He set his drinking bowl down, suddenly realizing how foolish he'd been to leave it in the tent unattended. "How did you pay for them?"

Rauxana pointed to the small chest she kept her face paint and personal things in. "All of the ingredients are the same ones that I use to ensure I do not conceive without your permission. I have simply mixed a stronger dose. It will unseat the babe if taken early enough."

Witchcraft.

Jacques rubbed his beard as he contemplated his pet.

Oh, she was his pet, his creature to play with and toy with. Yet it would seem that she was more intelligent than he'd noticed.

"I would give you sons, master," she offered, her eyes brightening. "Strong sons, and I will smother any daughters that come, if that is your will."

He believed her. For the first time he noted her ruthlessness. He dangled the little pouch from his fingers. "How does this concoction work?"

She fluttered her eyelashes to conceal her disappointment.

"Mix it in the lady's drink, but make sure she consumes all of it."

He closed his hand around it and nodded. "If it works, I will consider your offer."

He was lying.

Not that it mattered. She wasn't a Christian. No one would judge him for slitting her throat. His men whispered about her—not that he cared what they thought. He was the master.

Rauxana smiled, enjoyment brightening her dark eyes. She withdrew to the bedchamber, settling herself in the doorway and allowing her robe to open. She trailed her fingers across her flat belly. "I will give you strong sons, my lord, and anything else you require. I will be the most loyal wife."

Jacques felt a tingle on his nape again. This time he knew without a doubt that he had a viper in his tent.

The time was coming to be rid of her.

But the pouch in his hand was something he needed.

So he'd let her live today.

∾

It was evil.

Donald felt as if the leather lying against his palm were burning his skin. He stared at it, trying to decide what to do. The line between right and wrong was blurring. What he'd known so well his entire life had suddenly become something that he wanted to question.

To question his lord was the same as questioning God. How many times had he heard it said?

He couldn't count the times he'd heard it said, because that was what the church preached. A baron was given his title because God had decreed it, just as the king was in his place because of divine choice. He was a squire for the same reason. To question was to spit on God's will.

The leather pouch stung his palm.

He neared Thistle Keep and looked at the new keep. He was sure he could hear the echoes of the celebration that had taken place during the day. Now, the darkness was there to steal away that happiness, and he was the demon sent to snatch the soul of the innocent.

Why? He wanted to be worthy of taking a knight's vows. It was the hope of every squire. Loyalty and dedication were the tools that would turn him into a man who was strong enough in both body and will to be a knight.

Yet tonight, he found his loyalty wavering.

Was it a test from heaven?

Did he obey his master? Or throw the pouch on the ground and never enter the forest again?

He was tempted.

The pain stung him with every step he took and

tempted him further. The starlight illuminated the pouch, proclaiming his guilt, so he tied it onto a length of leather and put it around his neck, hiding it inside his tunic.

He needed to think. Needed to listen to his conscience's warnings. Needed to find some way to justify disobeying his master. The problem was he had no idea if he would succeed.

In which case, he'd have to perform his duty.

⁓

"What are you doing?" Her nurse sounded and looked horrified. Isabel looked up at Mildred in surprised.

"Sewing. As I said I would be."

Mildred hurried into the chamber, with two other women behind her. "It's what you're sewing I question."

Mildred snatched the fabric from her hands and shook her head. "You cannae be making things for the babe. Why, the demons will learn of it and set out to steal its soul before it can be baptized."

The other women nodded in agreement and made the sign of the cross over themselves.

"It was but one cap," Isabel protested. "I might be making it for another woman."

Mildred was busy picking out the stitches. "We'll not be taking any chances."

"Best course of action," one of the other women agreed. "With the way the fever took your last husband, best not to tempt fate."

"You'll wait until the baby is baptized," Mildred said firmly. "Don't fret, everyone will come and shower you with the things you need."

Isabel wanted to argue but she'd been raised on such lore. Was it superstition? Perhaps. In truth, the real question was, did she want to risk not respecting tradition?

She did not.

Her babe was already the most precious thing in her life besides Ramon. She hadn't felt it move yet but she felt it in many other ways. She smiled ruefully. She felt it in the way that she couldn't keep anything but porridge in her belly, and even that had to be consumed in small amounts, as well as after noon.

"You are likely right."

Mildred nodded. The other two women were making good use of the table Ramon had placed in the chamber, spreading out a new piece of linen. Mildred pulled a measuring ribbon from the sewing box.

"Up with you now, so we can measure."

"Make sure you leave room for me to grow," Isabel said as she stood.

Mildred's face crinkled as she smiled brightly. "I will, my lamb. Happily so."

❧

Jacques paced the confines of his tent.

Too much time had passed. The days had turned into a week and then a fortnight as he waited for Donald to return. Rauxana watched him but kept her mouth shut. She'd retreated to an oversized pillow near the foot of his bed to wait. He'd struck her for speaking out of turn a week ago; she'd been silent ever since. She knew something. He could see it glittering in her eyes, but he was the master.

He turned around but ended up facing the table where his father's letter rested.

"How long?" he asked as he turned back toward her. "How long does that concoction take to work?"

"Once consumed, it works very quickly, my lord. Within hours."

Jacques snarled.

"It must be done soon or nothing will unseat the growing babe," Rauxana continued.

He stopped pacing and cursed. "Then I must make sure that boy knows what I expect of him. Or see to the matter myself."

❧

It would snow soon.

The rain was bitterly cold, freezing during the night and not thawing until noon. Jacques growled as icy mud made its way into his shoes with every step. He needed to look like a peasant, so his boots were back at his tent because they were the mark of a man with money.

His worn shoes and tunic did little to keep him warm. A woodsman's hood helped a bit, but more importantly, it hid his features. He felt naked without his sword, but the weapon was the mark of a knight. Segrave's men would never let a knight close enough to the keep.

He gritted his teeth against the icy mud in his shoes. He tried to change his walk into more of a trudge as he stooped. People didn't look long as he passed them, just curious looks as they hurried to make their way to someplace warmer. He moved around the new keep, hiding his approval behind the hood. At least Segrave had done a good job of improving the estate. He'd proven Isabel fertile as well.

The skies opened up before he made it to the kitchens.

Jacques smiled at his turn of good luck. What few people there were scattered as the rain turned to sleet. The wind was cutting and he entered Thistle Keep without anyone noticing. He settled into a corner storeroom and waited for the evening shadows to offer him the opportunity to achieve his goal.

❦

"Come in, lad."

Donald looked up and found one of the kitchen cooks waving to him.

"It will snow tonight." She was an old crone but smiled kindly at him. She beckoned to him again. "I'll find you a spot to call your own for the winter. You've earned it."

Donald felt his lips splitting in a grin. A rush of achievement went through him as he nodded and gathered up the bedroll he called his own. The cook guided him through the passageways of the older keep. The rooms were stuffed full, ready for the long winter.

"Mind you," the woman warned, "I'm trusting you to keep your hands out of the stores. I don't need the lady or head cook angry with me."

"I'll mind my place. I'm not a thief, only born to a poor mother. I'm God-fearing," he promised and realized that he meant it. Tucked into the inside of his tunic, he felt the little leather pouch of poison. It felt as though it were smoldering, burning a hole through his tunic so that everyone might see it.

He was going to bury it in the woods tonight. In a deep hole, where no one would ever find it.

And he would beg God to forgive him for breaking his oath to Baron Raeburn. Because he wouldn't poison the Lady of Camoys.

He was going to serve her. Maybe he'd never be a knight, but he found it more to his liking than pouring poison into her cup. At least as a peasant he might be a good man.

"Here." The cook stopped and looked at a pair of bunks made of stone along the side of one room. They were built right into the arches that helped support the next floor. "It is nae the warmest."

"Far warmer than the yard," he offered cheerfully.

She nodded. "It is that. I'll see if there are any spare tunics, yours is tattered. Even a worn one will give you some more warmth."

"I'd be grateful."

And he would be.

Her expression became soft with memory. "I had me a boy. He'd be about your age now, but he marched away on the Crusade some eight seasons ago and I've not heard from him or me husband."

She smiled at him, showing off gaps in her teeth. "My hands ache when the cold sets in. You can help me haul the water and I'll make sure this is your place. The masons won't be needing you so much now that it is winter. My hands ache most in the snow."

"I will haul as much as you like," he promised quickly. "Any time that you call."

"That's a good lad." The way her voice cracked with happiness twisted his insides.

No one had ever been pleased to have him near.

She turned away and her feet shuffled down the passageway.

Donald smiled at the bunk as the woman moved away. He reached out and ran a hand over the stones. They were worn from years of being used but that just made them smooth. He sat down and enjoyed the lack of wind cutting through his clothing. For the first time in days, his toes felt as though they weren't going to freeze. He placed his bed roll in the bunk and settled onto his knees to thank God for guiding him to such a place.

The stone of the floor was hard against his knees but he folded his hands and concentrated.

A hard hand closed over his mouth.

"You'd better be praying for word that the lady has lost her child." Donald tried to fight but Jacques was far stronger. The man must be a demon to be so strong. Donald flailed against him but to no avail. "When did you give her the concoction?"

Donald gasped when the baron lifted his hand from his mouth, but he felt the cold touch of steel against his throat.

"Keep your voice low, boy, or I'll slice you from ear to ear."

Donald swallowed. "Aye."

Jacques frowned. "Aye…what?"

Donald shook his head, refusing to utter "my lord."

"You dismissed me."

Jacques growled, his eyes becoming slits as his

expression turned vicious. "You have nothing without me. Everything here will be mine."

He patted the boy's tunic down, growling when he found the bulge beneath it. He reached inside the tattered collar and yanked the pouch free.

"You will regret failing me."

Jacques lifted the dagger high but turned it and cracked the handle against Donald's temple. The boy went limp. Jacques lifted him and tossed him into the bunk. The impulse to kill him was strong, but it would be too simple a death. Once he was lord of Thistle Keep, he'd stake the boy out in the yard and watch him freeze to death as a warning to anyone thinking about disobeying him. He looked both ways before leaving the storeroom and walked toward the kitchens. He pulled his hood down low and stooped as he moved. He shuffled his feet when passing others and didn't much care if he was being deceitful. Claiming the prize was what mattered.

It was time to make his father proud.

❦

The first snow fell just as supper was ending.

The children laughed and went outside to play in it. Isabel stood on the steps of the new keep, watching the moonlight turn everything into a silver landscape. The flakes came down in feathers that floated back and forth on their way to the ground.

"And the season changes." Ramon stood at her side.

"Do you miss your place at the king's side?"

"Not one bloody bit," Ramon growled. "Canvas tent walls fail to cut the winter wind." He looked up at the new keep. "I am going to enjoy what we have built together."

"Your men built the keep, my lord."

He reached out and grasped her hand. "Yet you will fill it with life."

She smiled. "I am not the only one."

At the tables there were couples now. Ramon's men sitting beside women. The priests had turned a blind eye to it, for everyone knew most of the men who had marched off on the Crusade would never return. It was imperfect as far as Heaven went, but it felt very right. They had to make a life out of what they had.

The wind whipped and they hurried back inside where it was warm. A few candles were lit, offering a cheery welcome as they consumed the last of their supper. Isabel's drinking bowl was full again. She reached for it, not because she was thirsty, but because she couldn't bear to waste the beer. Tonight the snow was welcome, but soon the long months of winter would become a burden as everyone waited for spring and a new harvest. Everything would be measured and their stores stretched to last until new crops were grown. Everyone would be a bit thinner by then.

She drank down the brew, wrinkling her nose because it tasted somewhat bitter. Carrying a babe was twisting her senses. The scent of roasting meat made her run for the privy to retch, while she craved milk like a child. She finished off the rest of the beer and ignored the way her belly felt unsettled. Her babe needed nourishment.

Donald had something important to do.

He rolled over and tried to open his eyes, but it felt impossible. His head ached, making consciousness unappealing.

Still, something needled him.

Something important.

Jacques Raeburn's face surfaced in his foggy brain. The glow of evil intent pulled Donald from slumber. He flopped onto the floor as he grabbed his head. Agony threatened to keep him from his feet but he stumbled to the wall and used it to stay upright.

He had to warn…warn the lady.

⚬⚬

"Christ's mercy," the cook exclaimed. "What happened to you, lad?"

Donald stumbled into the kitchen, causing a stir as the maids who were settling down for the night saw the blood running down the side of his face.

"Come here and let me tend that for you."

"The lord…the lord is here."

The women clustered around him, urging him toward a stool.

"Nay. The lord is in the new keep."

The cook pressed a wet cloth against his temple. Pain shot through him, threatening to steal away his consciousness.

"Lord Raeburn is here."

The cook lifted her hand from his head. "What did you say, boy?"

Donald stood up but his knees were weak. "Baron Raeburn was here…" He patted his tunic and felt a wave of horror go through him. "He plans to poison the lady. To make her lose her babe. I must warn Lord de Segrave."

Eleven

SOMEONE RANG THE BELLS IN THE CHURCH.

Isabel rolled over but it was still dark. She bit her lip because she ached. A deep ache that curled her up into a ball.

She heard a pounding on the chamber door a second before someone shoved it in. "Ramon!"

Ambrose didn't stay behind the wall separating the bedchamber from the receiving chamber. Ramon was on his feet, his sword in hand before he realized who was in the chamber.

"Raeburn was in Thistle Keep."

Isabel blinked; her thoughts were moving slowly.

"I'll run him through if I find him," Ramon announced.

"Stay here," Ambrose insisted. "It is your lady he wanted to poison."

Ramon looked toward her. "Isabel?"

She tried to answer but her mouth was dry and all she ended up doing was moving her lips.

Mildred walked into the room, as Ramon lifted Isabel up from the bed.

"Drink this now…we have to purge you," Mildred said firmly.

Mildred's concoction was foul but it soothed her throat. Ramon held Isabel up, cupping her neck with one hand to keep her in place.

"There now," Mildred soothed.

Isabel gasped as her belly clenched violently. She flopped over and vomited.

Isabel had no idea how long it lasted, only that she had never hurt so much in her life. Every muscle felt strained and sore and even her insides burned. Ramon cradled her, smoothing her hair back from her face. She succeeded in locking gazes with him, but there was no peace there. Only a burning rage that nearly scorched her.

"The babe might yet be lost," Mildred said.

Isabel looked at Mildred, horrified. Her nurse had tears glistening in her eyes. "The boy says that devil Raeburn has himself a woman of the east with him. Says she brewed up a poison to make you lose the child."

Tears fell down Mildred's cheeks. Isabel wanted to cry but there was no moisture in her body.

"I am going to kill that bastard," Ramon swore. "To hell with the law and the barons' council."

"But…you…cannot…risk your position…"

"For myself, I would not. But for you, I will choke the life from him with my bare hands." His teeth were bared, his eyes bright with the need for vengeance. "I love you."

Ramon stroked her face and she grabbed his hand, pressing it tightly against her cheek.

"The barons…might demand your life if you kill a baron. Do…*not*," Isabel beseeched him.

He leaned down and kissed the back of her hand. "That is the only thing I cannot grant you, my love. I will not allow him to harm you."

He pulled away from her and it felt as if he were being ripped from her. He gripped his sword and began calling for his men before he left the outer chamber. Isabel curled into a ball, willing her womb to cradle her child. She would not lose it.

She would not.

❧

He wanted blood.

The fever burned brightly as Ramon led his men through the night. Jacques had moved his men a few times, but the land was scarred where their camps had been. The newly fallen snow made it simple to follow the tracks to where he nested now.

Jacques was just making it back to his men when Ramon found him.

"Raeburn!" he snarled, taking in the woodsman hood and common clothing. "I am not surprised to see you using trickery to gain your way."

Jacques's men jumped from their beds, running to support their lord. Ramon pointed his sword at him. "I will have satisfaction."

Jacques laughed and threw his arms out wide. "If you strike me down, the barons' council will have your head for it, as I am unarmed!"

"I have your squire to swear that you poisoned my

wife," Ramon declared. "Dishonorable action deserving of a dishonorable death."

"The word of a whore's whelp?" Jacques spat on the ground. "My captains will speak the truth. That you cut me down while I had no sword. Which testimony do you think will carry more weight?"

"He is right." Ambrose grabbed his shoulder and held him back. "As much as I wish it were otherwise."

"Get your sword, Raeburn!" Ramon ordered. "Face me."

Jacques shook his head. "I think not. In fact, I plan to live long enough to hear that your heir has slipped from his mother's womb."

Ambrose growled. "You have no honor."

"None," Jacques answered easily, gaining several snorts of amusement from his men. "I prefer profit, as do my men. I have always been better at planning, which is why my men follow me. That is why they will swear you cut me down in my own camp. Kill me and you'll end up hanged in the spring by the barons' council."

Ramon felt his bloodlust rising further, but he had to think. Rash actions often led to mistakes, and mistakes cost lives. His own master had taught him that as a young squire. Time and time again he'd witnessed the truth of it on the battlefield. Today, he struggled for the discipline to keep his head. Because he had far more to lose than ever before.

"I challenge you, Baron Raeburn. On the field."

"Why would I meet you?"

"Men do not follow cowards. For a coward will sacrifice his men when there is enough profit in it,"

Ramon declared in a clear voice that carried through the morning air. "Fail to meet me tomorrow and you are a coward. Every man behind you will know it and know that you might sell them out."

Jacques was still arrogant and sure of himself, but the men behind him lost their smiles. They stiffened as they cut looks between themselves.

Ramon looked up at the men behind Jacques. "And I will cut every man in this camp down while they sleep. Such is the death deserved by those who follow a coward and poisoner of women. Meet me or ride away. But be assured that I will find you if you stay too near."

❧

"Fool!" Jacques yelled as Ramon turned his stallion and rode away. "I will enjoy fucking your woman when my next arrow puts you in your grave!"

He certainly wouldn't be meeting anyone on the field of valor. Such was for fools who wasted their days devoting themselves to chivalry. He had profit to gain.

When he turned around to face his men, they were silent, looking at him with hard glares that even he couldn't shake off. By the time he arrived at his tent, he realized there wouldn't be an easy way to dismiss Ramon's challenge. Jacques sat in his chair and refused to be bothered. He snapped his fingers and Rauxana brought him his drinking bowl.

No, he would not be answering Ramon de Segrave's challenge.

His captains arrived within an hour to question him.

"The men want to know—"

"If I will meet Segrave at the tiltyard?" Jacques sneered at them from his chair. "Why should I? There is no profit in it."

"Then are we to leave?" the second captain asked. "If we stay here, the snow will make it simple for him to find our camp."

"My father has charged me with wedding Isabel of Camoys." Jacques stood up. "I will not be the first son to lose land."

"Then meet Segrave on the field," his captain said flatly. "Kill him on the field and the widow will be yours to claim."

"You do not tell me how to act."

His captain narrowed his eyes. "I'll not follow a coward or wait to be slaughtered in my sleep. You poisoned the man's wife. His challenge is just. So too will be his retribution on us if you don't face him."

Jacques felt the first stirrings of uncertainty. "Have you forgotten how much gold I have placed in your hand?"

"I risked my life for that gold," his captain answered clearly. "And a dead man has little use for coin."

There wasn't a hint of fear in the man, which was why Jacques had chosen him. Now, the same qualities he'd seen as beneficial were becoming a noose.

"Tomorrow," Jacques snapped, "I'll kill Segrave on the field and hang you by nightfall for this disloyalty."

The two captains didn't look away. Jacques felt a chill on his neck that he hadn't experienced since the last time he saw his father. Both men left the tent as Jacques sat back down.

So be it.

He lifted his drinking bowl and drained it.

Segrave was a hulk of a man, which made him slow.

It would be a pleasure to kill him on the field where his men would see who was the stronger baron to follow. By tomorrow night, he'd be sleeping in a keep.

With Ramon de Segrave's head by his bed.

That thought gave him pleasure. For if Rauxana's potion had failed to do its work, looking at her husband's severed head certainly would.

❧

"He could ride for London," Ambrose said.

Ramon nodded at Ambrose. "Let him."

Ambrose gave him a menacing look. "I would rather take some men and wait on the side of the road for the maggot."

Ramon stopped on his way across the yard. "Nay." He looked around the yard, with all its openings and outer buildings. "All are needed here. It is time to secure this keep until walls can be built. We must think of those looking to us to safeguard them."

Ambrose surveyed the two keeps and the people moving around the yard. The sun was up and the snow still fell. The keeps would now be the center of everyone's lives. If the food was poisoned, they would all die.

"Aye," he agreed. "I'll see to posting sentries."

Ramon should have been more pleased by Ambrose's words. But all he could think about was the fact that he might have acted too late. He looked up at the new keep. It was impressive, a true marvel, but it would be nothing if Isabel was lost to him.

Nothing.

❦

Ramon rose with the dawn and went to the church. Isabel wanted to go with him but her body refused. When she woke again, it was to the sound of Thomas bringing in her husband's armor. The harsh sound of metal clanking against metal threatened to drive her insane.

"Do not ask me not to go." Ramon gave her a firm look.

"Be mindful of…" Isabel tried to sound strong, but her voice was only a husky shell. Her throat was still raw. She struggled to conceal it, to show her husband only a happy expression.

The sides of her lips felt like they were cracking.

"Save your breath, Isabel." He tempered his tone, and that was worse than hearing him press his will upon her.

"I am strong," she protested. "The king…the king might demand your head if you ride against another baron."

"Richard would not. I have a confession."

"From a boy, who never had a choice in who he served."

Ramon sat on the edge of their bed and covered her lips with his hand. There was a hard certainty in his eyes. A glimpse of the man she'd first faced when he'd ridden up to her keep.

"He had a choice." There was a firm note in his

tone that she knew she could never argue with. "He might have come to me. Each man must accept when his honor is more important than those he serves. Just as every man must answer at the day of judgment for his lies. The boy made his choice and will answer for it. I will let him live a day longer than his master, but no more."

He pressed a kiss against her cheek and stood up. His squire was ready with the padded under tunic that went beneath his mail. There was grim focus in his motions, a determination that she felt radiating from him.

"Jacques has no honor," she said.

Ramon flexed his fingers as his squire slid a gauntlet into place. "Which is why I must ride against him. Only a baron has the right."

"I cannot bear to lose you."

Ramon waved his squire away. "I will join you in the yard."

The squire and his assistant gathered up the remaining pieces of armor and headed out of the chamber with them. Ramon came close again, sitting beside her and reaching out to smooth his fingers across her cheek.

"As I cannot bear to lose you. As long as Jacques draws breath, you remain his target. I could never be worthy of you if I did not face this threat. Pray for me, tell me you understand, but do not ask me to be a coward. You could never love a coward."

And he wanted to be worthy of her love…

It was there in his eyes. A need as great as her own. Her breath was frozen for a long moment as she found her secret yearning fulfilled.

"No, you are not a coward, nor could you ever be."
She blinked away the tears stinging her eyes. "I am
proud to be your wife. I want to continue being your
wife more than anything else. You let him be after he
wounded you, so let him be now. Let us live in peace."

His eyes brightened, his expression softening for a
moment. He stroked her cheek.

"An attack against myself, I could ignore." His
expression hardened. "Against you? I will fight to the
death. You are the keeper of my heart. I can deny you
nothing except this."

"You could die," she argued. "And I will be here
without you."

"I cannot live knowing the man who harmed you
draws breath. Forgive me for that failing." He kissed
her cheek before he left.

She was sure that her heart left with him.

∽

"What are you doing?" Mildred was horrified, but
Isabel only waved her into the chamber.

"Hurry. I must go to the tiltyard." But her legs
weren't cooperating. They quivered so badly Isabel
was learning against the wall next to her wardrobe.
"Help me dress, Mildred."

"I will not," Mildred stated firmly. "'Tis back to
bed that I will be helping you with."

"I must go," Isabel beseeched Mildred. "I cannot lie
here while he dies."

"I do not think the baron will be the one dying,"
Mildred informed her.

"You have never seen Jacques Raeburn," Isabel

whispered. "He lacks all honor. Do not deny me every moment with my lord. Besides, I never gave him my favor to carry…"

Isabel held up a long ribbon. It was green and fluttered from her hand. "I must make sure he has it."

But she didn't have the strength to do it. She looked at Mildred, desperate to find assistance. Yet her hope was fading as the moments stretched out and Mildred contemplated her.

"Well then," Mildred said at last, "if we're going to the tiltyard, we'll be needing a few more hands."

She went back to the door and spoke to one of the men standing guard. Isabel heard him walk down the steps before Mildred turned and came to the wardrobe.

"Now, let's find you something worthy of the wife of Baron de Segrave."

ॐ

The tiltyard was still decorated from the harvest festival, but the garlands were wilting now and the mood subdued. The snow had melted, leaving the ground muddy.

Isabel rode in a cart, Mildred beside her, and another woman who was strong enough to help hold her up. The curious looked at her as she passed and more than one cheered. Her driver took her to the tilt field. People were already swarming into the stands. Colorful pennant flags were flying in the morning breeze, set up for the tournament by the people of Thistle Keep and Ramon's men.

They looked out of place, just as the faces in the crowd were not covered in excitement, but deadly anticipation.

Jacques Raeburn had taken the north side of the field, his flag flying above the stands. Only his men were there to cheer him on. Yet they were great in number and Ramon's men watched them from the south side of the yard. Only the fact that their masters were set to battle kept them from charging at one another.

Her belly clenched tight with horror. There would be blood spilled today; the only question was how much? Ramon might prove the champion, only to be attacked by Raeburn's men.

Isabel raged against the unfair nature of fate.

On the south side, the stands were so full Isabel feared they might collapse. More people were still arriving and pushing their way up the stairs and crowding in. Her driver pulled onto the field and she heard a huge cheer. People balled up their fists and shook them as they shouted.

Ramon was behind the gate, but Ambrose rode out and slid off his horse in front of her.

"Lady?" His tone was deadly as he offered her a hand out of the cart. "My lord needs no distraction."

"I am here to stand firmly in the box as a loyal wife should and make certain Jacques sees that I am well." She gave him a hard stare. "Let Jacques be the one to worry that everything is not as he wants it to be."

Ambrose looked her up and down. "You lie better than most ladies do. I believe the wind might blow you off your feet."

"It will not," she informed him tightly. "Besides, there is a chair in the box, is there not?"

He offered her a slight curving of his lips, so slight she wouldn't call it a grin. "You have courage, lady."

He reached past her hand and grasped her wrist to help her rise. He hooked his other hand around her back and actually lifted her up most of the steps while keeping her feet only an inch from the ground. A box was built on the first tier of the stands for the nobles. Ambrose settled her in the high-backed chair and inclined his head.

"I would tell you to have my lord come for his favor, but I fear Jacques will not respect the rules of chivalry and allow me the time to tie it on his arm." She pulled the ribbon from her sleeve and held it out. "Yet I would have him wear it. And have Jacques see it."

Ambrose took the ribbon, but there was still doubt clouding his blue eyes. Isabel sat up straight.

"You will see no weakness from me," she assured him. "Yet I must be here. I must see with my own eyes."

"Then you shall, lady."

It was a hard compliment, but a compliment nonetheless. Ambrose took her ribbon and disappeared behind the closed gate. Time began to creep by, each moment stretching until it was a torment she couldn't endure much longer.

Yet she didn't want the time to arrive, because it might be Ramon's last.

Mildred was praying beside her, softly beseeching the saints to intervene.

Isabel wasn't sure anyone in Heaven had anything to do with what was about to happen. This would be a battle of flesh against flesh.

The sun shone overhead but the gates did not swing wide. People strained to see what was happening, but nothing did. At last, Jacques rode onto the tilt field, his stallion's hooves kicking up the mud.

"Segrave!" he bellowed. "Who is the coward now?"

He beat his chest armor with his sword and roared.

In the distance, the sound of approaching riders came. It grew louder and louder as Isabel felt her heart accelerating. At the far end of the field, a group of riders appeared, another baron's pennant flag fluttering in the breeze. There were two dozen knights at his back, all of them in full armor.

"Another baron?" Mildred asked.

"My lord is no fool," Isabel said softly, because it was the only way to hide the fact that she wasn't relieved. There was still a challenge to be fought.

The newcomers rode onto the field. One of them stopped and faced the crowd. He reached up and pushed his face guard up.

"I am Baron Smyth." His stallion danced in a circle, the huge beast snorting as his master pulled him up. "I will stand witness to this challenge."

His men rode to the four corners of the yard. The baron rode to the stands and dismounted. He climbed to the box where Isabel sat and paused before her.

"Lady."

She should rise.

Isabel bit her lip and rose from her seat. She felt Mildred watching her as Baron Smyth offered her his hand. She placed hers into his but he didn't raise her hand to his lips. He grasped her wrist and supported her as her knees gave out.

"Your husband was wise to send a rider to Havenworth. I see his report of poison is no lie." He turned and braced his hands on the rail. "Let this challenge be done with honor! Else face my judgment!"

His men pulled their swords, the blades flashing in the noon sun. The gates hiding Ramon opened with a groan as he rode onto the field.

"You are the coward, Raeburn!" Ramon accused clearly. "You deal in poison, and I will have satisfaction."

The crowd howled with outrage. Curses filled the air as Ramon beat his chest plate with his sword.

"You shall have my steel!" Jacques shouted as he pulled his face guard into place and guided his stallion forward.

Her heart stopped at they charged toward one another, their stallions pawing up the mud and flinging it out in dark clouds behind them, their nostrils flaring as the powerful beasts charged forward.

Each knight leaned forward, focused on one another. They collided with a clash, a horrible meeting of metal as the stallions shrieked and reared up.

They turned and swung their swords at each other again, the deadly blades bouncing off their armor. Jacques twisted around and drove his sword through the neck of Ramon's stallion.

The horse screamed and collapsed, rolling over Ramon as it died.

Isabel's heart stopped. People in the stands cursed, but Jacques pulled his horse around and sent it charging toward Ramon as he struggled to free his leg.

Jacques swung low, leaning far out to make sure his blade would reach. Ramon rolled out of the way and at the last moment came up onto his feet.

The crowd cheered but Jacques had the advantage

now. He guided his horse up the field and turned to run Ramon down. There were other horses, but weighted down by his armor Ramon would never be able to mount one in time. Ambrose sent something sailing through the air.

Ramon plucked it from the mud and turned it with a smooth motion. The sunlight flashed off the head of the spear before Jacques ran into it. The tip slipped beneath Jacques's shoulder plate and breast plate. He howled as he tumbled from the saddle to land in the mud.

"Well done," Baron Smyth said beside her. "Finish him!"

But Ramon didn't take the opportunity to plunge his sword into Jacques's back.

He waited while Jacques scrambled in the mud, fighting to get to his knees and onto his feet.

"I'll see your face when I kill you, Raeburn," Ramon declared.

"You will be the one losing his head!" Jacques snarled as he swung his sword in a wide arc designed to decapitate.

Ramon dodged the attack and reached in to deliver a hard punch to his jaw. The smack echoed around the field to another cheer rising from the stands.

Isabel didn't join in.

Neither did Baron Smyth, and that was what terrified her the most. He had gray eyebrows and age lines on his face. He knew the fight might go either way.

Just as she feared.

It was the worst fear she had ever known, holding her so tightly she could barely draw a breath.

Jacques stumbled and came back with an overhead swing. Ramon took the blow on his shoulder, snarling as he pushed up and punched Jacques in the face again. The sound was brutal, the scent of blood filling the air.

This time, Jacques stumbled when he tried to swing his sword. Ramon sidestepped easily, before smashing his foot into the back of Jacques's knee.

He crumpled, cursing, and the people in the stands howled with approval.

"Confess and be forgiven before your death," Ramon offered.

Jacques growled on his knees, looking beat, but suspicion tingled through her.

"Finish it!" Smyth yelled.

Ramon looked up and Jacques took advantage of his inattention. He pulled a dagger from his forearm and lunged at Ramon's neck.

Isabel bit her own hand as she smothered her cry. The people in the stands surged forward. Ramon pulled back, Jacques following him. They hit the ground, their armor clanking as the mud splashed up and coated them. For a moment, they were nothing but a tangle of limbs, straining as they struggled. Time felt as if it weren't moving, trapping her in a moment where her worst fears were reality.

There was a harsh grunt and a gurgle as one knight proved the victor. One set of legs stiffening in death spasms before slumping to the ground. Everyone held their breath as they waited for the victor to rise.

"Holy Christ…" Isabel prayed. "Sweet holy Christ…"

Ramon rose from the mud and she honestly wasn't sure if it was real or the sight of her husband rising from his body. He stood and pushed his face shield up, the dagger still in his hand.

The midday sun illuminated the blood on its blade.

The crowd roared with approval, shaking the stands.

All Isabel could do was collapse back against the seat in relief. "Thank God."

"Aye," Baron Smyth muttered. "Thanks be to God, for that was a nasty bit of business that might have ended badly."

He stood up and held up his hand. "The challenge is finished! Any man who does not go in peace will face justice!"

There was a pounding of hooves. Raeburn's men began spilling into the yard, herded by Baron Smyth's men. They were ruthless as they drove them into the tiltyard to join their master's fallen body.

The crowd started howling, their blood lust running high.

Ramon climbed up to the first level where a platform stood for a master of ceremonies. He pounded the wooden rail with his fist.

"There will be no lawless men in this county."

"Or in mine!" Baron Smyth added.

"Give up your swords or kneel and swear loyalty to a new master," Ramon declared. "Or you shall be cut down where you are."

Raeburn's men looked around, searching for escape, but there was none. Smyth's men had them surrounded and Ramon's men mixed with them, making the numbers unbeatable. They would be slaughtered.

They pushed one of their captains forward. He held up his hand to quiet them.

"What man do we kneel to?" he asked of Ramon.

"Ambrose St. Martin." Ramon pointed toward his second in command. Ambrose sat on the back of a stallion, his armor as solid as the grim look in his eyes. "I will personally ask the prince to raise him to the station of baron."

Many of the men nodded, for only a baron could have armed men.

"Kneel or throw down your swords and leave in peace. Make no mistake. Unrest will be dealt with swiftly and harshly."

Snow started falling again. Just a soft sprinkle, but the men surrounded in the yard looked up at it with horror. There was no place to go where hungry mouths would be welcomed during the long months of winter. Perhaps in the spring they might have had a chance of making a place for themselves. Now, they were dependent on Ramon's good will.

"I will kneel."

It was the captain who spoke. He turned to face Ambrose and hit his knee. The men behind him followed, until they were all on one knee.

Would it be the solution they all craved?

Isabel didn't know, but all she cared about was looking at her husband standing at the rail. Ambrose rode out, his new men rising and following him.

Only Jacques's body was left behind.

Isabel didn't give it a single glance.

Instead she ran into the arms of the man she loved. Ramon clamped her against him, burying his face in her hair.

For once, fate had been kind.

She planned to treasure the gift until her days
were done.

∽

"I have done you no favor with this," Ramon warned
his friend.

Ambrose grinned in spite of Ramon's grim tone.
"You have offered me an opportunity. Never let
it be said that I am not a man to make the most of
such occasions."

Ramon looked over Raeburn's men. They stood
waiting for Ambrose to lead them back to the camp.

"This lot will be unruly."

"Aye," Ambrose agreed. "I plan to make sure they
have enough tasks to do, that by nightfall, they will
lack all strength to plot against me."

"I am leaving you a dozen knights for your personal
guard, else you will never be able to close your eyes.
Do not eat anything without having it tasted. Let no
one into your bed without careful consideration."

Ambrose nodded. "It seems you have your wish,
my friend. You now have the means to curtail my
roving ways."

Ramon slapped him on the shoulder.

"We'll ride for London tomorrow," Ramon
decided. "You need the prince's seal."

There was no guarantee that he would get it, but
Ambrose felt his blood igniting. He was full of anticipation, dreams he'd cradled close to his heart for most
of his years finally within reach.

He'd get that seal.

There was no other outcome he'd consider.

His gaze fell on the men that were now his. Their strengths and their weaknesses. Every transgression would reflect on his name. It was the burden he'd coveted, and he fully intended to shoulder it. He wanted to earn their loyalty, for that would be a far stronger bond than fear-inspired oaths.

Yet his first test was one that confounded him.

"The witch is inside." Ambrose eyed the captain who had spoken. The man nodded. "Raeburn brought her from the east. She brewed up the poison."

Men were whispering, asking to burn her. Ambrose held up his hand and they fell silent. They eyed him, waiting to see what he'd do.

"I will be the one to decide the matter."

Ambrose stiffened but lifted the tent flap out of his way and entered. The floor was covered with Persian carpets and the table held expensive glass from the Holy Land. There was a huge throne-like chair facing the entrance of the tent and an overlarge bed for campaigns behind it.

At the foot of the bed lay a huge pillow. The woman was on it, lying across its expanse and watching him with dark eyes. Her only clothing was a robe that lay across her curves like molten gold.

Her hand moved, lowering from her lips as she swallowed something. She blinked and drew in a deep breath. "I am not a witch."

"Did you brew the poison?" he asked.

She blinked again. "What men label a poison, women call an easement for bringing their courses."

"To the Lady de Segrave, it was a poison."

She blinked again, this time slower. "I obeyed my

master. For one such as myself, there is no other path. He bought me…in the market."

Her eyes slid shut. Ambrose moved closer as her breathing became softer and softer. Her hand relaxed, the small pottery cup she'd drunk from rolling over the edge of the pillow and onto the floor.

He picked it up and sniffed it. A bitter scent clung to it, a dark ring marking the inside.

Poison, no doubt.

A draft blew through the tent as his captain entered. "Do you want us to take her?"

"Not just yet." Ambrose stood and placed the cup on the table.

"She should be burned."

Ambrose turned to look at the man. "Have compassion. She will be dead soon enough and by her own hand. You'll take some men and bury her."

The captain's expression darkened.

"You will," Ambrose insisted. "There will be order in this camp and Christian values." He aimed a hard look at the man. "Every man will be judged by what he does from this day forward, and they will extend that mercy to one another as well as this woman. No man will be faulted for the obedience he gave to Raeburn. Neither will she."

"Aye, my lord. Well spoken."

Ambrose turned around and watched as the woman drew her last breath. It was soft and slow, her face serene as life left her body.

He lowered his head and offered prayer for her, beseeching mercy for a soul who had found little of it in life.

Ramon's men were building something in the yard.

Isabel looked at it as she was brought back to the keep. Their mood was somber, unlike it had been when they labored to raise the new tower. Their expressions were grim and she felt a chill on her nape.

"What is that?" she asked.

Ramon cradled her as he carried her up the stairs to their chamber, his arm tightening instead of giving her an explanation.

"Ramon?" she pressed. "You are avoiding my question. Why?"

He settled her into their bed, holding his tongue until he had made sure she was settled on two plump pillows and the bedding was tucked up to her chest.

"It is a gallows," he said in a hard tone.

Thomas arrived to help Ramon take his armor off. She wanted to help but she was weak. The bedding helped restore warmth to her toes and she tightened her grip on the blankets, but she kept her eyes on Ramon. His squire poured some water into a pan. Ramon happily cupped it in his hands and splashed it onto his face. Mud and blood washed away and he braced his hands on the table before speaking again.

"The boy must pay," Ramon said softly, but with a firm tone she recognized well.

Thomas's lips were set in a hard line as he handed his lord a towel to dry his face. Ramon stood and walked toward her. "It is the duty of a lord to enforce the law on his land. He'll be hanged in the morning. It will be quickly done."

"Could you not banish him?"

Ramon shook his head. "His crime is too great. He'll spend his last night in the dungeon."

"The what?" She sat up. "There is no such thing on my land."

"In the keep I built, there is a dungeon for times when the law must be enforced. Or someone held because they might do harm to others. He might have tampered with the food stores instead of just your drink."

Her belly tightened; things might have been so much worse. Yet she couldn't fathom that beneath her very bed was a place designed for nothing but torture. "I cannot bear the idea of sleeping above such a place of pain and torment."

"There is only a set of chains in there, to keep those who have proven themselves untrustworthy from harming others."

"He didn't poison me."

Ramon was washing his hands and forearms. "He carried the poison into this keep and failed to tell me. Our child might be dead because of it."

She cradled her belly, trying to protect the tiny life inside her. Yet she knew it was true. No one had a will strong enough to start life once it had stopped.

Life could so often be quickly gone.

"I am going to bathe. There is a man at the door in case you need help."

She was suddenly tired. Every bit of strength bled away and left her grateful for the bed supporting her.

She was grateful for a lot of things.

So many things.

Yet she hungered for more favor from fate. Just one

more miracle. She covered her belly with her hands, trying to protect and soothe the baby inside her.

Just one more gift.

Isabel slept, waking when Ramon returned from bathing. He gathered her close and kissed her temple.

She sighed and rested her hand on his chest, absorbing the proof of his life. Willing it to travel through her body to their child.

❧

Isabel woke in the early hours of the night. The moon was only a sliver in the sky, the chill of winter tightening. Ramon lay beside her, his breath soft and even. Her nose was cold but the man holding her was so very warm.

Something moved inside her.

It was only a soft motion, but within her womb. She lay still, framing the small mound of her belly with her hands. Waiting as she held her breath, sleep losing its hold on her instantly.

Was she imagining things?

It moved again, and again. A soft thump against the inside of her womb. Like the motion of a butterfly's wings. And then it came again, a little stronger now, like the tapping of a finger against the back of her hand.

A smile brightened her face.

Their child lived…

Joy burst inside her, sending two tears of happiness down her cheeks.

Alive.

It was such a gift. Such a blessing. She would raise

her child with love and never forget to tell him how much joy his presence brought to her.

The poor little boy named Donald had never heard such words from his mother.

Isabel felt her joy ebbing as she contemplated the gallows standing so newly built in the yard. Everyone pitied the boy, but that would mean nothing when the sun rose and he was taken to his execution.

She sat up, not even sure what she'd decided to do. Only that Donald's face refused to leave her thoughts. The bed itself was no longer welcoming.

The keep was quiet, the guard no longer at her door. She walked down the stairs in her bare feet and kept going until she made it to the chamber beneath the great hall. She opened the door she hadn't realized led to another level and went down the narrow steps. Here, there was no heat from a hearth, no scent of smoke. Only a lingering smell of mortar. The stairwell was narrow and the only way down into the dungeon. Once on the ground floor, she felt the walls closing in on her for the ceiling was low.

The huge collar Ramon had once threatened her with was now secured around Donald's throat. The boy wasn't sleeping. He watched her as she entered the room, his face looking much older than the last time she'd seen him. His eyes were sunken back in his head, dried blood still on the side of his face.

"Lady..." he rasped and fell to his knees. The chain shifted, sending noise through the chamber that echoed in a horrifying way.

"Be still," she warned and looked at the door above her.

When she looked back at him, he'd clasped his hands and held them up to her. "Forgive me. The priest said I'd burn in hell if you didn't forgive me. I beg you, have mercy on my soul."

What are you doing?

She wasn't entirely sure. Only that she'd ended up there without fully deciding to go. It had been an instinct of some sort. Something she was powerless to ignore. Another flutter of motion stirred in her belly and she knew what she was about.

Life. Aye.

"I forgive you."

Relief covered his face. He collapsed onto his haunches and cried silently. His expression became one of acceptance. "I'm grateful to you. I am indeed."

It turned her stomach to see him.

She lifted the key from the hook on the wall and moved toward him. He watched her, biting his lower lip to suppress the question he wanted to ask. When she fitted the key into the lock, he quivered, his entire body shaking as a light entered his eyes.

"Lady?"

She twisted the lock free and stepped back, suddenly unsure if she had made a mistake. Donald collapsed on the floor, flattening himself and reaching forward with one hand. He caught the edge of her robe with two shaking fingers. He drew the fabric to his lips and kissed it.

"Go," she said as tears filled her eyes. "I cannot do more for you. My husband will hang you if you are caught."

He lifted his head and looked at her, his eyes

swimming with tears. "You have done everything, lady. I cannot thank you enough."

"Yes, you can," she said as he drew back onto his haunches and stood. "Become a man of honor. Prove my actions right by never doing harm again, for in truth, I am not sure why I am here. Perhaps goodness is a chain, for Rauxana cut my bonds and without that mercy, I would have suffered greatly. So now I release you. Show your gratitude with your actions. Become a good man."

"I shall," he whispered before he looked toward the door. Hope brightened his eyes and he showed a hunger for life. He crept across the floor quietly, pausing in the doorway to look at what was on the other side before disappearing through it.

She'd have to confess to Ramon.

Isabel replaced the key and drew in a deep breath.

She could not lie. No, there was nothing for it but confession.

"I wondered if you would make it through the night without coming down here."

She gasped and jumped as Ramon appeared in the doorway. Her husband contemplated her as she lifted her chin.

"I planned to tell you," she said firmly.

He nodded. "Aye, I believe you would have. No matter how much you know I feel that boy is a threat to you."

"Only so long as Jacques was alive."

Ramon came down the stairs and picked her up. "The Raeburns have other sons, Isabel. They will always consider this land theirs. Land is the only true wealth. They will not abandon what they see as their claim."

He carried her up the stairs.

"They will have to." She spoke firmly. "Our child lives."

He froze with her still in his arms. Need flickered in his eyes.

"I felt it move," she whispered, "inside my womb."

He let her feet down and cupped her belly, seeking proof.

"Mildred says you will be able to feel it in time. When my belly rounds."

Disappointment flashed across his face, but he nodded.

"I couldn't stomach the thought that blood would be spilled at sunrise on the day that I learned my child still lived. Forgive me for that."

Her husband stood silent for a long moment.

"I love you, Isabel."

"Yet that is not saying you forgive me," she argued softly.

He laughed softly. "I understand you. Why do you think no one stopped you?"

She lifted her head. "You know me too well."

He offered her an arrogant chuckle.

"I am surprised none of your captains questioned you on the matter."

Ramon opened the door and started to carry her through it. Two of Ramon's captains stood there, Donald held between them.

"They did not question, because they were here." Ramon hooked his hands into his wide belt. "Where is the old woman who claims this boy?"

"I am here, my lord."

An old woman made her way from where she'd been sitting at one of the tables. Ramon stared at her. "You claim this boy?"

"Indeed I do. Adopted him, I did, for me own son is lost on the Crusade."

Ramon nodded. "You would have mercy for him?"

"Aye. He came to me, my lord, and told me about the poison. If he'd not, the babe would have been lost by morning. It is a woman's knowledge, you see. Have mercy, for if he'd held his tongue, everyone would have thought it naught more than misfortune."

Ramon looked at Donald. He nodded at his men and his captains released the boy. Donald stumbled but corrected himself and stood tall.

"Do you want to be adopted, boy?" Ramon asked.

Donald blinked, the question catching him by surprise. He turned to look at the cook, his lips twisting into a giddy smile. He cleared his throat and looked back at Ramon. "Aye, my lord."

"And swear loyalty?"

Surprise flashed across Donald's face a second before he fell to his knee. "Forever, my lord!" His voice was so loud, several of the men sleeping on the floor of the hall woke and sat up to see what was happening.

Isabel held her breath. But Donald looked up at Ramon with a glitter of satisfaction in his eyes. She realized she'd never seen the boy so happy. Ramon didn't miss it. He tightened his lips to keep them in a hard line.

"Done." Ramon turned his head toward the cook. "Now stop keeping your mother up so late with worry. She needs her rest, my men eat a lot of food."

Donald sprang up, his feet barely touching the floor. "Aye," he answered as he put his arm out for the cook. She took it as tears made shiny tracks down her wrinkled cheeks.

Ramon shook his head but his lips curved before he turned and scooped Isabel off her feet. Once she was settled into their bed he grunted at her, "My men are taking bets on how easily you will bend me to your will."

"They would not." She slapped his shoulder before he pressed her head back down. "Admit you enjoyed seeing that boy happy."

"I'll run him through if he steps out of line." There was a hard note of finality in his tone. She smoothed her hand along his chest.

"Sometimes, all any of us need is a second chance at life. I am grateful for my second chance with marriage."

"As am I."

It was simple to slip back into sleep now. Ramon's embrace cradled her as she felt her child move again.

Aye, she was grateful for the chance to know love.

❦

The White Tower was imposing, just as it was intended to be. Prince John sat inside it with his brother's barons. Occupying the head of the table, king in everything but name, which vexed him because it meant each baron had a vote. They also had the right to wear a baron's coronet with eight points on it. No one except a royal was allowed a crown. It was Richard's seal on their position, his blessing on their rulings.

John didn't care to share the crown with anyone, but he was only a prince. He would need the support of these men if he wanted the crown. The people of England were growing tired of Richard's Crusades and the cost they had to shoulder for his glory, both in gold and lives. That dissatisfaction was something John might use to his advantage. No one wanted to be ruled by a king who didn't want to be in the country.

"You killed Baron Raeburn."

"In a fair fight," Ramon de Segrave answered clearly. "He poisoned my wife. My challenge was just."

Two of the other barons nodded in agreement. "Raeburn bought his title," Baron Smyth said. "He was no true baron."

"But your action caused his army to fall under your command," John argued. The rest of the barons' expressions tightened. None of them wanted any baron to have more resources than they had.

Ramon stared at him. "The army in question is under the command of my captain, Ambrose St. Martin. He is worthy of the title of baron."

John stroked his beard. Ambrose St. Martin was a huge, golden-haired beast of a man. He stood behind his lord with a solid stance.

"His task will be greatly vexing if you elevate him. Raeburn's men lacked discipline and honor. But to disband them would have flooded the borderlands with villains. The Welsh lairds would have been happy with that. More men to use against us. Even if only half of them are salvaged, it is better."

"I see the worth in your actions," the prince

muttered. "Ambrose St. Martin, you are raised by my hand to the title of baron."

There were a few narrowed eyes, but John enjoyed knowing that not everyone was pleased. It was important to keep every baron guessing. They'd think to rule him otherwise. But there was one thing that John intended to do.

And that was to rule in his own right.

He'd be the king of England, and soon too.

As for Richard, well, John doubted his brother would ever return from the Crusade. It was an added bonus that his brother had done nothing about ensuring he had an heir.

That left the throne of England for him, and John was going to be very happy to accept it. More than one of the barons had noted how things were going to be. Segrave and St. Martin would now be indebted to him as well.

England was as good as his.

৯৯৯

Isabel looked up as the church bells began to ring. There were shouts of joy in the kitchen as everyone hurried out to greet the returning lord.

She moved slower, her belly big and round.

It was the heart of winter, the trees frozen and everything covered in white. A terrible time to travel, but she enjoyed watching Ramon as he led the way back into the yard.

He would never put off his duty because the road was too cold. She wondered how she had ever dreaded his arrival.

He pushed his face plate up and aimed his dark stare at her.

"I seek the Lady of Camoys!"

"Only Lady de Segrave is here," she replied.

His lips curved into a satisfied grin. He slid from his stallion and marched up the steps, his armor clanking with his motions.

He cupped her chin, his fingers cold, but she rubbed her cheek against them to warm them.

"I am here, my lord."

"And I have come to be your devoted husband, madam."

He leaned down and kissed her, to the delight of those watching. Mildred snorted, but Isabel was far too absorbed in the kiss to pay attention to her.

❧

Isabel's toes were warm now. The ice of winter was gone as warmer air surrounded them all. The scent of newly turned earth was thick.

"Bear down now…harder."

Mildred was showing no mercy.

Isabel groaned, feeling as if she must be splitting in two. She couldn't seem to draw in enough breath, but Mildred had no sympathy.

"Bear down, Isabel! Harder, I tell you, you must do it with the pain."

"I am trying…" Isabel panted.

"Harder!" Mildred's voice snapped like a whip.

The birthing table was hard against her back but Isabel curled up and grabbed her knees. Two maids pressed their hands into her back to help keep her there as she bore down. Her body was splitting again, opening as the pressure built until it burst, and her baby slipped through into the world. She felt it moving, passing from her womb to where the midwife waited.

The midwife caught the baby with steady hands and eased it free. "A son," she declared as she swung the baby by its heels and thumped it firmly on the back twice. When she turned him up, she rubbed the infant briskly with a length of fabric. His tiny body shook, his hands opening and closing before he gulped air and let it out in a wail.

Isabel sobbed, reaching out for her baby. The maids all cried out, helping her to cradle the baby because her arms were shaking from the effort of the birth. Mildred tucked the fabric around him, her face crinkled up with her joy.

Isabel's son screamed, the sound echoing through the kitchen and out into the great hall. A cheer went up from those waiting beyond the closed door. Ramon's squire began pounding on the door.

"Lady…lady…my lord waits," he called. "What word?"

He wouldn't actually enter the birthing area, for it was a woman's place, but he flattened his hand and hit the door frame.

"A son!" the midwife called to him. The pounding stopped as the sound of the boy running through the hall echoed into the kitchen. A moment later, there was a roar that Isabel recognized very well.

After all, it was the man she loved.

The baby drew in a shaky breath and opened his eyes, locking gazes with her.

Love was a fine thing indeed.

A very fine thing.

Read on for an excerpt from

The Highlander's Bride Trouble

Scottish Highlands, 1487

"Ye may be dismissed for the night."

Abigail Ross, the Earl of Ross's daughter, didn't really look at her maid, Nareen Grant. She was too busy breaking the wax seal on the letter she'd just received. Her cheeks flushed and her eyes sparkled as she unfolded the parchment. Its crinkling echoed loudly in the quiet chamber. She was well past the blush of youth, but it was clear affection had no time limit. Even in her late twenties, Abigail was excited by her love letter.

Although, perhaps "liaison letter" might be a more appropriate description. Abigail enjoyed her lovers, and she enjoyed knowing she didn't owe them the obedience a wife would.

"Go on, Nareen. I know ye like yer sleep."

Abigail drew out the word *sleep*. She looked up for a brief moment, making it clear she knew what Nareen would be doing under the veil of night.

Abigail knew Nareen's weaknesses too. It was the

only reason Nareen served her, so she might enjoy
freedom as well.

"The moon is full," Abigail muttered before looking back at the letter. There was a subtle warning in
her tone, indicating she would turn a blind eye only if
Nareen returned the favor.

Nareen inclined her head before leaving the bedchamber. Once she passed through the arched doorway that separated the bedchamber from the receiving
chamber, she allowed her pace to increase.

She wasn't interested in sleeping, and luckily, her
mistress didn't have any issues with her nighttime
rides. Of course, in return, Nareen was expected to
ignore the unmarried lady's lovers. So it wasn't luck,
it was an agreement. One Nareen enjoyed benefits
from as well.

She shuddered, a tingle of fear rising from the dark
abyss where Nareen had banished several memories
she never wanted to think about again. Sometimes it
was very hard to forget her cousin Ruth and the hor-
rors Nareen had suffered while with her kinswoman.

Yes, the arrangement made it possible for Nareen
to escape being under the care of her kin, and the
unsavory plans Ruth had been making for her.

Nareen turned her attention to the moon. She
could see it glowing through the seam in the window
shutters. Just a faint sliver of yellow light, it was like
a beacon, drawing her toward joyful abandon. The
whisper of chilly night air coming through didn't
bother her a bit. In fact, it was invigorating.

Outside, she didn't have to worry about being
trapped within stone walls.

Nareen steeled her expression as she went through the doors that led to the stairs. Two Ross retainers stood there, making sure the earl's daughter was well guarded throughout the night. They each held a five-foot-tall wooden staff topped with a wicked and deadly looking spear top. The metal gleamed in the moist Highland air. Their gazes followed Nareen as she left, and they stiffly pulled on the corners of their knitted caps.

No one really spared her much attention as she made her way through the partially lit passageways. Several of the torches had been blown out by the vigorous wind.

Nareen skipped down the stone steps, making the three stories to the ground floor in a flash. Abigail would be traveling again soon, if the letter held an invitation. That meant Nareen would be on a tighter leash once the highborn lady found a way to wheedle her father into granting her permission to return to court. The earl had sworn he wouldn't allow it, but Nareen knew he'd soften. Once the wine began to flow, the Earl of Ross lost his will. Abigail always exploited her father's weakness to suit her whims.

So tonight, Nareen would ride.

Many would tell her it was the demons causing the gusts of wind. Nareen scoffed at them. There were legends that went back farther than the Church. Tales of Celtic lore that were still told around the winter fires. She preferred the stories that told of strength and daring, to the Church's teachings that tried to convince her to fear the witching hours.

Nareen pulled her arisaid up from where the length

of Grant tartan draped down her back, and laid it over her head. During the day, the piece of wool was secured at her waist, and of little use except to make it clear she was proud to be a Grant. But at night, it would shield her from rain and keep her warm. She pulled it around to cover her shoulders before venturing into the yard. Most of the Ross retainers taking their ease in the yard looked her way, but they returned to whatever they were doing once they recognized the Grant colors.

She was just the mistress's attendant.

That position suited Nareen well. She didn't regret leaving her cousin's keeping, not even when it reduced her to being a personal servant. At least she need not worry about Ruth selling Nareen's maidenhead.

Nareen shuddered. The woman held no power over her now. Nareen had seen to that.

The horses greeted her when she entered the stable. Her mood improved as she reminded herself that she was free of Ruth and her unsavory plans.

Her mare tossed its mane in greeting. Nareen murmured softly to it in Gaelic as she eased the bridle on. Her mare pawed at the ground, eager to stretch her legs.

"Me thoughts exactly," Nareen said as she slid onto the back of the animal. The gate watch raised the gate for her, but not without a stern look of disapproval.

Nareen didn't bother to look back. She leaned low over the neck of her mare and let the animal have its freedom. The horse picked up speed, chilling Nareen's cheeks as they raced across the open land that surrounded the Ross castle.

❧

Saer MacLeod turned his head, listening to the night. He kicked dirt over the small fire he'd built to cook his dinner, and it died, leaving him in darkness.

It wasn't that dark. He'd endured nights that were as black as a demon's eyes, and this one wasn't anywhere near that deep.

But there was something—someone—riding toward him. There was no way he was going to greet that stranger anywhere but on the back of his horse.

There was a whistle from his man. Baruch held up one finger.

Saer didn't reach for the pommel of the sword strapped to his back. A lone rider wasn't that much of a threat.

"I thinks it's her…" Baruch rode up close to his laird's side. "Just like the Ross lad told me, she's riding by moonlight…"

"Good," Saer muttered. He felt a surge of impending victory and savored it.

Nareen Grant had turned him down and dismissed him the last time he'd seen her.

He intended to make sure she knew he was not so easily brushed aside.

❧

Nareen was sure her heart was beating as fast as her mare's. The animal slowed, having spent its first burst of speed. Her arisaid had fallen back, baring her head, but she enjoyed the bite of the night air. She laughed, at ease for the first time all day. But her elation evaporated when her mare's ears lifted. Nareen tightened her grip on the reins as she searched the shadows. "Who is there?" she demanded.

"Ye take a risk by riding out at night, lass."

Her company emerged from the shadows cast by the edge of a woodland patch, where the forest trees thinned and gave way to the slope.

"But yer command of the mare is impressive, Nareen Grant."

He was a large man. She could describe him as huge, but resisted the urge because there was already a chill tingling on her nape. If he knew her name, it was possible he was an enemy of the Grants. She tightened her knees, making ready to flee.

"Ye have naught to fear from me." He nudged his horse farther away from the shadows. Her heart froze as the moonlight illuminated his hard body. There was no mistaking his prime condition, and his voice was deep and young enough to confirm she might be in true peril if he turned hostile.

"Name yer clan," she stated boldly. She lifted her chin and stared straight at him. A weak plea would never do.

There was a husky chuckle from the stranger. "Are ye sure ye are in a position to demand things of me, lass? Most Highlanders do nae care for a lass who spits fire."

"I do nae care for anyone who will nae speak the name of their clan without hesitation. Such actions mean ye have no honor."

He rode a full stallion, the horse just as impressive as its master. The animal was prime quality, telling her he had coin in his purse, but that fact didn't reassure her. Many times, noble lords were far more unscrupulous than a common villain. The law favored them in every way, and they took advantage of it.

He nudged the beast with his knees until it turned and the moonlight washed over his face. She gasped, recognizing him instantly. And a little too well for her liking. A rush of heat flooded her cheeks, for she had just accused a laird of having no honor.

"What are ye doing riding on Ross land in the dark of night, Saer MacLeod?"

He moved his horse closer to her mare and leaned down to pat the neck of the sturdy beast he rode. Her attention was drawn to his hand, fixating on the way he stroked the animal. There was a confidence in his motions that sent a tingle across her skin. He was more than bold, he was supremely at ease in the night—so much so, she envied him.

More heat teased her face, this time flowing down her body.

"This is hardly dark," he said at last.

She jerked her gaze up to his face to find him grinning at her. She tossed her long braid over her shoulder, detesting the way he made her feel vulnerable. "Ye're right, it is hardly dark, which is why I am enjoying it. Good-bye, Laird MacLeod."

She tightened her grip on the reins and sent her mare in motion again. She wasn't running away; it was simply a matter of doing what she pleased. Aye, indeed it was.

Abigail already told her what to do most of the day. Of course, it was far better than answering to a husband or to her cousin Ruth.

Her dark memories stirred again, so she leaned low

over the neck of the horse and felt the wind pulling the shorter strands of her hair from her braid. The steady beat of the mare's hooves filled her head, but there was something else too, a deeper pounding. She turned her head to find Saer MacLeod keeping pace with her, an amused grin on his lips.

She kneed her mare, urging the animal to go faster. It was an impulse that irritated her because she was letting herself be goaded. There would be no responding to Saer MacLeod.

She pulled up, the mare settling into a slow walk, tossing her head as Nareen worried her lower lip. "I'm sure ye have important things to do, Laird MacLeod."

He guided his stallion in step beside her mare. "Ensuring ye do nae get set upon by the MacKays is important. I hear they have no love for the Ross. They claim the earl killed their laird and have vowed vengeance."

"I am a Grant."

"But ye serve the earl's daughter," Saer countered. "There would be more than one man who would consider that enough to include ye in their feud."

Her heart was beating faster. She drew in a deep, slow breath to calm herself. "I do nae need yer protection." Her tone was far from smooth, further irritating her. She didn't need the man hearing how he unsettled her.

He grinned more broadly in the face of her temper, a cocksure, arrogant, full curving of his lips that sent a tingle through her belly. She was amusing him and nothing else.

"I do nae need yer permission to ensure ye come to

no harm, Nareen. Just as I did nae need yer brother's consent to let me ride along with him to deal with yer cousin Ruth."

She jerked, involuntarily pulling on the reins. The mare stopped, snorting with frustration. Saer reached out and stroked the animal's neck again. The horse quieted immediately and made a soft sound of enjoyment.

Nareen's mouth went dry at the way his touch pleased. She wondered… "Let me mare be."

Nareen tried to pull the horse away. Saer reached out and captured her hand to keep her from commanding the mare.

The contact was jarring, his warm flesh shocking her. Her own fingers were chilled from the pace of her ride, but his were warm and inviting. More than a warmth that chased away the night temperature, this was a heat that touched something deep inside her. She licked her lower lip because it was too dry, drawing his gaze to her mouth.

She jerked her hand away.

"I told ye at court, I want naught to do with ye." At last, she'd grasped enough of her composure to say what she truly needed to.

"Aye, ye did." He patted her mare's neck, stroking the velvet surface of her skin with a long motion before answering. "Look at me, Nareen Grant, and tell me if ye see a man who is easily told what to do."

His tone was soft and menacing, carrying a warning that even the mare sensed. A chill shot down Nareen's back, her gaze locking with his. She was keenly aware of him, her lips tingling with anticipation. She felt like there was something inside him that was drawing her closer, some force that reached out to stroke her, entice her to do his will.

He jerked the reins right out of her slackened grip. "What are ye doing?"

Saer didn't answer her. He held the reins, and her mare began following his stallion as he sent the beast forward. Her only option was to drop down the side of the animal while it was in motion. One look at the ground warned her against such a rash action. Moonlight illuminated the rocky ground they rode across, promising her a rough landing.

But she was still tempted, because Saer's back promised her something else. His shirtsleeves were rolled up and tied at his shoulder. She was as fascinated by his back as by his keen gaze. A long sword was strapped across his back at an angle so the pommel was behind his left shoulder and easy to reach with his right hand. There was nothing ornate about the weapon, just solid purpose. He was bastard-born and raised among the isles. The Highlanders called him a savage, and his actions proved he was exactly that.

He took what he wanted, just as he was taking her.

She looked at the ground again, but the sound of water drew her attention to where he was leading her. The noise grew until it was loud enough to drown out the steps of the horses. He guided them around a granite outcropping and down to where the moonlight shimmered off a river. It was swollen from rains farther up in the Highlands, the moonlight lighting the white peaks raised by the current.

There was a fire burning near the face of the outcropping they had just come around. It was completely hidden from the open space. Over six dozen horses and men were taking their ease near the fire, the scent of roasting rabbit floating in the air. The orange flicker from the fire showed her the colors of the MacLeod plaid in their kilts. They looked up, but turned their backs once they realized their laird had returned with a female.

"Ye would never see trouble coming, lass. The Ross have no idea we are on their land."

Saer let out a whistle, which was answered in kind. She didn't care how much truth there was in his words. He slid off his horse and handed the reins to a younger boy who had come up to serve his laird. Saer handed off the reins of her mare to another lad before dismounting.

"Will ye dismount, or shall I assist ye, lass?"

Nareen lifted her leg and slid to the ground. She did it too fast, and her ankle bent, but she recovered, welcoming the twinge of pain, because it gave her something to focus on besides his unsettling presence. Once on the ground, she battled the instinct to feel small next to Saer MacLeod.

She would not be made to feel anything by the man, and that was final.

"Ye have no authority over me, Laird MacLeod." She reached for the reins of her mare, but the lad was leading the horse away. "I'll be going where I please."

"Go into the night, and I'll follow ye." His eyes flickered with a warning. "As much as I admire the wild streak in ye, it will nae protect ye from men set on feuding. Yer brother is me friend and ally. 'Tis me duty to see ye protected." His tone was firm.

She bristled. "I do nae wish to be under yer protection," she insisted. "I've made me own place. Ye may tell me brother I absolved ye of any responsibility."

"I've clasped yer brother's wrist and called him friend. Honor is not absolved by words." He stepped closer. "But that is nae the only reason I will ride out after ye, Nareen Grant."

His voice had deepened and his tone made her knees go weak. She detested the reaction, willing herself to ignore it. Yet it persisted, turning and twisting through her like some sort of dark suggestion she couldn't ignore because it was inside her.

"I must return to me mistress."

"Ye're hiding in yer position," he accused softly. "Ye are the daughter of an ennobled laird, nae a serving lass."

"I made a place for meself when the one me noble family sent me to was sordid," she defended.

"Something ye are to be admired for." His expression changed, the hard set of his lips softening as he moved even closer. She lost the battle to ignore her response. He was too near to ignore completely; the soft night breeze carried the scent of his skin to her.

She stepped back. His lips parted, flashing his teeth as victory filled his eyes.

"Ye intrigue me, Nareen Grant. Ye are noble-born, yet ye did nae meekly accept yer plight with yer cousin."

"Of course I did nae, I am a Grant," she answered with pride. His dark eyes brightened with approval and something that looked like intent. "Do nae be intrigued." She stepped to the side, to place more space between them. "For I am nae interested in ye a bit."

One of his dark eyebrows rose. "I'm willing to wager I can change yer mind, lass."

Her eyes widened, a sickening twist of nausea shooting through her belly. "I am nae something to be made sport of."

And she couldn't bear it. The need to retch was growing as she battled the image of him taking her on the ground while his men ignored them.

There was nothing to stop him. Once more, she had only her wits, and it shamed her to know that was by her own doing. Reckless choices often delivered harsh consequences. But she was nae going to submit easily.

"Ye claim me brother is yer friend," she reminded him. "I believe he would nae care to know ye are trifling with me."

His expression hardened. "Yer cousin Ruth has paid for her deeds, but I wonder if stripping her of her freedom and placing her and her entire estate under the guardianship of a trusted man was enough. She bred a fear in ye. For that, she has nae been punished enough."

It was true, but she couldn't share such a thing with him. Not with anyone.

"Ruth no longer rules her estate?"

Saer shook his head. "Her choices are limited to what fare she might enjoy from the kitchen and what dress she may wear."

For a moment, Nareen recalled the gleam that always brightened her cousin's eyes when she was laying out her plans. The staff lived in fear of being singled out by their mistress. "Ruth thrived on control. She'll hate having none."

"Then it was well done."

His voice had a deep timbre that struck her as too familiar, too kind, too focused upon her. She recoiled from it, shaking her head because she didn't want anything about Ruth to matter to her. "I do nae care what became of her. She means naught to me."

He reached out and stroked her cheek. "'Tis a sad thing to see how hard yer feelings are. But there is naught more to fear, she'll nae have the opportunity to inflict such ills again."

Nareen jerked away from the contact. She even took a swipe at his hand, but he moved faster, withdrawing in time to avoid being struck. Someone chuckled from where his men clustered near the fires, but Saer was watching her from narrowed eyes.

"I am nae afraid of anything," she assured him.

"Is that so?" Saer inquired in a silky-smooth tone.

Nareen nodded. Satisfaction began to fill her, but it was cut short as he reached out and stroked her face again. She jumped, completely unable to control her reaction.

"Ye are making sport of me in front of yer men, like a savage."

His eyes glittered, but it wasn't with the outrage Nareen had intended to provoke. Instead, there was an unmistakable pleased looked in those dark orbs.

"I *am* a savage, Nareen." He stepped forward, placing himself within touching range again. "I do nae let words stand alone. If ye truly have no interest

in me, there is no reason to avoid me touch. Stand
steady and prove ye are nae moved. I have no taste
for a frigid woman."

She laughed at him but stepped back again. "Then
it seems we have a common ground, for I crave no
man's touch."

His lips thinned. "Now that is something ye shall
have to prove as well."

"I will nae. Me word should be enough on the
matter, if ye truly are me brother's friend." She didn't
care to hide behind her brother's name, but the circumstances offered her few alternatives.

"As ye noted, I am a savage, and I always demand
proof before I believe."

This time, she was ready when he reached for her
cheek. She stepped aside, avoiding him. She was just
beginning to smile with her victory when he closed
his hand around her wrist. He really was huge. His
fingers closed easily around her smaller wrist, clasping
it in an iron grip. She braced herself for pain, but there
was none, only a secure hold that defied her attempt
to break it.

"Release me." Her voice had risen, and she
shut her mouth before revealing any more of her
unsettled state.

"Prove ye are unmoved, lass, and I shall be content
to accept yer dismissal." His tone had deepened,
becoming something hypnotic.

"I am irritated." And remaining still was proving
too difficult. She twisted her hand, trying to break his
hold again.

"Aye, ye are that." He lifted her hand to his face

and pressed a kiss on the delicate skin of her inner wrist. She shuddered, the touch intensely intimate. She'd never realized her skin might be so sensitive. The simple touch of his lips unleashed a bolt of sensation that shook her all the way down to her toes. His eyes filled with satisfaction.

"But ye are also affected."

He released her, and she stumbled back a pace because she'd been resisting his hold so greatly. Laughter erupted from his men. Saer stiffened, and he crossed his arms over his chest.

"What?" she said. "Are ye trying to impress me by controlling yerself now that ye see yer men are enjoying the sport ye are making of me?"

"Aye, I am," he answered darkly. "I am nae the one who chose this setting for our meeting, Nareen. Ye should nae have refused to see me again at court. That left me no choice but to chase ye."

"Ye have no right to chase me, nor take me mare's reins."

He offered her only a slight tilt of his head. "Riding through the night hours is nae safe."

"Ye were doing it," she pointed out.

He reached back and grasped the pommel of the long sword that was strapped to his back. "I am more prepared than ye, lass."

"So ye think," she warned.

His eyes narrowed again, this time sweeping her from head to toe. He wouldn't find her dagger. At least, not until it was too late.

"I can see to meself," Nareen assured him, her confidence was high when it came to protecting herself. The knowledge restored her balance, and it was a relief.

She turned and made to go after her mare. She felt his gaze on her, but he didn't try to stop her. The young lad who had taken her mare watched as she untied the knot that secured her bridle to the other horses. No one spoke a word, but they watched her, some of the retainers stroking their beards.

Nareen mounted and turned her mare toward the path that led away from the hidden campsite. She pressed her knees into the sides of the mare to get her moving.

Saer was no longer in sight. The urge to look around for the MacLeod laird was almost irresistible, but she lifted her chin and headed up the path. Her jaw was aching by the time she gained the high ground, because she was gritting her teeth.

But she was satisfied.

She was on her way, going where she wished.

Once out of the woods, her mare picked up speed, crossing the open space that allowed the Ross fortress to see invaders coming—the site for the castle had been chosen because of the natural clearing. The gate watch made her wait while they scanned the land. She glanced behind her, looking back toward the wooded area. For a moment, something moved, and Saer emerged for just a split second.

"Open the gate," she called up.

"Ye'll wait on the captain's word," a retainer called back down. "Do nae say the Grant leave their gates open in the dark of night."

Of course they didn't. No one did. The only

reason she was allowed out was because the Ross truly did not care if she returned. A servant was replaceable, especially one from another clan. She'd taken solace in that fact, but now, she realized how foolish she had been.

Saer MacLeod could have kept her, and no one would have bothered to send out even a single rider to look for her. As much as she detested the facts of the world, she could not deny that the Grants had enemies—every clan did. Even on Ross land, she might find herself under attack from one of her brother's enemies. If Saer could find her, so could others.

It was time to think about her circumstances.

"It's clear," the captain of the watch called from the top of the corner tower.

The portcullis was raised just enough for her to enter. But the moment the gate closed behind her, she realized she was there only because Saer had allowed it. His stallion was capable of running her mare to ground.

He'd allowed her to return.

That knowledge unleashed several emotions she wanted to ignore. But as she returned her mare to her stall and rubbed her down, there was no way to hide from her own thoughts.

Saer MacLeod had allowed her to decide what she wished. His fellow Highlanders might call him a savage, but he was far more accommodating than she expected of a man.

It was what he wanted, no doubt. All men craved the same thing from women.

It was more than a word. The idea whispered

through her thoughts and along her skin, raising goose bumps. She shivered, but realized she was actually trembling. She hissed, letting her temper flare in the hopes it would burn away the memory of his touch.

Another emotion teased her, warm as a flash of temper, but it wasn't anger. She frowned as she failed to understand it. Even if she detested the man and everything about him, the memory of his lips against her wrist filled her thoughts, leaving behind a slight sting on her cheeks.

She shook her head and made her way toward her bed.

She would not think about his touch or the way it made her feel. There would be no lament over the choice she had made to reject him.

There would not be.

◈

"I'm surprised ye let her go back into that fortress," Saer's captain remarked when he joined him at the edge of the clearing. "I do nae think she'll be making it simple for ye to catch her again."

"I hope not."

Baruch chuckled. "Are ye sure ye want that one, Laird?"

Saer cut his captain a hard look. "That is what I'm here to discover. She intrigues me, and I confess I've never been impressed with a lass's strength before."

"Her brother agreed to yer suit," Baruch reminded him. "It would be a lot simpler to learn what it is ye want to know if ye had kept her."

Saer looked back at the Ross fortress. "If I did

that, she'd be able to dismiss me the same as those her cousin allowed to make sport of her." His tone betrayed his anger. "She will come to me."

"And how do ye figure to make that happen?"

Saer turned his stallion to head back to the camp. "She craves freedom. Nae the inside of that fortress."

Baruch slowly smiled. "And ye've cleverly made it so she is the one who has caged herself. Well played, Laird. Even a spitfire cannae claim ye forced her inside that gate."

"She will not," Saer confirmed. "Nareen Grant will notice exactly what I did. She is no simpleton."

Baruch let out a low whistle. "Careful, Laird, a spitfire is often more trouble than she's worth. Once the passion cools, ye'll be stuck with a harpy for a wife. One that will have the care of yer daughters."

"Or I might just have found a woman who is nae afraid of me."

Which was what he truly craved. Now that he was Laird, there were offers of brides, but he didn't have the stomach for a shivering woman in his bed. His father's bride had been one of those, a daughter offered up by her father, and white as a ghost on the day of her wedding. His father had turned to Saer's mother for passion when the years went by and his noble wife never warmed toward him.

Saer wanted nothing to do with a marriage like that.

Nareen trembled, but she also spat at him. What he really wanted to know was would she reach for him once she surrendered to passion?

It was a gamble, one that carried a large risk. Saer wasn't blind to the facts. But he also couldn't ignore the way Nareen blushed for him. Her cheeks had been hot, even in the cold night air, just as they'd been when he'd encountered her at court.

Every moment they'd shared was branded into his memory. If he was given to superstition, he'd suspect her of casting spells. Court ladies had reputations for bewitching men with their wiles.

He grinned, the burn of a challenge warming him. If Nareen had enchanted him, he was going to make sure she suffered the same fate.

"Where are ye going, Laird?" Baruch inquired.

"To introduce meself to the Earl of Ross," Saer answered without looking over his shoulder. "It would be terribly rude of me to cross his land and nae clasp his hand. Such an action might start rumors about me lack of social graces."

"Well now, we wouldn't be wanting that," Baruch agreed as he followed his laird toward the castle. "But ye know, ye do nae have to spend the night inside the fortress. The summer night is fine."

"Aye." Saer continued toward the gate.

Baruch snorted behind him and abandoned further argument. "She's under yer skin," he groused instead.

"Perhaps." Saer ignored the temptation to wait until morning to enter the castle. There was one thing he disliked more than being surrounded by stone walls, and that was ignoring a challenge. "Since I plan to claim her, it matters not."

"Aye," Baruch answered.

Whether or not Nareen was teasing him was not the reason he moved closer to her refuge. He wanted to know why she invaded his dreams. He'd stand in her path until she faced him. The answer would be revealed only when she stopped running.

The Highlander's Bride

Highland Trouble

by Amanda Forester

❧

Their attraction is forbidden

All Highland warrior Gavin Patrick wants is to get back to
his native Scotland. But before he can leave the battlefield,
he's given a final mission—escort Lady Marie Colette to her
fiancé. Under no circumstances is he to lay hands on the
beautiful, clever-tongued heiress…no matter how desperate
the temptation.

Their desire, undeniable

Forced to pose as a married couple to make their escape
from France, Gavin and Marie Colette find themselves
thrown into peril…and each other's arms. As the danger
mounts, so does their forbidden passion. But it isn't until
Marie Colette is taken from him that Gavin is forced to
decide—is he willing to lose the woman who stole his heart,
or will he jeopardize his honor, defy his promise, and steal
her in return?

❧

Kilts and Daggers

Highland Spies

by Victoria Roberts

❧

When Fagan Murray is charged with escorting Lady Grace Walsingham back to her home in England, he expected tension with the headstrong lass. But he didn't expect to be waylaid by Highland rebels. Fagan soon realizes he'll do anything to protect Grace, even if he has to protect her from himself.

Lady Grace Walsingham hated the Scottish Highlands— well, one Highlander in particular. Ever since she discovered her sister was a spy for the Crown, Grace has yearned for adventure. But the last thing she wanted was to encounter danger in the Highland wilderness, needing the one man she despises to protect her.

❧

Praise for *My Highland Spy*:

"An exciting Highland tale of intrigue, betrayal, and love." —Hannah Howell, *New York Times* bestselling author of *Highland Master*

For more Victoria Roberts, visit:
www.sourcebooks.com

The Highlander's Prize
by Mary Wine

❧

Clarrisa of York has never needed a miracle more. Sent to Scotland's king to be his mistress, her deliverance arrives in the form of being kidnapped by a brusque Highland laird who's a bit too rough to be considered divine intervention. Except his rugged handsomeness and undeniable magnetism surely are magnificent…

Laird Broen MacNichols has accepted the challenge of capturing Clarrisa to make sure the king doesn't get the heir he needs in order to hold on to the throne. Broen knows more about royalty than he ever cared to, but Clarrisa, beautiful and intelligent, turns out to be much more of a challenge than he bargained for…

With rival lairds determined to steal her from him and royal henchmen searching for Clarrisa all over the Highlands, Broen is going to have to prove to this independent-minded lady that a Highlander always claims his prize…

❧

"[The characters] fight just as passionately as they love while intrigue abounds and readers turn the pages faster and faster!" —*RT Book Reviews*, 4 Stars

For more Mary Wine books, visit:
www.sourcebooks.com

The Trouble with Highlanders
by Mary Wine

❧

With her clan on the wrong side of the struggle for the Scottish throne, heiress Daphne MacLeod, once the toast of the court, is out of options…

Norris Sutherland once helped Daphne, but she walked away from him without a backward glance. Now she's in deep trouble and needs him more than ever. But he may be lost forever…unless she can somehow convince him to forgive her.

❧

Praise for Mary Wine's Highland romances:

"Mary Wine brings history to life with major sizzle factor." —Lucy Monroe, *USA Today* bestselling author of *For Duty's Sake*

Hot enough to warm even the coldest Scottish nights…With a captivating leading lady and terrific pacing." —*Publishers Weekly* Starred Review

"Not to be missed." —Lora Leigh, *New York Times* #1 bestselling author

"One gripping plot twist follows another…kilt-tossing, sheet-incinerating lovemaking." —*Publishers Weekly*

For more Mary Wine, visit:
www.sourcebooks.com

How to Handle a Highlander
by Mary Wine

❧

In a land of warriors playing a deadly game...

Moira Fraser has been given an ultimatum—marry the elderly Laird Achaius Morris, or risk another deadly clan war. She vows to do the right thing, as long as she can steer clear of the devilish charms of one stubborn Highlander...

How do you avoid becoming a pawn?

Gahan Sutherland knows there's a dangerous plot behind Moira Fraser's wedding, and will stop at nothing to foil it. But where a hotheaded, fiery Highland lass is involved, trust and honor clash with forbidden attraction, threatening to blow the Highlands sky-high.

❧

"Well-written and filled with delightful repartee, this is a feast for medieval fans." —*RT Book Reviews*

"Mary Wine weaves a tapestry of a tale with adrenaline-pumping action, political manipulation, sweet and spicy love scenes, clan culture, and a touch of humor." —*Long and Short Reviews*

For more Mary Wine, visit:
www.sourcebooks.com

The Highlander's Bride Trouble

Book 4 in The Sutherlands series
by Mary Wine

❧

Her clan is in chaos

Nareen Grant is strong, confident, well-educated—and skilled with a bow and dagger. Betrayed by her family, she makes her way alone, until she lands in the lap of Saer MacLeod. But she wants no help from a savage man of the Isles.

And rivalries are deadlier than ever

Saer MacLeod is considered fierce even by Highlander standards, but he's enchanted by the headstrong Nareen. When an old feud endangers her life, Saer feels a ferocious desire to protect her…and claim her for himself.

❧

"Wine's rip-roaring ambushes and beddings make for a wild ride through fifteenth-century Scottish eroticism." —*Publishers Weekly*

"The rapid pace, wonderful prose, and deeply emotional scenes make this book a marvelous read." —*RT Book Reviews* Top Pick, 4.5 Stars

For more Mary Wine, visit:
www.sourcebooks.com

About the Author

Mary Wine is a multi-published author in romantic suspense, fantasy, and Western romance. Her interest in historical reenactment and costuming also inspired her to turn her pen to historical romance with her popular Highlander series. She lives with her husband and sons in Southern California, where the whole family enjoys participating in historical reenactment.